Letters From Gronow

OTHER TITLES PUBLISHED BY ERIC FLINT'S RING OF FIRE PRESS

Bartley's Man
Blood in Erfurt
Essen Defiant
Essen Steel
Gloom Despair and Agony on You
Incident in Alaska Prefecture
Joseph Hanauer
Letters Home
Love and Chemistry
Medicine and Disease after the Ring of Fire
Muse of Music
No ship for Tranquebar
Second Chance Bird
Storm Signals
The Battle for Newfoundland
The Danish Scheme
The Demons of Paris
The Evening of the Day
The Heirloom
The Masks of Mirada
The Play's the Thing
The Persistence of Dreams
The Society of Saint Philip of the Screwdriver
Turn Your Radio On

Letters From Gronow

By

David Carrico

Book Title Copyright © 2018 by David Carrico.
All rights reserved. No part of this book may be reproduced in any form or by any electronic or mechanical means including information storage and retrieval systems, without permission in writing from the author. The only exception is by a reviewer, who may quote short excerpts in a review.

Eric Flint's Ring of Fire Press handles DRM, Digital Rights Management, simply: We trust in the **_Honor_** of our readers.

Cover art by: Laura Givens

This book is a work of fiction. Names, characters, places, and incidents either are products of the author's imagination or are used fictitiously. Any resemblance to actual persons, living or dead, events, or locales is entirely coincidental.

David Carrico

Visit my website at https://davidcarricofiction.com/

Parts of this work have been previously published in the _Grantville Gazette_ volumes 70 to 75

First Printing: 2018

Eric Flint's Ring of Fire Press

ISBN-13 9781982978969

Dedication

To the memory of my wife Ruth, who was my Ella in truth.

Contents

Letters From Gronow Episode 1 1
Episode 2 19
Episode 3 39
Episode 4 71
Episode 5 103
Episode 6 139
Episode 7 189
Dramatis Personae 301

Letters From Gronow Episode 1

Magdeburg
From the Journal of Philip Fröhlich
16 October 1634

> Monday
> Breakfast–
> > *2 barley rolls 1 pfennig*
> > *1 cup small beer 1 quartered pfennig*
>
> Supper–
> > *1 wurst 1 pfennig*
> > *2 mugs beer 1 pfennig*

id the cash entries in Master Gröning's accounts today, then reviewed Saturday's entries. Found two errors in Thomas' work and took them to Master Schiller. He boxed Thomas' ears, then made him recopy the entire page, watching over his shoulder the entire time. Later Thomas tried to stab me with his pen, but the quill nib barely scratched me before the quill broke. Master Schiller gave him his hand for that as well and would not give him a good right wing quill to replace it but forced him to take one of the left wing quills. Serves him right.

After work and before supper I slipped into Syborg's Book Store to dream. There on the table with the oldest hardest-used books was one I hadn't seen before, larger than the others, but thinner, wrapped in heavy paper rather than boards or leather. My hands were cleaner than usual, so I picked it up.

The cover was a block print of a great black cat, and I almost dropped it, but the title was *Der Schwarze Kater – Eine Zeitschrift*. I opened the cover to discover that this book contained several poems and prose stories. I turned the page, and began reading a work called *The Cask of Amontillado*.

Nine pages later, I closed the book, wide-eyed. This story had gripped me as nothing had before. I must have this book.

Evening prayers recited, so now to bed.

From the Journal of Philip Fröhlich
17 October 1634

> Tuesday
> Breakfast–
>> *1 barley roll 2 quartered pfennigs*
>
> Supper–
>> *1 barley roll (old) 1 quartered pfennig*
>> *1 cup small beer 1 quartered pfennig*

Dreams last night were strange.

Checked incoming bills of lading against contracts all day, found one error. Gave to Master Schiller. He double-checked and gave me a pfennig as a reward along with today's pay.

Thomas looked hungover. Tried to stay out of his way.

After work, ran to Syborg's Book Store. *Der Schwarze Kater* was still there. I pulled it out and laid it flat atop the other books on the table and looked around. The Masters Syborg Elder and Younger were not present, but Georg their clerk was, and he came to the table when he saw my lifted hand. When I asked him how much for the book, he picked it up and looked around. "Master Matthias took this on as a trial, and they sold very quickly. People want more, except for the old woman who brought this one back claiming it was filled with demonic filth and we should be ashamed of selling it in the same shop with Augustine and Melanchthon and Calvin. Master Johann told me to get whatever I can for it since the old lady tore some of the pages. So, what can you do?"

I took two pfennigs out of my pocket and held them out to him. He shook his head. I added another pfennig. He shook his head. I added the last coin in my pocket, a quartered pfennig. He shook his head, but this time with a smile and held his hand out. I poured the coins into his hand, picked up the book and hurried back to my room.

Began the next story, *The Dunwich Horror*. Sadly, have not finished but cannot keep eyes open. Besides, candle is guttering.

Stumbled through prayers. Bed.

From the Journal of Philip Fröhlich
18 October 1634

>Wednesday
>Breakfast–
>> *1 barley roll 2 quartered pfennigs*
>> *1 cup small beer 1 quartered pfennig*
>
>Supper–
>> *1 barley roll (very old) 1 quartered pfennig*
>> *1 winter apple 1 pfennig*

Dreams last night were very strange.

Spent most of the day drawing columns on pages for Master Schiller. Hate that. Wish Master Gröning would buy the new-fangled preprinted forms the up-timers made so useful. Old miser.

Thomas hungover again today. Wasn't in a mood to deal with him today, so when he snarled at me I told him to leave me alone or I'd kick him in the stomach. He wrapped his arms around his middle and groaned. Never seen anybody turn green before. Almost laughed.

Took today's pay in candle stubs. Master Schiller looked surprised, but said nothing.

Finished *The Dunwich Horror* tonight. Think I finally understand what the up-time word wow means.

Evening prayers recited—twice. Now to bed.

From the Journal of Philip Fröhlich
21 October 1634

>Saturday
>Breakfast–
>>*2 barley rolls 1 pfennig*
>
>Supper–
>>*1 wurst 1 pfennig*

Woke up several times last night from dreams.

Finished *Der Schwarze Kater* tonight. Started over at beginning.

On last page of book, Master Johann Gronow, the editor—whatever that is—says that *Der Schwarze Kater* is looking for people to write stories.

I know what I want to do now.

What's an editor? Must find out.

Recited evening prayers—three times. Now to bed.

From the Journal of Philip Fröhlich
22 October 1634

>Sunday
>Breakfast–
>>*Fasted*
>
>Lunch–
>>*1 wheat roll 3 pfennigs*
>>*1 sausage 2 pfennigs*
>>*1 cup small beer 1 quartered pfennig*
>
>Supper–
>>*1 wurst 1 pfennig*
>>*1 cup sauerkraut 1 pfennig*
>>*2 mugs beer 1 pfennig*

Lord's Day, Lord's work.

No dreams last night.

Church this morning. St. Jacob's had more people in the nave than the last few weeks. More people made it a little warmer, which was good.

Music was as bad as usual. Sang anyway. I like the old songs.

Sermon was better than usual. No one fell asleep, although old man Schickelgruber was breathing so loud he might have been snoring while standing.

Broke my fast after church. Spent the afternoon reading *The City of God*. St. Augustine is hard to understand, and my Latin is not as good as it should be, but I'll keep trying.

Was supposed to meet Cousin Johann at The Green Horse tonight, but he didn't come, so spent the evening meditating on St. Augustine.

A productive holy day.

Recited evening prayers, so now to bed.

From the Journal of Philip Fröhlich
23 October 1634

Monday
Breakfast–
2 barley rolls 1 pfennig
1 cup small beer 1 quartered pfennig

Supper–
1 wurst 1 pfennig
1 mug beer 2 quartered pfennigs

No dreams last night—that I remember, anyway.

Did Master Gröning's cash entries. Not very many this time. Hope that doesn't mean Master G will be running out of money.

Reviewed Saturday's entries. Found three errors in Thomas' work. Master Schiller was not happy. Unfortunately, found an error in my work as well. Master Schiller even unhappier. Should have shown him mine first, I think. Had to recopy my whole page. Thomas had to recopy two pages, but he still laughed at me. Miserable son of a spavined donkey and an ugly sow.

After work, went to Syborg's Books. Master Syborg the Younger—Master Johann, that is—talked to me about *Der Schwarze Kater*. He says this is supposed to be modeled after an up-time thing called a magazine. Another case where the up-timers appear to take a perfectly good word and make it mean something very different from its usual meaning. An up-timer magazine is not a storehouse, but is something like a book that is published periodically, and they sometimes have a common theme or element. Master Johann says *Der Schwarze Kater* will print stories by two up-timer writers, Master Poe and Master Lovecraft, and maybe others who would write the same kind of stories.

I asked Master Johann what an editor was. He says that is the person who puts together the different stories to make the magazine. Which explains why the book says to send new stories to Master Gronow, the editor.

Came home. Finished rereading *The Dunwich Horror.*

Recited evening prayers. Told God I want to be a writer. Asked Him to make that happen. And now to bed.

From the Journal of Philip Fröhlich
26 October 1634

>Thursday
>Breakfast–
>> *2 barley rolls 1 pfennig*
>> *1 cup small beer 1 quartered pfennig*
>
>Supper–
>> *1 cup cabbage soup, 1 wheat roll 4 pfennigs*
>> *1 cup small beer 1 quartered pfennig*

Don't remember dreams from last night, but awoke tired.

Thomas was discharged today. Master Schiller caught him taking a swig from the wine bottle we're not supposed to know that Master Schiller keeps hidden in his desk drawer. When Master Schiller shouted at him, Thomas dropped the bottle and it broke. Master Schiller chased him around the office four times swinging Master Gröning's old walking stick at him. I ducked under my table. Thomas yelped every time the stick hit him, and he finally tried for the door. He couldn't get the door handle to turn, and Master Schiller caught him by the collar just as the door began to open. After giving Thomas several licks with the stick on his back and butt, all the while yelling that he was a thief, Master Schiller threw wide the door and kicked him down the steps, shouting that Thomas should never show his face here again, just before he slammed the door.. By that point I had mopped up what little wine was left and was sweeping the glass up. Master Schiller said nothing, just closed the drawer on his desk and climbed back up on his stool. Put the pieces of glass in a box, got back up on my own stool, and drew forms the rest of the day.

Master Schiller gave me an extra pfennig with today's pay. Not sure why, but he still looked angry, so I didn't ask questions.

Stopped at Syborg's Book Store. Master Matthias himself made time to speak with me—but only because we were the only ones in the store. He asked me what I was reading. I told him *The City of God*. He looked a little surprised and asked me how I was doing with that. Told him it was hard, that I wasn't at all sure I was understanding it. He smiled, leaned closer, and whispered that he hadn't finished reading it either, and I should just keep slogging away at it.

Made so bold as to tell Master Matthias that I really like *Der Schwarze Kater*, and asked if there was anything else like it. He said, no, not exactly like it, although there were a couple of people trying to produce what the up-timers call "science fiction". Then he told me something that drove all other thoughts out of my head.

There will be a new volume of *Der Schwarze Kater* available next week! With newly translated stories by Masters Poe and Lovecraft!

Don't recall much after that. Hope I was polite when I left. I really don't remember. Don't remember walking back to my room. I just remember sort of waking up, sitting on my bed, holding a newsletter talking about *Der Schwarze Kater*. It's all wonderful until I see the price—two dollars.

I may be skipping some more meals.

Took three tries to recite evening prayers. Now to bed, and sleep—I hope.

Letters From Gronow

From the Journal of Philip Fröhlich
30 October 1634

Monday
Breakfast–
1 barley roll 2 quartered pfennigs
1 cup small beer 1 quartered pfennig

Supper–
1 barley roll 2 quartered pfennigs
1 cup small beer 1 quartered pfennig

Master Schiller brought a new boy into the office this morning. His name is Martin Niemoller. He's younger than I am, smaller, and very skinny. He doesn't talk much, either.

First thing I showed him how to do was draw forms. His first few lines weren't very straight, but he finally got the knack of it.

Reviewed the entries from late last week, found two errors in Thomas' last work. Showed them to Master Schiller. He took a deep breath, and muttered "Good riddance!" Then he took his own pen knife and scraped off the ink of those entries and rewrote them himself. We're not allowed to do that, but I guess Master Gröning lets Master Schiller.

Stopped at Syborg's Book Store after work. No, *Der Schwarze Kater's* new volume is not available yet.

Very unhappy and angry. After I got back to my room, decided that the anger was wrong. Made myself read an extra page from *The City of God* as penance.

Re-read *The Cask of Amontillado* to provide a sop for my hunger for the new volume.

Recited evening prayers. Then recited again to calm myself further. And now to bed.

From the Journal of Philip Fröhlich
1 November 1634

> Wednesday
> Breakfast–
>> *1 barley roll 2 quartered pfennigs*
>
> Supper–
>> *1 barley roll 2 quartered pfennigs*
>> *1 cup small beer 1 quartered pfennig*

No dreams last night.

Hungry, but saving pfennigs.

Martin asked me today if I read any. Told him yes. When he asked what I read, I told him *The City of God*. He said that was good. Then I told him about *Der Schwarze Kater*. He frowned and said that sounded demonic, or pagan at best. He spent the rest of the day drawing forms while humming hymns loudly—and badly.

Stopped at Syborg's Book Store after work. No, *Der Schwarze Kater's* new volume is not available yet.

Made myself read Leviticus Chapter 23 to draw down my frustration.

Recited evening prayers. And so to bed.

From the Journal of Philip Fröhlich
2 November 1634

> Thursday
> Breakfast–
>> *1 barley roll (old) 1 quartered pfennig*
>
> Supper–
>> *1 barley roll (very old) 1 quartered pfennig*

Dreamt I was being bricked into a room that I had been tricked into entering because I was told the new volume of *Der Schwarze Kater* was there. Had it in my hand when I awoke and discovered that it was a dream. Said several words I shouldn't have.

Master Schiller had me doing cash entries all day. Guess they were late in arriving or something. More than usual, too, which I guess is good. If Master Gröning has cash, he'll be able to keep paying me.

Tired after work. Wanted to just come back to my room, but made myself go by Syborg's Book Store. All of them were there when I walked in—Master Matthias, Master Johann, and Georg. Georg waved me over as soon as I came in. He had a big grin on his face, and he pulled something out from underneath the counter and put in my hands a copy of the new volume of *Der Schwarze Kater*. I started shaking.

"That's our last copy," he said. "Hope you've got the two dollars."

Very excited, told him I'd be right back with the money. He kind of frowned, said something about he didn't know, there were other people who wanted it. Master Matthias heard him and came over, told him to quit tormenting me, told me to go get my money and it would be here when I got back.

Ran back to the room as fast as I could. Dodged around walkers, under wagons, over crates and barrels, leapt over a donkey, tripped over a cane, rolled, and came up running. Heard some yelling behind me, kept going. Made it to my rooming house with no further mishaps and tore up the stairs to my room. Pried up the loose floorboard and pulled out my coin sack, ran back downstairs and back to Syborg's, if not quite as fast. Was panting heavily when I got there.

Counted out two dollars' worth of pfennigs on the counter. Master Matthias himself handed me my new volume of *Der Schwarze Kater*. Hurried home, not quite as recklessly as before. Didn't want to drop it. Lit a candle stub, began reading *The Fall of the House of Usher*.

Candle is dying, can't keep eyes open, want to finish story, but can't. So frustrated almost weeping.

Stumbled through evening prayers. Bed.

From the Journal of Philip Fröhlich
3 November 1634

>Friday
>Breakfast–
>>*2 barley rolls 1 pfennig*
>>*1 cup small beer 1 quartered pfennig*
>
>Supper–
>>*1 cup cabbage soup 2 pfennigs*
>>*1 barley roll 2 quartered pfennigs*
>>*1 cup small beer 1 quartered pfennig*

Exhausted this morning. Don't remember dreams, but must have had some, because I was so tired. Felt hungover, but wasn't drunk.

Head hurt all day. Wish I had some of Dr. Gribbleflotz's little blue pills.

Martin was humming hymns again today. Badly. Finally told him that if he couldn't do a tune better than that in public, he should be silent, as hymns were supposed to be a praise to God, and what he was doing was an insult. He looked at me shocked and almost on verge of tears, I think, but he shut up. Master Schiller frowned at me, but said nothing. It was worth it, because it was quiet the rest of the day.

Didn't visit the bookstore after work. Just ate supper and went home. Felt better after the soup.

Finished *The Fall of the House of Usher* by Master Poe. Master Lovecraft's story is *The Doom That Came to Sarnath*. Forced myself to not read it tonight so I can make the magazine last longer.

Recited evening prayers. Decided I was rude to Martin. Will apologize. Recited evening prayers again.

Now to bed.

Letters From Gronow

From the Journal of Philip Fröhlich
5 November 1634

> **Sunday**
> **Breakfast–**
> > *Fasted*
>
> **Lunch–**
> > *1 wheat roll 3 pfennigs*
> > *1 sausage 2 pfennigs*
> > *1 cup small beer 1 quartered pfennig*
>
> **Supper–**
> > *1 wurst 1 pfennig*
> > *2 mugs beer 1 pfennig*

Lord's Day, Lord's work.

Muddled dreams last night. Woke up twice.

Church this morning. St. Jacob's had fewer people in the nave. Gossip is that some people have been sick, rumors of plague were whispered about, even though it's winter.

Music was even worse than usual. Sang anyway.

Sermon was no better than usual. No one fell asleep, but suspect that may be because with fewer people, the nave was colder than usual. Old man Schickelgruber wasn't there, so it was a bit quieter.

Broke my fast after church. Spent the afternoon reading more of *The City of God* and thinking about it. St. Augustine is still hard to understand.

Did meet Cousin Johann at The Green Horse tonight, and he explained one of my problems with St. Augustine, but told me he would have to think about the other one.

Even so, a productive holy day.

Recited evening prayers, and now to bed.

From the Journal of Philip Fröhlich
6 November 1634

>Monday
>Breakfast–
>>*1 barley roll 2 quartered pfennigs*
>
>Supper–
>>*1 barley roll 2 quartered pfennigs*
>>*1 winter apple 1 pfennig*
>>*1 cup small beer 1 quartered pfennig*

I apologized to Martin Niemoller for being rude to him last week. Then I told him he still needed to learn his hymns better, as it's disrespectful to God to sing them badly. He tried to tell me that he's doing the best he can. I told him he needs to learn better, but not here. It's distracting.

Master Schiller commended me for apologizing, then told Martin I was right, and set him to work drawing more forms. He is getting the lines straighter than he was.

Reviewed the entries from late last week, found no errors. Pleasant surprise after following behind Thomas for so long. Showed the pages to Master Schiller. He looked somewhat glad. He said Master Gröning would be pleased.

Have an idea for a story! It came to me while I was looking at the entries, and almost distracted me from the work.

Was so involved in thinking about the story idea this evening, didn't even read any of the new *Der Schwarze Kater*. Was surprised when I noticed that.

Eventually recited evening prayers. Then recited again to calm myself more. Now to bed.

Letters From Gronow

From the Journal of Philip Fröhlich
11 November 1634

    Saturday
    Breakfast—
        1 barley roll 2 quartered pfennigs
        1 cup small beer 1 quartered pfennig

    Supper—
        1 barley roll 2 quartered pfennigs
        1 cup small beer 1 quartered pfennig

Master Gröning only hires us for a half day on Saturdays. Old miser. But he still expects near a full day's ledger entries from us.

Today I was glad to leave after noon, as it gave me a chance to run to my room and work on my story. And I finished it.

That felt good. That felt really good. I was almost dancing in the room when I got done.

After a little while, I picked it up and read it. I like it.

So, I will fold it up and put the address on it and take it to Master Gronow's offices and submit it.

∞ ∞ ∞

Back. Found Master Gronow's office in the building where the magazine said it would be. The door was closed and locked, which did not surprise me, but there is a slot cut in the door with a sign above it that says "Submissions", so after a moment I dropped the story through the slot. And as soon as I let go of it I wanted to take it back, but my hand wouldn't reach through the slot far enough to pick it up where it fell. So I leaned against the door and prayed about it.

Ate supper on the way home.

When I returned to my room I treated myself to *The Doom That Came to Sarnath*. Very fine.

Still I worry about my story.

Recited evening prayers. Now to bed.

From the Journal of Philip Fröhlich
15 November 1634

>Wednesday
>Breakfast–
>>*1 barley roll 2 quartered pfennigs*
>>*1 cup small beer 1 quartered pfennig*
>
>Supper–
>>*1 barley roll 2 quartered pfennigs*

No dreams last night.

Today a messenger stepped inside the office. Master Schiller held out his hand, but the messenger stood and said, "This here message is for nobody but Philip Fröhlich."

Master Schiller frowned, but pointed at me, and the messenger stepped over to hand me an envelope before he ducked his head in a bow—to me!—and turned and left.

"If that is not part of the business of Master Gröning, you will leave it alone until your day is done," Master Schiller said. His face looked like he was tasting something sour. I stuffed it inside my shirt, and didn't open it until I got back to my room.

14 November 1634
Master Philip Fröhlich

I have received what appears to be a story submission to *Der Schwarze Kater* magazine with your name and contact address on the outside. Unfortunately, at this time I cannot publish your story, mostly because I cannot read the blasted thing.

Letters From Gronow

First, I do understand if you are not able to afford one of the new Goldfarb und Meier typewriting machines. You will notice that, as much as I personally lust after one, this response is written with pen and ink. You will also notice that my letter is perfectly legible, with well-formed characters inked on the page. Sadly, your story was not. Pencil written on cheap tan paper does not make for a readable page, and the smudges and attempted erasures simply make it illegible.

Second, your handwriting, from what I could detect of it, is execrable. Your school teacher would be chastised if I knew who he was.

Third, it is simply not permitted to spell the same word three different ways on one page. I suggest you pay attention to the Bible as translated by Martin Luther. However he spelled a word is how it should be spelled in writing.

I hesitate to say this, but if you can find a way to improve the presentation of your story, whose title I cannot decipher, you may resubmit it.

Good day to you.
Johann Gronow
Editor and Publisher
Der Schwarze Kater

David Carrico

Episode 2

Magdeburg
From the Journal of Philip Fröhlich
19 November 1634

> Sunday
> Breakfast–
> > *Fasted*
>
> Lunch–
> > *1 sausage 2 pfennigs*
> > *1 wheat roll 3 pfennigs*
>
> Supper–
> > *1 barley roll 2 quartered pfennigs*
> > *1 wurst 2 pfennigs*
> > *1 mug beer 1 pfennig*

ave not written in journal other than noting expenses since Wednesday afternoon.

No dreams last night. No dreams since Tuesday night.

Forced myself to go to church today. Didn't want to go. Haven't wanted to get out of bed since Wednesday. Haven't wanted to do anything since Wednesday. The message from Master Gronow crushed me. I had so hoped that I would see my story in *Der Schwarze Kater*, and it left me broken when it was rejected.

Master Schiller noticed it, and asked me what was wrong. All I could do was shake my head.

Even Martin could tell something was amiss, and found the courage or the charity to ask what was wrong and if he could do anything. Again, all I could do was shake my head.

Thursday. Friday. Saturday. Broken inside. Avoided Syborg's Books. Came home. Ate bites of bread that were dry as dust and bitter as wormwood. Sat in the dark until sleep overcame me. Offered meaningless prayers.

Today, didn't want to go to church. Pulled the blanket over my head and resisted getting up so strongly, but a voice in the back of my mind—my conscience, my guardian angel, my patron saint, who knows—told me that it was when I least want to assemble with the body as St. Paul instructed that I most need to. I could not argue with that, and so, slowly, reluctantly, I forced myself to arise, and wash, and don my best clothing.

At church the music seemed dreary, and I did not sing. The reading was meaningless to me, and I did not listen. Then came the homily, from old Pastor Gruber who sometimes fills the pulpit at St. Jacob's. The leaders really need to appoint a new pastor for us. I know the church is small and poor, but we need a regular pastor as much as the other churches do.

Pastor Gruber talked about making our lives a pleasing offering to the Lord. He talked about how craftsmen and artists and musicians spend years learning and practicing and honing their crafts and arts and skills so they could make things of beauty. He even talked about a famous musician from the future of Grantville, one of the greatest musicians ever, who wrote "Soli Deo Gloria"—For the Glory of God Alone—on the manuscripts of his greatest works. He ended by quoting a verse from

Ecclesiastes. He said, "Whatsoever thy hand finds to do, do it with all thy might."

It was like I woke up. It was like Master Schiller slapped the back of my head and said, "Pay attention!" After that moment, I could only think of that verse, even after church as I was eating my lunch.

When I got home, I read through Ecclesiastes in my Bible until I found the verse in chapter 9, and it said exactly what Pastor Gruber had said.

Thought about that the rest of the day, even as I read a few more pages from *The City of God*, and as I ate supper.

Decided that I was a writer—that I am a writer—and if it takes me years to learn my art, so be it. Master Gronow will be my judge, but always Soli Deo Gloria.

Recited evening prayers. And now to bed.

From the Journal of Philip Fröhlich
20 November 1634

> Monday
> Breakfast–
>> *2 barley rolls 1 pfennig*
>> *1 cup small beer 1 quartered pfennig*
>
> Supper–
>> *1 wurst 1 pfennig*
>> *2 mugs beer 1 pfennig*

Vague recollections of dreams, but obviously nothing strong if can't recall them.

Felt better at work. Caught Master Schiller looking at me with his eyebrows raised. When I grinned at him, he nodded and returned to his work.

Reviewed last week's work. Only found one error on one of Martin's pages. None on mine, which I don't understand how that is. I was so lost after Wednesday. *Deo gratias*, nonetheless. Master Schiller must be in a good mood, because when I showed him the error, he didn't shout at Martin or beat him with the ferrule, he just told him to copy the page over.

At the end of the day, told Master Schiller that I wanted to take today's pay in candle stubs and quill feathers—left wing ones, because they're cheaper. He didn't quite frown, but asked me why. Told him I'm going to be a writer, and I need to practice my writing so that the editor will take my work. At that, his eyebrows went up again, but he just said, "St. Paul guide your hand, then," and let me pick my own quills.

Tonight I took Master Gronow's letter and practiced writing some of the words from it. This may take longer than I thought it would. Endure. Persevere. Perfect.

Recited evening prayers. And now to bed.

From the Journal of Philip Fröhlich
21 November 1634

Tuesday
Breakfast–
1 barley roll (old) 1 quartered pfennig

Supper–
1 barley roll 2 quartered pfennigs
1 cup small beer 1 quartered pfennig

Dreams last night were strange.

Posted Master Gröning's cash entries today. Looked odd. Not very many entries, but one of them was large.

Otherwise did what Master Schiller told me to do.

Did ask Master Schiller if I could help with the writing that has to be done. He gave me a funny look. Told him it had been so long since I had written regularly, that I was afraid I was going to forget how. He laughed, then said that the hand I had learned in school was probably different than what was used by the factors and merchants and masters like Master Gröning. I said I would try. He gave me an old letter and some scrap paper. Wasn't so different from what I saw in school or what Master Gronow's letter looked like. Spent the rest of the day at copying parts of the old letter, showed the best of it to Master Schiller, he nodded and said I might be useful at that.

Went home. Re-read part of the new volume of *Der Schwarze Kater*, looked at the last page where it says how to send stories to Master Gronow. Looked different. Got out the first volume, compared the two pages. It is different. And now I know why Master Gronow did not send my story back to me.

Took a deep breath. Recited evening prayers. Now to bed.

From* Der Schwarze Kater, *Volume 2
Black Tomcat Magazine Submissions

We recommend you keep a personal copy of your story. All submissions become the personal property of the publisher upon receipt, and will not be returned, regardless of ultimate decision about publication. Allow for six months of mail and processing time before querying as to the publication decision.

From the Journal of Philip Fröhlich
22 November 1634

>Wednesday
>Breakfast–
>>*None*
>
>Supper–
>>*2 barley rolls 1 pfennig*
>>*1 cup small beer 1 quartered pfennig*

Dreams last night. Woke up twice.

Overslept this morning. Somehow the church bells didn't wake me. No breakfast. Threw on clothes, ran through streets, down alleys, jumped a fence to run across a lot and jumped another fence on other side, arrived at work just after Master Schiller had unlocked doors and entered. Came in on heels of Martin. Master Schiller raised one eyebrow when he saw me, but shook his head and said nothing.

Martin was set to logging the orders today. Watched over him for a while, then started doing the cash entries. More of them than usual again. Said that to Master Schiller. He nodded, said that the war was creating opportunities.

Reminded Master S about wanting to write more. He pulled a document out of the stack on his desk, told me to make a copy. Six pages! Spent rest of day copying it, only got first two pages done. Think he did that on purpose. Lots of words I did not know.

Starting writing my story again tonight, with ink. Being careful about letters. Taking longer the second time because of that, and because I have to stop and think after every few sentences about what I had done in the story or how I had said things. Understand now why I should keep a copy for myself, but that's going to almost double the time it takes to prepare a story. But I need to know what I've done, and no one in

Magdeburg has any of the incredible Grantville machines that can automatically make pages of book stuff. Which is too bad. I think that must be really neat.

Read parts of the new *Der Schwarze Kater* again. The other stories are good, but not as good as Master Poe or Master Lovecraft. I shiver when I read their work. I am not as good as the others, but I will be one day. I will be better, one day. Maybe not as good as Masters Poe and Lovecraft. But to be almost as good as them would be a fine thing.

Recited evening prayers, and now to bed.

From the Journal of Philip Fröhlich
24 November 1634

>Friday
>Breakfast–
>>*1 barley roll (old) 1 quartered pfennig*
>>*1 cup small beer 2 quartered pfennigs*
>
>Supper–
>>*1 barley roll 2 quartered pfennigs*
>>*1 cup small beer 1 quartered pfennig*

Had dreams last night. Woke up thrice, gasping.

Martin was logging more orders today. I made some cash entries, then finished the last two pages of the document Master Schiller told me to copy. He looked at it, pointed out words where my hand was not regular, told me to copy it again. All of it. Joy.

Did ask him what the words I didn't know mean. He told me some of them, told me the rest were lawyer's words and even he wasn't sure what they meant. Seems like it would be a fine thing to be a lawyer and get to use words that other people don't know.

Looked at what I've been writing when I got home tonight, decided my hand with the story wasn't any better than my hand at work. Started over with that as well. Joy.

Recited evening prayers. Now to bed.

From the Journal of Philip Fröhlich
10 December 1634

> Sunday
> Breakfast–
>> *Fasted*
>
> Lunch-
>> *1 sausage 2 pfennigs*
>> *1 wheat roll 3 pfennigs*
>
> Supper–
>> *1 barley roll 2 quartered pfennigs*
>> *1 wurst 2 pfennigs*
>> *1 mug beer 1 pfennig*

No dreams last night that I remember, although I woke up a bit weary.

Went to church at St. Jacob's this morning. Music was better than usual, but I would have sung anyway. Reading was for Advent. Couldn't help but think that Herod was a greater monster than anything from the minds of Masters Poe and Lovecraft.

Homily was by Pastor Gruber again. I like him. He's pretty old—white hair, anyway—and his mind wanders a bit, and his voice keeps getting softer every time he preaches, but his homilies are always interesting, and about people, instead of just about big theology words. I know the theology is important, but sometimes I just need to hear how people are supposed to be. Including me.

Read more of *The City of God*. Does anyone really understand St. Augustine? I'll keep trying. Johann is having trouble getting it all into my head. Not sure he really understands it, though.

After having started my story over twice, I think my hand at writing is finally where it needs to be. Master Schiller said as much for the latest document he had me write. So when I get this version done, I'll be ready to submit it back to Master Gronow. After I make a copy for myself, that is.

Recited evening prayers, and now to bed.

From the Journal of Philip Fröhlich
13 December 1634

>**Wednesday**
>**Breakfast–**
>>*1 barley roll 2 quartered pfennigs*
>>*1 cup small beer 1 quartered pfennig*
>
>**Supper–**
>>*2 barley rolls 1 pfennig*
>>*1 cup small beer 1 quartered pfennig*

Woke up sweating. Usually means I dreamt, even though I don't remember any.

Master Schiller had me copying documents all day, new documents these were, that I hadn't seen before. Some new words I hadn't seen before in them, but when I asked Master S about them he said they were more lawyer words and to just copy them as they were. The amount of money mentioned in them made me gulp. I didn't know anyone had that much money, even Master Gröning. But he wasn't the only person mentioned, so it must be something they're all sharing in, or something. Still, had to concentrate extra hard to keep my hand steady for a while.

Stopped at Syborg's Books after work. Master Matthias himself was there and greeted me with a smile. He asked me if I was still reading St. Augustine. I said yes, and that I was still struggling with it. He laughed and said so was he. I asked him if there was going to be another book of *Der Schwarze Kater,* and he said yes, but probably not until February.

So I need to start saving my pfennigs now, to have my two dollars ready when the next book comes out.

Maybe I can have my new story turned in before that. Wouldn't it be fine to see it in those pages?

Recited evening prayers, and now to bed.

From the Journal of Philip Fröhlich
16 December 1634

Saturday
Breakfast–
>*2 barley rolls 1 pfennig*
>*1 cup small beer 1 quartered pfennig*

Supper–
>*1 wurst 2 pfennigs*
>*1 mug beer 1 pfennig*

Dreamt I was sitting in a classroom and St. Augustine was teaching. Woke up in the middle of him about to apply the ferrule because I couldn't explain *The City of God.* Was really glad that I woke up.

Master Schiller told me today that he was going to make me clerk over the contracts and agreements, and I would have to keep them straight and organized and make all the copies and things. It will also raise my pay by two dollars a day. I will be getting twelve dollars a day starting next Monday. That means I'll be able to buy the next *Der Schwarze Kater* and still eat something every day. That will be nice.

Was so excited about that it was hard to concentrate on finishing the story, but I was able to do that tonight. All done, and in my best hand. And I think I spelled the words right—or at least the same way. Something to thank God for in church tomorrow.

Recited evening prayers. Now to bed.

From the Journal of Philip Fröhlich
18 December 1634

    Monday
    Breakfast–
        2 barley rolls 1 pfennig
        1 cup small beer 1 quartered pfennig

    Supper–
        1 sausage 2 pfennigs
        1 cup small beer 1 quartered pfennig

First day as contracts clerk. Had to make copies of two agreements. Had to find them first. What a mess. Going to have to figure out how to make sense out of the contracts. All scattered around, all in different drawers and stacks and kinds of folders. Hard to make sense, even harder to find. Now I know why he wanted me to become the clerk. *Scheisse.* I mean, I know that's rude and vulgar and St. Paul says not to be that way, but honestly . . .

Also had to review the entries from last week. No errors. Master Schiller was pleased by that.

Martin is doing pretty well. Not sure he's going to be able to keep up with everything after I start spending more time on contracts, though.

Started writing out my copy of my story tonight. Slow going, because I want it to be as good as the original that I will give to Master Gronow. Don't have to think as much about what to write, but keeping my mind on the copying is just as hard as copying a contract, even though I wrote what I'm copying. Haven't figured out why, yet.

Read *The Fall of the House of Usher* from the second *Der Schwarze Kater* again tonight. Even though I have read it at least twice before, Master Poe still strikes sparks in my soul. Will I ever be able to touch someone like he touches me? I don't know. I hope so. To know that I can touch another soul with my words and make them feel what I feel, that would be wonderful.

But enough for tonight. Recited evening prayers. Now to bed.

From the Journal of Philip Fröhlich
21 December 1634

Thursday
Breakfast-
2 barley rolls 1 pfennig
1 mug beer 1 pfennig

Supper–
1 wurst 2 pfennigs
1 mug beer 1 pfennig

Dreams last night, mostly running with someone chasing me. Didn't get caught, but was sweating again when I woke up.

Have set aside the two dollars for the next *Der Schwarze Kater*. Able to afford more food after paying the rent, paying a tithe to the church, and putting a little back for an emergency and for a new coat. This one is about to unweave itself, it is so old and so threadbare. It's like it invites the wind to come in rather than holds it off. If I wanted to, I could probably net fish out of the river with it. Mother would be ashamed to see me in it.

Finished figuring out what I want—or need—to do to get Master Gröning's contracts and agreements organized. Had a long talk with Master Schiller about it. He finally agreed, but really resisted at first because he didn't want to spend the money for the new folders and labels and shelves. Not going to list the details here, but it's going to take some work to get everything pulled together and sorted and put in new folders and labeled.

Almost halfway done in copying my story, but it's going slow. Have been really tired in the evenings this week. Haven't even gone by Syborg's Books. May have to try the coffee I hear everyone talking about, but it's so expensive.

Done for the night. Recited evening prayers. Now to bed.

From the Journal of Philip Fröhlich
22 December 1634

>**Friday**
>**Breakfast–**
>>*1 sausage 2 pfennigs*
>>*1 mug beer 1 pfennig*
>
>**Supper–**
>>*1 wheat roll 3 pfennigs*
>>*1 mug beer 1 pfennig*

Dreams last night. Dreamt I was flying through the air, arms spread out like wings. Could look down and see Magdeburg below. Could tell it was Magdeburg because of the river and the Dom. Wonder if angels look down on us like that? That would be so fine a thing, to see the world from the eye of a soaring bird—an eagle, maybe, or a raven or cuckoo.

Master Schiller announced that Master Gröning had decided to follow the up-time practice of closing for Christmas Day. Will enjoy the day, attending the mass at St. Jacob's. Will miss the pay, though.

Master Schiller brought a small gift for Martin and me: a small package of raisins for each of us. I tried a few. They were tough and chewy, but sweet, so sweet. It was all I could do to not devour them all right then, as Martin did. I wrapped the rest of mine back up in the paper and placed them in my kerchief and brought them home. I shall try to only eat a few at a time, so that I can savor them for a long time. So sweet, even with the crunchy seeds in them.

Read Matthew Chapter 1 tonight. Will read Luke Chapter 2 tomorrow. Will probably hear one or the other as the reading at mass Sunday, but that's fine.

Spent some time copying my story. Almost done with the copy.

Just ate a couple of raisins.

Recited evening prayers. Now to bed.

From the Journal of Philip Fröhlich
24 December 1634

>**Sunday**
>**Breakfast–**
>>*Fasted*
>
>**Lunch-**
>>*1 sausage 2 pfennigs*
>>*2 wheat rolls 5 pfennigs*
>>*1 mug beer 1 pfennig*
>
>**Supper–**
>>*1 barley roll 2 quartered pfennigs*
>>*1 wurst 2 pfennigs*
>>*1 mug beer 1 pfennig*

Dreams last night. Awoke twice, but don't really remember them.

Attended St. Jacob's this morning. Music was pretty good, but it usually is during Advent. Sang with a will. Reading was for Advent again—or still, I should say. Homily was not as good as Pastor Gruber's last homily. Found myself thinking about Joseph, the husband of Mary. He must have been an unusual man.

Read five pages in *The City of God* this afternoon. Either I'm starting to figure St. Augustine out, or that was a section where he took it easy on the readers, because I think I may have understood what he was trying to say. Which means I probably have it all wrong. Will have to wait until Johann returns to Magdeburg from his trip to find out.

Ended up falling asleep in the middle of the sixth page. Woke up when the Vespers bells were ringing.

Copied half a page of the story. Have decided to wait until after Epiphany to send my story to Master Gronow. I'm sure he's a busy man during the holidays, and I would rather have his full attention. I think. Maybe. Surely.

Can't keep my eyes open.

Recited evening prayers. Now to bed.

From the Journal of Philip Fröhlich
28 December 1634

>Thursday
>Breakfast-
>>*1 wheat roll 3 pfennigs*
>>*1 mug beer 1 pfennig*
>
>Supper--
>>*1 wurst 2 pfennigs*
>>*1 mug beer 1 pfennig*

Dreams last night. Woke up at least twice. Don't remember them, though. Frustrating.

Martin came to work today. Got sick not long after he came in. Master Schiller managed to get him to the door before he puked. Then he shat his pants, nasty watery stuff from the stain it left. Master Schiller threw a few pfennigs at him and told him not to come back until he was well. Hope whatever he has is not catching. According to the up-timers, it is important to keep clean when sickness is around. Found some soap and took a little of our water to wash my hands. No towel, so had to wipe my hands on my trousers. Cold, but if it keeps my guts in place, worth it. Master Schiller saw what I was doing, and came and did the same thing.

So, ended up doing Martin's work instead of mine today. Or maybe I should say alongside mine, as I still had to do at least a few contract things in addition to all the entries. Master Schiller gave me a couple of extra pfennigs at the end of the day. Should have been more, but I'll take what he can give.

Stopped at Syborg's Books on the way home. According to Georg, the next book of *Der Schwarze Kater* is still going to be published in February. Frustrating. Want it NOW! Came home and re-read parts of the first one. Wish I could mend the torn pages. I know that's why I got it so cheaply, but I would really like to fix them before they get damaged more. I keep hearing about up-time stuff called 'tape', but probably isn't available in Magdeburg, and would probably cost a lot more than I can afford.

Finished copying my story. Compared it to the original version. Didn't see any differences. Just waiting for Epiphany now.

Ate some raisins.

Recited evening prayers. Now to bed.

Letters From Gronow

From the Journal of Philip Fröhlich
5 January 1635

    Friday
    Breakfast–
        1 wheat roll 3 pfennigs
        1 mug beer 1 pfennig
    Supper–
        1 sausage 2 pfennigs
        1 mug beer 1 pfennig

Martin came back to work today. He is very pale and skinny, but seems able to work. I will have to review his work closely, I think. But because he was there, I was able to spend a lot of time working on the contracts. Got a bunch of them put in their new folders and labeled and put in their right places on the shelves. Starting to make a difference in how the office looks, to not have piles of contracts just lying around.

Epiphany Eve tonight. Had the story with me, tucked inside my shirt. Address and stuff was on it. After work, ran to the building where Master Gronow's office is. The door was closed and locked again, which did not surprise me. The slot was still cut in the door, and it still had the sign above it that says "Submissions," so the story went into the slot. And just like last time, as soon as I let go of it I wanted to take it back, but too late. So I leaned against the door and prayed about it again.

Ate supper on the way home.

When I returned to my room I treated myself to *The Dunwich Horror*. Very fine.

Trying not to worry about my story. Hard.

Recited evening prayers. Now to bed.

From the Journal of Philip Fröhlich
12 January 1635

> Friday
> Breakfast–
> > *1 barley roll 2 quartered pfennigs*
> > *1 sausage 2 pfennigs*
> > *1 mug beer 1 pfennig*
>
> Supper–
> > *1 wurst 2 pfennigs*
> > *1 mug beer 1 pfennig*

No dreams last night. Was still nervous when I awoke.

Was right to be nervous. Today a messenger stepped inside the office. Same one as last time. Master Schiller held out his hand, but the messenger shook his head and said, "Master Philip Fröhlich."

Master Schiller waved his hand at me and turned back to his ledger. The messenger stepped over to hand me an envelope before he ducked his head in a bow and left.

Master Schiller said nothing, but when he looked back at me his face had a bit of a frown on it. So like last time, I stuffed it inside my shirt and got back to work. I didn't open the message until I got back to my room.

10 January 1635
Master Philip Fröhlich

It appears to me that you are going to be persistent. I can admire that in a man. It is, however, better to have something worthwhile to be persistent about.

I have received your most recent submission of a purported story for consideration of publication in *Der Schwarze Kater*. It is an improvement over your previous submission. I can at least read this one. Mostly. Your use of the local secretary hand is acceptable. Your executing it in a very small size, I assume so you can get as many lines on a page as possible, is not. Nor is filling the page from edge to edge, top to bottom and side to side. I am not going to ruin my eyesight trying to read this.

I see I must educate you on the practicalities of writing for a publisher.

When you submit a story, you are making a presentation to the publisher, in much the same way that an artist or a musician is making a presentation to a patron. It should represent your best work, and should be done so well as to make as good an impression as possible. You want to make it easy for the publisher to read it. The more things you do that hinder the reading of the work, the less likely the publisher is to buy your work—as you have now discovered twice.

So, first of all, use good quality octavo-sized paper of the same size no larger than eight inches wide by ten inches high. I found the multiplicity of paper sizes in your submission to be confusing at best and irritating at worst.

Second, space the lines at least 1/4 inch apart—3/8 inch would be better.

Third, leave blank margins of about one inch on all sides of each page.

I did not read the story. A few things caught my eye as I looked over the pages, though. It appears that your spelling has improved. Alas, it is now more evident that your grammar also needs work. I refer you again to the Bible as translated by Martin Luther. Model your grammar on his.

Finally, your title, *The Perils of Portia*—to quote the up-timers, lose it. Think of a better title.

I again hesitate to say this, but if you can correct the issues in your story noted above, you may resubmit it.

Good day to you.

Johann Gronow

Editor and Publisher

David Carrico

Der Schwarze Kater

Episode 3

Magdeburg
From the Journal of Philip Fröhlich
14 January 1635

    Sunday
    Breakfast—
        Fasted
    Lunch-
        1 sausage 2 pfennigs
        1 wheat roll 3 pfennigs
    Supper—
        1 cup sauerkraut 2 quartered pfennigs
        1 wurst 2 pfennigs
        1 mug beer 1 pfennig

Only noted expenses yesterday. Was dealing with message rejecting story.

No dreams last night. Don't remember any from the night before, either.

Attended church today. With Christmas and Epiphany concluded, music wasn't anything special. Did sing, but it was dull. Reading and homily weren't much better. Missed Pastor Gruber. But still felt better after it was over.

Master Gronow's letter did not crush me like the first one. Guess having been hit once, the second time was no surprise, or something. Learning the writing is going to take longer than I thought. Just means I am more determined to see my story in *Der Schwarze Kater*. Will have to work harder, is all. Pinned both letters to the wall where I can see them all the time.

Read three pages from *The City of God*. May be starting to understand this. That kind of scares me. Johann still in Jena, so no one to talk to about it.

I am a writer—new-born, perhaps—or newly-fledged—and definitely not far along the path to success. But I will get there. Will sell something to Master Gronow some day.

Recited evening prayers. And now to bed.

From the Journal of Philip Fröhlich
15 January 1635

    Monday
    Breakfast–
> *1 sausage 2 pfennigs*
> *1 wheat roll 3 pfennigs*

    Supper–
> *1 sausage 2 pfennigs*
> *1 mug beer 1 pfennig*

Dreams last night sort of pleasant. Met my guardian angel. Name's Max. Carries an up-time style rifle like the broadsheets show Julie Sims has. Says modern demons require more firepower. That's where I woke up. Wrote that down. Might could be a story someday.

Martin looked better at work today. Still way too skinny, but didn't look so much like a walking skeleton. His hands were steadier. Spent some little time praying that he will be well, and that whatever made him sick does not come my way.

Master Schiller looked at me closely when I came in. Said nothing, but I saw him look hard at me a couple of times in the morning. Finally asked him why. He said the last time I got a private message, I spent the next three days walking around and looking like someone standing ankle-deep in Hell with the tide rising, and he was wondering if I was going to do it again, because he wasn't paying me for that.

Told him no, that I was fine and that nothing in the messages would affect me like the first one did. He raised his eyebrows. Told him the editor refused my story, but told me that I could fix it and submit it again. Master S lowered his eyebrows and almost frowned, said I needed to do that. Told him I was. He nodded, turned back to his ledger, didn't look at me again.

Spent most of evening thinking about story. Glad I have a copy this time. Think I can see a way to make it work better. Will have to rewrite almost all of it, though. Start over, in other words. That will not be okay, but it is what Master Gronow was telling me to do. Sort of. I think. Yes.

Recited evening prayers, and now to bed.

From the Journal of Philip Fröhlich
16 January 1635

>Tuesday
>Breakfast–
>>*2 wheat rolls 5 pfennigs*
>>*1 mug beer 1 pfennig*
>
>Supper–
>>*1 sausage 2 pfennigs*
>>*1 mug beer 1 pfennig*

Dreams last night. Think I talked to Max again, but don't remember for sure.

Reviewed last week's entries. No errors, which was good, since Master Schiller and I did all the work last week. Martin started making cash entries again today. Let me get back to working on the contracts. Getting close to being halfway done with the reorganizing. Piles around the office and stuffed into drawers getting smaller. Good. Master S kind of smiles when he looks around.

Stopped at Syborg's Books tonight after work. Master Johann was there, and Georg. Asked them if new *Der Schwarze Kater* book was on their shelves yet. They both laughed. Master Johann said no, it will still be middle of February before it's out. Georg said that it isn't a book, that because *Der Schwarze Kater* is a magazine, they call it an issue, and this will be the third one. More up-timer weirdness with words, I guess.

So I have to wait another month, I told them. That's not fair. I want it now. They laughed, and told me I'd have to get in line, that there were a lot more people, and a lot more important people, who wanted it just as much as I did. I said my two dollars was just as good as anybody else's. Master Johann laughed again.

True, though. Doesn't matter if it's me, or Princess Kristina, or Prime Minister Stearns, or Emperor Ferdinand, when we're reading *Der Schwarze Kater* we're all the same.

Still thinking about how to recraft my story. Ideas rolling around in mind, but nothing has settled yet.

Enough for today.

Recited evening prayers. Now to bed.

From the Journal of Philip Fröhlich
19 January 1635

Friday
Breakfast–
1 cup sauerkraut 2 quartered pfennigs
1 barley roll 2 quartered pfennigs
1 cup small beer 1 quartered pfennig

Supper–
1 sausage 2 pfennigs
1 mug beer 1 pfennig

No dreams last night. Don't remember any, anyway. Probably good, as I'm not sure I'd want to see Max three nights in a row. Too strange.

Found real mess in office today. Box back in back room had a bucket sitting on the lid. Martin picked up bucket and knocked lid askew. He saw papers, and called me.

Six contract files. Such a mess. Somehow they had gotten wet sometime before. Dry now. Pages were stuck together in the folders, moldy. Stunk. Eeeeough. Made stomach churn at first.

Called Master Schiller to come see. He turned white when he saw the box, and even whiter when he saw the files. Old contracts, very important contracts, Master Gröning will not be happy if they are lost.

Green mold, not black. Could separate pages with some care. Have very thin-bladed knife in back room, old, not used for anything, but long enough to reach past mid-page of the contracts. Used it to pass between pages, gently gently gently to separate them. Got first folder separated, looked at mess. Master Schiller gave me ten dollars, told me to go buy a bottle of Genever and some clean rags.

Came back with Genever, moistened rag, dabbed at page. Master S told me not to scrub, it might rub the letters off. After several dabs, mold began to loosen and come off the page. Page is stained, but can read the words. Took close to half an hour to do one page front and back. Set it aside to dry. Whooph. Genever has strong odor, but is better than mold smell. Guess I know what I will be doing for several days. Master S wasn't so white after that, but he looked nervous. Kept looking at the door. Guess he was hoping Master Gröning wouldn't walk in or ask for those agreements.

Tired when I got to my rooms. Didn't try to start story writing. Just read parts of the second *Der Schwarze Kater*. After that, thought about story a bit, think I have way to start it.

Tired.

Recited evening prayers, and now to bed.

From the Journal of Philip Fröhlich
20 January 1635

    Saturday
    Breakfast–
        2 barley rolls 4 quartered pfennigs
        1 mug beer 1 pfennig

    Supper–
        1 sausage 2 pfennigs
        1 mug beer 1 pfennig

Dreamt in color last night. Max was in one of the dreams. His wings were blue. He still had his up-time rifle. Black rifle. Said he was sad because Julie Sims was a better shot than he was. Woke up at that, laughing.

Managed to get the first file's pages cleaned up in the half-work day today. Should be dry by Monday, will be able to put file back together, start cleaning the next one.

Genever is strong. Master Schiller says not to drink it. Wouldn't want to. Hurts my nose just to clean the pages with it.

Started writing the new tale for my story today. Changed title to *Portia's Lament*.

Started reading parts of the Bible again. Genesis, Exodus, Joshua, Samuel, Kings, the Gospels, Acts of the Apostles. Those parts where there are story-like sections. Looking to drink in how Martin Luther would tell stories. Master Gronow says that's the mark I need to hit. Best I'd learn from the best.

Also read more of the second *Der Schwarze Kater* again. Really want third issue. At least three weeks. Bah.

Recited evening prayers. Now to bed.

From the Journal of Philip Fröhlich
23 January 1635

> Tuesday
> Breakfast–
> > *1 sausage 1 pfennig*
> > *1 mug beer 1 pfennig*
>
> Supper–
> > *1 wheat roll 3 pfennigs*
> > *1 mug beer 1 pfennig*

Dreamt last night. Woke up twice. No Max this time.

Finished cleaning second file. More pages, more moldiness. Took longer. Had to buy another bottle of Genever. Moldy parts of pages don't look like the not moldy parts. Obvious stains. But can read the words pretty well. Must be good ink, soaked into paper. Will put second file back together tomorrow, start third file. Even more pages. Getting tired of smell of moldy paper and Genever. Master Schiller glad to see this done, anxious to finish all of them. Can only do so much at a time.

Reading through Samuel. Strong stories about strong people. Think I'm starting to see why Master Gronow told me to read the Bible. Master Luther's words simple, clear, but strong. Need to learn from that. Tell the story.

Wrote more on *Portia's Lament* tonight. Trying to shape it like Martin Luther would. Not as easy as it seems it should be. Will keep working on it.

Recited evening prayers. Now to bed.

From the Journal of Philip Fröhlich
26 January 1635

Friday
Breakfast–
> *1 cup sauerkraut 2 quartered pfennigs*
> *1 wheat roll 3 pfennigs*
> *1 cup small beer 1 quartered pfennig*

Supper–
> *1 wurst 2 pfennigs*
> *1 mug beer 1 pfennig*

Dreamt last night. Woke up three times, twice panting. Think it was because I reread both Lovecraft stories from the first two issues of *Der Schwarze Kater* again last night. Really wish third issue was out.

Finished cleaning the third file today. Three more to go. This is taking a lot longer than I wanted, but Master Schiller says it's very important and needs to be all I work on until they're done. He actually has been reviewing the daily work by Martin, so guess he's serious. Old contracts, old paper is all I know. Must be something special.

Reached a place in *Portia's Lament* where I saw why my first version didn't work. Or at least one reason why. Thought about it all evening. Think I understand why. Will try to fix tomorrow.

Read the story of David and Bathsheba from Samuel tonight. Hard story. David was stupid. But people are stupid sometimes, even smart people and good people. So I need to think about that for stories. Heroes can't be too good, or too smart, or too strong, or too anything, I guess, because real people usually aren't. Even saints aren't perfect. Think about that.

Enough for tonight. Recited evening prayers, and now to bed.

From the Journal of Philip Fröhlich
29 January 1635

Monday
Breakfast–
1 wheat roll 3 pfennigs
1 mug beer 1 pfennig

Supper–
1 fish stew 4 pfennigs
1 mug beer 1 pfennig

Dreamt last night. Don't remember anything, except Max was there. Funny how having a name can make something seem more real.

Never would have thought that Genever would be part of my work, but had to buy a third bottle today. Close to half-way through cleaning the fourth file. Not as much mold as the first three. That's good. Getting tired of doing this. Ready to get back to regular work. And really getting tired of the stink of old mold and old paper mixed with Genever. Eeeough. Makes my nose itch.

Worked on *Portia's Lament* tonight. Think I'm getting the story better. Have some ideas about how to make the copy I submit work better. Think my hand is getting finer. Spelling is good. Grammar . . . I need to be more careful.

Still reading in Samuel. David was a horrible father, his sons were mostly fools, and his wives weren't much better. How did he get to be king? If I tried to write a story like that, would anyone believe it? Maybe, maybe not. From all accounts the Romans were just as bad, if not worse. Dear God, how can You put up with us?

Recited evening prayers. Twice. Once for me, once for the emperor. If Gustavus Adolphus is no better served than David was, he's in trouble.

And now for bed.

From the Journal of Philip Fröhlich
2 February 1635

> Friday
> Breakfast–
>> *1 cup sauerkraut 2 quartered pfennigs*
>> *1 wheat roll 3 pfennigs*
>> *1 mug beer 1 pfennig*
>
> Supper–
>> *1 sausage 2 pfennigs*
>> *1 mug beer 1 pfennig*

Dreamt last night. Woke up sweating, so must have been a good one. But don't remember it.

Finally finished the last of the file cleanup today right before end of day. Hurrah! Master Schiller gave me five extra dollars with today's pay and thanked me for the hard work. That will pay for the next issue of *Der Schwarze Kater*, and then some.

Was on the fourth bottle of Genever. Master S took that. Fine with me. I never want to see or smell that again.

Portia's Lament is crawling out from under the tip of my quill. Slow, slow, slow. Think it is taking shape, though. Very different from *The Perils of Portia*. Having trouble believing what I wrote before, and thinking it was good. Eeeough.

Ash Wednesday before too long. Lent is coming.

February. New issue of *Der Schwarze Kater* should be out soon soon soon. Syborg's Books is going to see me every day from now until it does appear. I'm ready.

Excited. Anxious. Hard to calm down. But must calm down.

Three pages of *The City of God*. That weighted me enough for tonight.

Recited evening prayers. Now to bed.

From the Journal of Philip Fröhlich
4 February 1635

Sunday
Breakfast–
Fasted

Lunch-
2 sausage 4 pfennigs
1 wheat roll 3 pfennigs
2 mugs beer 2 pfennigs

Supper–
1 barley roll 2 quartered pfennigs
2 wurst 4 pfennigs
2 mugs beer 2 pfennigs

No dreams last night.

Attended church today. Attendance was light due to the blowing snow. Music was about as good as usual. Sang with feeling. Reading was good and clear. Pastor Gruber did the homily and talked about how the saints of old persevered in doing good even when those around them persecuted them. Didn't like that one as much as some of his others because it was so general. Like it better when he tells a story that has a point.

Pastor Gruber talked to me afterward. Everyone else left so quickly that it was only a moment before it was just him and me. He asked me what I thought of the day. Told him the truth about the homily. He sighed and said sometimes he had to preach what the Dom magister or the seasonal liturgy required, even if it didn't make for an engaging homily.

We ended up talking about St. Augustine, and Pastor Gruber invited me to eat with him. We ended up in a better tavern than I usually eat at.

He wanted to pay for my food, wouldn't let him. Told him to use it for someone who needed it worse than me. Food was good. Discussed *The City of God* almost all afternoon. He helped me understand some pieces that Johann hadn't been much help with. Enjoyed it.

Went home, spent more time with *Portia's Lament*. Another page done.

Reread *The Cask of Amontillado*. Almost didn't need to bother. Almost have it memorized, I think.

Ready for Issue 3. Now.

Recited evening prayers. Now to bed.

From the Journal of Philip Fröhlich
7 February 1635

> Wednesday
> Breakfast–
>> *1 sausage 2 pfennigs*
>> *1 wheat roll 3 pfennigs*
>> *1 mug beer 1 pfennig*
>
> Supper–
>> *1 wurst 2 pfennigs*
>> *1 mug beer 1 pfennig*

Dreamt last night. Woke up once for sure, maybe twice. Don't remember dreams, though.

Work was regular. More time spent getting agreements and contracts sorted, filed, and labeled. Maybe three-fourths done. Master Schiller likes what's happening. Says the office looks like a master's office should look, and he likes that I can find every contract in just a few minutes. Haven't seen any extra pay yet, but might. Regardless, will make my job easier, too, so good from that side of the table as well.

Martin still looks fragile from when he was sick, but puts in his full day and doesn't try to duck the work. Even when he is down he is better than Thomas was on his best days. Told Master S that. He agreed.

Stopped by Syborg's Books tonight, just like I did Monday and Tuesday. Wasn't really expecting anything when I went in, but Master Matthias waved me over as soon as I came through the door. Moments later, I was holding Issue 3! Swear my heart skipped beats. Dug out my two dollars and gave it to him, then left and ran back to my room.

Lit my candles, and settled in to read. Read Master Lovecraft's story first, *The Statement of Randolph Carter*. Felt the hair on my neck rising. Swallowed often. Found myself looking at shadows in the corners.

Then read Master Poe's story, *The Pit and the Pendulum*. Heart was racing when done. Could have sworn I heard a *swoosh* sound in the room.

Read both of them again. Just as good the second time.

Want to read again, but so tired. Can't keep eyes open.

Recited evening prayers. Twice.

From the Journal of Philip Fröhlich
8 February 1635

> Thursday
> Breakfast–
> > *1 cup sauerkraut 2 quartered pfennigs*
> > *1 wheat roll 3 pfennigs*
> > *1 mug beer 1 pfennig*
>
> Supper–
> > *1 sausage 2 pfennigs*
> > *1 barley roll 2 quartered pfennigs*
> > *1 mug beer 1 pfennig*

Dreamt last night. Really dreamt last night. Woke up four times, and was sweating from the first.

So tired this morning, but was worth it!

Thought of new stories all day. Not a good idea. Hard to focus on work. Don't think I made mistakes, but need to make sure tomorrow.

Read both of the new stories again, plus another of the other stories in the issue. It was good, if not equal of Masters Poe and Lovecraft.

Made myself set Issue 3 aside and work on *Portia's Lament*. Hard. Mind felt like a bee was buzzing around in it. Got maybe half a page done. Probably not any good . . . will look at it tomorrow; suspect will have to do over.

Looked at the page about how to submit stories. Requirements list is longer. Looks like I am contributing to the magazine. Just not the way I want to do it.

Enough for tonight.

Recited evening prayers. Now for bed.

From Der Schwarze Kater, Volume 3
Black Tomcat Magazine Submissions

Legibility is paramount. If we can't read your story, we won't buy it. To that end, we strongly recommend that your work be prepared with the new Goldfarb und Meier typewriting machine or something similar. If a true manuscript is presented, please use practiced penmanship and calligraphy. Standard Magdeburg and Thuringia secretary hands are acceptable.

Please use octavo-sized paper no larger than eight inches wide by ten inches high. All pages of a story submission should be approximately the same size.

If the story is typed, please insert a blank line between each line of lettering. If the story is written out, please space the lines about 3/8 of an inch apart. Either way, leave a blank margin of approximately one inch on all sides of each page. This facilitates both ease of reading and making comments or instructions on the page. Keep in mind that the easier it is for the publisher to read your work, the more likely it is to be published.

Our manual of writing style is Martin Luther's translation of Holy Scripture. All issues of grammar and word spellings will be decided in accordance with his practice. Note that familiarity with and practice of those guidelines improve your chances of having your story published. All things being equal, the story requiring the least amount of work on our part has the advantage.

Format the first page such that your name, contact address, and word count of your story are in the upper left hand corner, the story title should be in the upper edge center, and page number in the upper right corner. Subsequent pages should contain your surname and abbreviated title in the upper left corner and page number in upper right corner. Page numbers are important. If your work gets dropped, we need to be able to put the pages back in the right order.

We recommend you keep a personal copy of your story. All manuscripts become the personal property of the publisher upon receipt and will not be returned, regardless of ultimate decision about publication. Allow for six months of mail and processing time before querying as to the publication decision.

From the Journal of Philip Fröhlich
10 February 1635

> Saturday
> Breakfast–
>> *1 sausage 2 pfennigs*
>> *2 barley rolls 1 pfennig*
>> *1 mug beer 1 pfennig*
>
> Supper–
>> *1 wurst 2 pfennigs*
>> *1 barley roll 2 quartered pfennigs*
>> *1 mug beer 1 pfennig*

Dreamt last night. Really dreamt. Woke three times, last time confused as to where I was. Took a little while to realize there was no pendulum in my room.

Quiet day at work today. Got most of the remaining contracts reviewed and filed and labeled. Maybe one more day to be done. Not sure what I'll do after that, but Master Schiller will certainly think of something.

Stopped by Syborg's books on the way back to my room, told Master Johann how much I liked Issue 3 of *Der Schwarze Kater*. He smiled, said that was good, and that he would tell the publisher.

Wrote more on *Portia's Lament*. Got several pages done, actually. Surprisingly. Think I'm over halfway done. Will keep working on it. Not sure, but I'm beginning to think this is going to be longer than *The Perils of Portia* was. Think I have an idea that will make it better for Master Gronow. Need to look into it.

Recited evening prayers. Now to bed.

From the Journal of Philip Fröhlich
11 February 1635

>Sunday
>Breakfast–
>>*Fasted*
>
>Lunch–
>>*1 wurst 2 pfennigs*
>>*1 winter apple 1 pfennig*
>>*1 mug beer 1 pfennig*
>
>Supper–
>>*1 barley roll 2 quartered pfennigs*
>>*1 wurst 2 pfennigs*
>>*1 mug beer 1 pfennig*

No dreams last night that I remembered after I woke up.

Attended church today. Attendance thin. Probably due to the weather. Music was not very good. Sang anyway. Reading was good and clear. Homily was dull. Two or three men around me were snoring. Haven't figured out how they can do that while they're standing, but they do.

Read more from *The City of God* during the afternoon. Five pages, I think. Either it's starting to make sense or my mind is fading, because I think I followed the argument. Johann is supposed to be back next week. Will ask him or Pastor Gruber.

More pages written for *Portia's Lament*. This will be my copy. Cheap paper, and I have corrected a few mistakes on it. When I am done, then I will prepare the very nice copy for Master Gronow. Very nice.

Ended the day by reading one of the new stories from *Der Schwarze Kater*. Good story. Almost as good as Master Lovecraft. Almost. Only reading one new story per night. Lasts longer that way.

I'll let this one stay.

Recited evening prayers, and now to bed.

From the Journal of Philip Fröhlich
13 February 1635

> Tuesday
> Breakfast–
>> *1 cup morning broth 2 quartered pfennigs*
>> *1 barley roll 2 quartered pfennigs*
>> *1 mug beer 1 pfennig*
>
> Supper–
>> *1 wurst 2 pfennigs*
>> *1 winter apple 1 pfennig*
>> *1 barley roll 2 quartered pfennigs*
>> *1 mug beer 1 pfennig*

Finally found someone who makes broth like Mama's. Little place between The Chain and St. Jacob's Church. Old woman runs it. Scrawny. No teeth. Mean cast to her eye. Someone called her Mama Schultz. Held a long meat fork in her hand and looked like she wasn't afraid to use it. But her broth tastes like Mama's. I'll go back.

Dreamt last night. Only one I remember was Max, holding his gun and saying over and over that he was almost as good a shot as Julie Sims now, and no demons better be coming around me. Laughed. Think I told him that any angel worth his wings would be at least as good as Julie Sims, and he should keep practicing. Wings are still blue.

Finished organizing the last of the contracts today. All have been found, put in the same kind of folder, labeled, and stored on the shelves behind my desk. Good. Glad that's done.

Now I have to make the searching charts, so I can find them easily without having to look at every folder. I think I'll have one chart that lists all the contracts by the names of the people involved, and one that lists by the kind of contract it is, and maybe one that lists them by date. This may take a while. Just when I thought I was done with it.

But Master Schiller was really happy when I got done, and gave me an extra ten dollars when he handed me today's pay.

Stopped by Syborg's Books on the way back to my rooms. Georg grinned at me and told me that it would be over two months before the next issue of *Der Schwarze Kater* comes out. He was making fun of me, but I just laughed. It is kind of funny how attached I have become to the magazine.

Asked Georg if there are any other books or magazines like *Der Schwarze Kater*. He told me not yet, but that there are some rumors floating around of a couple of new ones that might come out before too long. Told him to let me know when they do. Also, if they get any English or American books or magazines like these, I want to know. He asked me if I could read English. I said I would learn.

And I would.

Wrote two pages on *Portia's Lament*. Story is approaching its . . . I'm sure there's a word for it, but Master Gronow hasn't told it to me yet. High point? Peak? Where things happen and make the story conclude. Feel like I've been climbing a big hill and about to reach the top.

So. Done for the night.

Recited evening prayers. Now to bed.

From the Journal of Philip Fröhlich
16 February 1635

> Friday
> Breakfast–
> > *1 cup morning broth 2 quartered pfennigs*
> > *1 wheat roll 3 pfennigs*
> > *1 mug beer 1 pfennig*
>
> Supper–
> > *1 sausage 2 pfennigs*
> > *1 wheat roll 3 pfennigs*
> > *1 mug beer 1 pfennig*

Stopped at Mama Schultz's for breakfast. Mean as ever, but broth still good. If I ran a tavern, I'd hire her to cook and to keep peace in the common room. One jab from her meat fork, and everyone would settle down.

Dreamt last night. Max showed up again. Told me he was worried. He'd been talking to Master Poe's guardian angel, and he says this business of being a writer may cause the demons to come flocking. He's not sure he can handle all that. I asked him was he my guardian angel or not. He said yes. I said God assigned him. He said yes. So God thinks you can do it, I said. And you can shoot as good as Julie Sims. He got this big smile, and then I woke up. Weird, as the up-timers say. Wonder if that's a portent?

Finished my searching charts today. Done. Showed Master Schiller. He liked it, and that it would make it easier to find contracts. Gave me a couple of extra dollars with today's pay.

Finished retelling *Portia's Lament* tonight. Think it's good. Better than it was, anyway. Tomorrow will start working on the nice copy to give Master Gronow. Very nice.

Read last new story from third issue of *Der Schwarze Kater*. Think the third issue was better than the second, by a little bit, but not as good as the first issue. And Masters Poe and Lovecraft are still the best.

Recited evening prayers. Now to bed.

From the Journal of Philip Fröhlich
26 February 1635

> **Monday**
> **Breakfast–**
>> *1 sausage 2 pfennigs*
>> *1 wheat roll 3 pfennigs*
>> *1 mug beer 1 pfennig*
>
> **Supper–**
>> *1 sausage 2 pfennigs*
>> *1 barley roll 2 quartered pfennigs*
>> *1 mug beer 1 pfennig*

No dreams that I remember last night. Didn't wake up, either. Dull evening, I guess.

Master Schiller had me reviewing entries from last week, since my contract work was done. Didn't find any errors, but a couple of pages were kind of hard to read. Showed him, and he had Martin recopy one and me recopy the other. Was okay with that. Kind of good to do some numbers again.

Spent all Saturday and Sunday afternoons and evenings copying the new tale of *Portia's Lament*. Wrote some tonight, too. So far it looks really good. Master Gronow should be pleased with it. I think. I hope. Please.

Did some reading tonight in Kings. Found the stories of King Ahab. Not a good man. Not even a nice man. Makes King David look like a saint. And his wife is worse. Wonder how many bad kings and evil men in history were driven by their wives? Story there? Think about it. Same could be true of good kings and good men, but bad kings and men would probably make more enthralling stories. Think about that, too.

Started rereading third issue of *Der Schwarze Kater* again. Good stories. Tired. Eyes blurring.

Recited evening prayers. Now for bed.

From the Journal of Philip Fröhlich
6 March 1635

> Tuesday
> Breakfast–
>> *1 cup morning broth 2 quartered pfennigs*
>> *1 barley roll 2 quartered pfennigs*
>> *1 winter apple 1 pfennig*
>> *1 mug beer 1 pfennig*
>
> Supper–
>> *1 wurst 2 pfennigs*
>> *1 barley roll 2 quartered pfennigs*
>> *1 mug beer 1 pfennig*

Dreams last night. Don't remember much, except I think Max was lurking around the edges. Guess a guardian angel has to do his guarding some time.

Saw Master Gröning today for the first time in a long time. Master Schiller made us brush our clothes and shoes this morning first thing, and sweep the floor. He even brought in a bottle of good wine. The master looked old and tired, and had a really bad cough. Hurt to listen to him. Fancy clothes. Looked around, smiled, told us we were doing well, then took Master S into the back office and closed the door. Took the wine, too. Spent most of the morning in there. Came out, handed me and Martin both a five dollar bill, told us to keep doing good, and left. Master S said good job and told us to get back to the accounts.

Angry. With myself. Very angry. Was copying *Portia's Lament* tonight. Being very careful, making a really nice copy, over half-way done. Then tonight, sneezed really hard three times in a row. Knocked over the inkwell. Landlord's stupid table doesn't have well for inkwell, was sitting on tabletop. Had just refilled it, full of ink. Splashed over four pages. Tried to wipe it off. Didn't work. Will have to recopy those pages. Again.

Angry.

Made myself read ten pages in *The City of God*. Took that many to bank the fires of my anger. Calmer now. Just very unhappy. Sad, maybe. Waste of time, paper, ink. Not cheap.

Recited evening prayers. Three times. Now to bed, hope to sleep.

From the Journal of Philip Fröhlich
12 March 1635

> Monday
> Breakfast–
> > *2 barley rolls 1 pfennig*
> > *1 cup small beer 1 quartered pfennig*
>
> Supper–
> > *1 wurst 1 pfennig*
> > *1 mug beer 1 pfennig*

No dreams. Woke up tired, weary. May be why.

Martin had new shirt on today. New to him, anyway. Could see where seams had been changed to fit him. Still looked good. Need to think about that for me. Most of my shirts getting very thin, worn. Not sure they can be patched. Will find out soon, I'd guess.

Took until today to gather the money to replace ruined paper and spilled ink. Not cheap. Started copying from point where pages had been ruined. Got three done tonight. One tomorrow, and I'll be able to start copying the story from the point where I left off. Will push to finish soon. Want this in Master Gronow's hands as soon as possible.

Re-read *The Gold of the Rhine* story from first issue of *Der Schwarze Kater* again. Good story. Felt more like Master Lovecraft than Master Poe, but good story. River dragon was scary. Written by Master Klaus Wolfenstein. Not a common name, but that's what the magazine said in two places. Even without the name, can tell writer is a down-timer. After reading the Bible so much, word choices and stringing together makes patterns. Up-timer patterns are different.

Tired.

Recited evening prayers. Now to bed.

From the Journal of Philip Fröhlich
13 March 1635

>Tuesday
>Breakfast–
>>*1 cup morning broth 2 quartered pfennigs*
>>*1 barley roll 2 quartered pfennigs*
>>*1 mug beer 1 pfennig*
>
>Supper–
>>*1 wurst 2 pfennigs*
>>*1 barley roll 2 quartered pfennigs*
>>*1 cup sauerkraut 2 quartered pfennigs*
>>*1 mug beer 1 pfennig*

Dreamt last night. Don't remember much, but woke up twice.

Weather is starting to warm up a little. Snow melts a little during the daytime sun, then freezes into crusty ice. Makes walking to work a bit chancy in places. Four years ago would have said fun. Now just want to get places without falling and getting wet or colder. Does that mean I'm growing up?

Nothing remarkable at work. Master Gröning's cash entries up. Made copies of two new contracts, made folders, added to the searching lists. Martin continuing to improve, both health and work.

Copied the last ruined page, added two more new page copies. Keep this up, will be done with the new fine copy with three more nights of copying. Ready to get it done and turn it in.

Read a little. Tired.

Recited evening prayers. Now for bed.

From the Journal of Philip Fröhlich
16 March 1635

>**Friday**
>**Breakfast–**
>>*1 cup morning broth 2 quartered pfennigs*
>>*1 wheat roll 3 pfennigs*
>>*1 mug beer 1 pfennig*
>
>**Supper–**
>>*1 wurst 2 pfennigs*
>>*2 barley rolls 1 pfennig*
>>*2 mugs beer 2 pfennigs*

Stopped at Mama Schultz's for breakfast. Not many people there when I walked in. She nodded at me when she handed me my broth. Told her that hers tasted like my mother's. She stared at me for a moment, then put her meat fork down and patted me on the cheek. Said I was a good boy. Then picked up the meat fork and told me to get out of the way of the men behind me. I like her. Trying to think of a story to tell she could be in.

Quiet day at work. Master Schiller hasn't yelled about anything in days. Makes me afraid something bad is going to happen. Hope not. I like quiet. Let's me think about what stories I can tell.

Copied last four pages of *Portia's Lament* tonight. All done. I think. Need to look at it tomorrow when I'm awake and make sure it's right. So tired now can't even see the pages.

Recited evening prayers. Now for bed.

From the Journal of Philip Fröhlich
18 March 1635

>Sunday
>Breakfast–
>>*Fasted*
>
>Lunch-
>>*1 sausage 2 pfennigs*
>>*1 wheat roll 3 pfennigs*
>
>Supper–
>>*1 cup sauerkraut 2 quartered pfennigs*
>>*1 sausage 2 pfennigs*
>>*2 mugs beer 2 pfennigs*

Dreamt last night. Woke up at least once, but don't remember anything about them.

Attended church today. Music wasn't bad, so sang with a will. Reading and homily were average. Hope Pastor Gruber will speak again soon.

Spent afternoon looking over *Portia's Lament* one last time. Seemed to be as good as I could make it. Thought the presentation, as Master Gronow called it, was very nice. So took it by the office. Door was closed, as usual. Dropped it through the slot in the door and said a prayer, as usual, adding to it that I hope the response isn't as usual.

Johann was back in Magdeburg today, so we met at The Green Horse. Talked for hours. He told me about what he is doing at Jena, I told him about my new work for Master Schiller and my writing. Then we got serious and talked about *The City of God*. I surprised him some with what

I said. I could tell. That was a strange feeling, to have someone I look up to treat me with respect over something I say. Strange . . . but I think I could learn to like it.

Read from *The City of God* tonight. Several pages . . . at least eight. And it flowed. I'm able to follow what the saint was saying. That doesn't make me a saint, does it? Hope not. If so, I need to rethink what I think about saints.

Feel good. Feel nervous.

Recited evening prayers, and now to bed.

From the Journal of Philip Fröhlich
23 March 1635

Friday
Breakfast–
1 cup morning broth 2 quartered pfennigs
2 wheat rolls 1 pfennig
1 mug beer 1 pfennig

Supper–
1 wurst 2 pfennigs
1 winter apple 1 pfennig
2 mugs beer 2 pfennigs

Dreamt last night. Saw Master Poe's pendulum. Heard it swoosh. Woke up three times, dream kept coming back.

Nothing different at work today. Martin getting better at work.

Very nervous. No answer from Master Gronow. Know the page in the magazine says allow six months, but always before he's responded in a day or so.

Tried to read, but couldn't focus on either the magazines or *The City of God*. Finally ended up reading in the Bible. Samuel again. King Saul. Very strange man. Chosen by God, but went so wrong. How? Why? And why would God allow His chosen king to fail like that? Think about that.

Recited evening prayers. Now to bed.

From the Journal of Philip Fröhlich
24 March 1635

> Saturday
> Breakfast–
> > *1 barley roll 2 quartered pfennigs*
> > *1 mug beer 1 pfennig*
>
> Supper–
> > *1 sausage 2 pfennigs*
> > *2 barley rolls 1 pfennig*
> > *1 mug beer 1 pfennig*

No dreams last night. Don't remember any, anyway, didn't wake up in the night.

Should be careful what I wish for. Messenger brought Master Gronow's response to work today. Same messenger. Didn't even look at Master Schiller this time, just brought the envelope to me, handed it to me with a nod, and left.

Master S didn't even look at me. Put it in my shirt until I got home. Hard not to rip it open right then.

Looks like I have more work to do.

23 March 1635
Master Philip Fröhlich

No. Just . . . no.

I must deliver more lessons in presentation, I see. If you still have my response to your previous submission, please reread it. Take special note of the section where I stated that you need to make it easy for the publisher to read your work, and that if you do things that hinder the reading of the work, the more likely it is that the publisher will reject your submission. Make an extra special note that among those things that will certainly cause a publisher to reject your work is submitting a manuscript written with scarlet ink on bright yellow-tinted paper.

The contrast between those hues was painful to observe. Even now, my temples throb. I am on my second glass of wine, and expect to do more. Alas, my tin of Dr. Gribbleflotz's Sal Vin Betula is empty, or I would have ingested several of those as well.

Your purpose in preparing a manuscript is to make it as perfect as you can in normal preparation, so that the publisher's eye can simply glide over the page, taking in the story without stumbling over the letters. To be perfectly clear, plain white paper. Of as good a quality as you can afford, of course, but <u>Plain White Paper</u>. Do you understand that? And black ink. Not artistic blue, or pretentious purple, or any pastel shade, or even (shudder) red. <u>Black</u>. <u>Ink</u>. White paper, black ink, for maximum contrast and ease of reading. The publisher needs to be astounded by your story, not by your calligraphic artistry.

Having said that, I will confess that your illuminated capital that began the story was interesting. Distracting, but interesting. However, the drawings you interspersed throughout the work were, shall we say, tedious at best, and execrable at worst.

The two paragraphs I managed to read before my eyes closed in self-preserving rebellion seemed improved. And *Portia's Lament* is a marked improvement as a title. Nonetheless, it is not adequate. Conceive of another, please.

It is now with some trepidation that I say this, but when you correct the issues noted above, you may resubmit it.

Good day to you.

Johann Gronow

Editor and Publisher
Der Schwarze Kater

Episode 4

Magdeburg
From the Journal of Philip Fröhlich
25 March 1635

>Sunday
>Breakfast–
>>*Fasted*
>
>Lunch–
>>*1 sausage 2 pfennigs*
>>*1 winter apple 1 pfennig*
>>*1 wheat roll 3 pfennigs*
>
>Supper–
>>*1 cup sauerkraut 2 quartered pfennigs*
>>*1 mug beer 1 pfennig*

Dreamt last night, but nothing that I remember. Just enough to remember I dreamt.

Attended church today. Music was surprisingly good. Sang with a will. Reading and homily were about like usual.

Must be getting used to rejection. Master Gronow's letter not a great surprise, not a blow. Disappointing, but not crushing. Pinned it up on the wall next to the others. So, will learn from it. Still determined to see my story in *Der Schwarze Kater*.

Read four pages from *The City of God*. St. Augustine uses—used—words well. Plus, my Latin is getting better. I need to learn from him as well as from Martin Luther. Was hoping to see Johann today, because he is supposed to have been back from Jena by now, but no word of his return yet, so spent the evening alone.

I am a writer. From what Master Gronow says, I am not very good yet, but I will learn. Wonder if Master Poe and Master Lovecraft had their stories rejected? Surely not. If they did, wonder how long it took them to sell? How many words did they write?

Will sell something to Master Gronow someday.

Recited evening prayers. And now to bed.

From the Journal of Philip Fröhlich
28 March 1635

>Wednesday
>Breakfast–
>>*1 cup morning broth 1 pfennig*
>>*1 wheat roll 3 pfennigs*
>
>Supper–
>>*1 sausage 2 pfennigs*
>>*1 mug beer 1 pfennig*

Dreams, dark at first. Reminded me of *The Ore of the Gods* story from *Der Schwarze Kater*, Issue 3. By Augustus von Hohenberg, I think. Another down-timer writer. Story wasn't bad, but was set in a mine, dark underground. Shivery. Dream woke me at least twice. Then it shifted and Max appeared. Slept easy after that. May be something to this guardian angel thing after all.

Was doing cash entries today, something looked wrong. Entry was linked to a contract but did not look right. Pulled contract from shelf behind me, read through to the part about payments. Note for payment did not agree with contract terms. Showed to Master Schiller. He agreed, said he would show to Master Gröning. Gave me an extra two dollars at the end of the day.

Stopped by Syborg's Books on the way back to the rooms. Master Matthias was there. Asked about the next issue of *Der Schwarze Kater*. He grinned, told me first part of next month. So, need to save the money for it. Really want to read it now.

Think I have an idea on how to change the story to make it work better. Will not try any more stuff to make it fancy. Should have realized that would not impress Master Gronow. Stupid idea. Make the story good. Make the copy good. Nothing else matters.

Read *The Gold of the Rhine* from Issue 1 again, by Klaus Wolfenstein. Mentioned before. Meh. Not very scary. Dwarves were more like comedians than evilness. Made notes about making characters.

Recited evening prayers. Now to bed.

From the Journal of Philip Fröhlich
30 March 1635

> Friday
> Breakfast—
>> *1 cup morning broth 1 pfennig*
>> *1 winter apple 1 pfennig*
>> *1 barley roll 2 quartered pfennigs*
>
> Supper—
>> *1 wurst 2 pfennigs*
>> *1 mug beer 1 pfennig*

Dreams last night. Didn't wake up. Only thing I remember is Max telling me I'm a good writer and he enjoys being my guardian angel. Dream ended before I said anything, I think.

Master Schiller had me reviewing the Hamburg contract, the one I found the problem with a couple of days ago, and looking back through the earlier cash entries to see if there were any other problems. Didn't find any today, but not done yet. Master Gröning not happy about the problem, Master S says, but is happy that I found it. Guess that's good.

Continued work on new version of the story. Is working so far. Considering new title—*Portia in Tauris*. Lines up with old play someone told me about. We'll see if Master Gronow likes this one. Long way to go before he sees it.

Weary.

Recited evening prayers. Twice, because fell asleep the first time. Now to bed.

From the Journal of Philip Fröhlich
1 April 1635

> Sunday
> Breakfast–
>> *Fasted*
>
> Lunch-
>> *1 cup sauerkraut 2 quartered pfennigs*
>> *1 winter apple 1 pfennig*
>> *1 wheat roll 3 pfennigs*
>
> Supper–
>> *1 bowl fish stew 3 pfennigs*
>> *1 barley roll 2 quartered pfennigs*
>> *1 mug beer 1 pfennig*

Lord's Day, Lord's work.

Began the day with church. Music was good again. Two Sundays in a row. Unusual, but enjoyable. Sang with a will. Reading was good, Pastor Gruber did the homily. He spoke on the young boy who gave the loaves and fish to the Savior for the feeding of the five thousand. Everyone talks about the miracle of the feeding, but what about the miracle of the boy being right there, right then, with just that much food, and being willing to give up all that he had? From the smaller miracle came the larger one. Small things come first. No one does great things without doing small things first, not even the saints. Must think on that. Think that's true about lots of things.

Still haven't heard from or about Cousin Johann. Though he was supposed to be back from Jena by now. Starting to get worried.

Five pages read from *The City of God*. Beginning to love St. Augustine's words. Not sure I understand them all, but the way they flow, the way he can say such grand things, makes a chill run up my backbone sometimes.

Spent some time reading in Kings in the Bible, finished the story of Elijah and the priests of Baal. Glad that he won. Think I'm glad he killed them. Had to be a bloody mess, though. But it wasn't enough. Elijah wasn't the king's favorite then. Should have been. Should have won the fight with that. But didn't. Had to run for his life. So sometimes the story doesn't end up the way that people think it should. Sometimes the story is dark, or hard. How do I apply that to my life? How do I apply that to my writing? Think about that, too.

Oh, no dreams last night.

Recited evening prayers. Three times. Needed that many to be calm for some reason. So now to bed.

From the Journal of Philip Fröhlich
3 April 1635

Tuesday
Breakfast–
1 winter apple 1 pfennig
1 wheat roll 3 pfennigs

Supper–
1 sausage 2 pfennigs
1 mug beer 1 pfennig

Dreamt I was sitting at the Green Horse and Master Poe was sitting across from me and we were talking about writing. Wish I could remember what we said. I'd write it down.

Finished reviewing cash entries at work that tied to the Hamburg contract. Found a couple of other entries that didn't look right to me. Showed them to Master Schiller. Could tell he wasn't happy that I'd found them, but he said he'd show them to Master Gröning. Gave me an extra dollar at the end of the day.

Stopped at Syborg's Books. Master Johann was there. Asked him about the next issue of *Der Schwarze Kater*. He said maybe in a month it will be in their store. Showed him my extra dollar from today, told him I had my money ready. He laughed and promised I would have a copy.

Worked on *Portia in Tauris* tonight. New opening is done. Think it works better at getting reader's attention. Think I know where the story is going next. Will work on that tomorrow evening. Must remember to get some more candle stubs.

Recited evening prayers, and now to bed.

From the Journal of Philip Fröhlich
6 April 1635

Friday
Breakfast–

1 cup morning broth 1 pfennig
1 barley roll 2 quartered pfennigs
1 mug beer 1 pfennig

Supper–

1 bowl fish stew 3 pfennigs
1 mug beer 1 pfennig

Dreamt I was listening to Master Lovecraft and Master Poe talking. Some about life, some about writing, remember that much. Really wish I could remember everything they said. Stupid dreams. What good are they if you can't remember anything from them?

Master Schiller told me today that Master Gröning was very pleased that I had found the other problems with the Hamburg contract. Proves that the bastards in Hamburg, as the master put it, have been cheating for some time. He was ready to sue for breach of contract before, but his regular lawyer died, and he wasn't happy with any of the regular lawyers in Magdeburg. But there is a new lawyer who has opened offices in the city now, and the master is impressed with him, so they will probably act on this.

Hope the master wins, and hope it doesn't affect me.

More work on *Portia in Tauris* tonight. Seems to be going well—but then, I thought that about the first three versions of the story. Only time and Master Gronow will tell.

Recited evening prayers. Now to bed.

From the Journal of Philip Fröhlich
9 April 1635

> Monday
> Breakfast–
> > *1 cup morning broth 1 pfennig*
> > *1 winter apple 1 pfennig*
> > *1 wheat roll 3 pfennigs*
>
> Supper–
> > *1 cup sauerkraut 2 quartered pfennigs*
> > *1 barley roll 2 quartered pfennigs*
> > *1 mug beer 1 pfennig*

Raining today. Cold rain. Dislike being wet, dislike being cold, really dislike being both wet and cold. Took a longer way to work so I could stay on the graveled streets rather than deal with the mud. Heard the city was going to gravel the rest of the streets before too long. Hope so. Really don't like the mud, but seems like cobble stoning it all would be expensive. The up-time finished roads are nice, but I heard they weren't cheap either.

Master Schiller made us clean and sweep this morning, because Master Gröning and his new lawyer were going to come by later. Since we got the contracts organized, lot easier to dust and clean and sweep. Good thing, because they arrived just a few minutes after we got done. Martin was putting the broom in the closet when they stepped through the door.

Was surprised. Expected lawyer to be big imposing serious man. Short, not much taller than me, very lean. Dark eyes, hair almost black, no beard. Wouldn't want to be facing him if he was angry, but he was laughing when they came in the door and smiled a lot during the conversations.

Master Wulff, the lawyer, wanted to talk to me about how I found the problem. Showed him the first cash entry I saw, showed him what looked funny about it, then showed him the contract and the part of it that the cash entry seemed to not match. He looked back and forth between them, then took the contract file and read through the entire thing. He read fast—a lot faster than I do. Then he went back to the part I had pointed to and read it again.

When Master Wulff got done, he put the file down. He had a serious expression on his face and gave me a nod. He told Master Gröning that I was right and that there were grounds to sue the Hamburg partners. Then he looked at me and wanted to know who had trained me to read contracts. I said Master Schiller had told me some things, and the rest I had figured out for myself. He looked very surprised at that and told Master G and Master S that I was really good and they should take care of me.

They left not long after that. Master S didn't say anything, but he gave me ten extra dollars at the end of the day, plus told me to take as many of the candle stubs as I needed.

So, long day. Stopped at Syborg's Books on the way home. Master Matthias told me before I could ask that it would be another few weeks before they would get the next issue of *Der Schwarze Kater*. Getting really anxious again.

Worked on *Portia in Tauris* a little. Slow going, as I am rethinking everything before I put it down again. Lots of stuff being changed. Different story now—very different.

Recited evening prayers. Twice. So now to bed.

From the Journal of Philip Fröhlich
12 April 1635

Thursday
Breakfast–

1 sausage 2 pfennigs
1 wheat roll 3 pfennigs
1 mug beer 1 pfennig

Supper–

1 wurst 2 pfennigs
1 winter apple 1 pfennig
1 mug beer 1 pfennig

Had a dream that Master Gronow was chastising Masters Poe and Lovecraft for not being better writers, not writing more and better stories. Couldn't see his face, but knew it was him because he talked about *Der Schwarze Kater*. He was pretty rude, too. If he's like that really, not sure I want to know him.

Spent today like yesterday, teaching Martin how to do the checking of the entries to make sure they were done right. He had a lot of trouble yesterday, but today, after the first couple, he caught on and was able to see what I was telling him and figure out what the error had to be. Smart kid. Looks healthier, too. Filling out a little. Doesn't look like a walking skeleton now.

Raining again when work was over. Not good. Not heavy rain—not much more than a mist, but wet and cold, with a bit of east wind blowing.

Recited evening prayers. Now to bed.

From the Journal of Philip Fröhlich
15 April 1635

Sunday
Breakfast–
Fasted

Lunch-
1 cup morning broth 1 pfennig
1 winter apple 1 pfennig
1 wheat roll 3 pfennigs

Supper–
1 wurst 2 pfennigs
1 barley roll 2 quartered pfennigs
1 mug beer 1 pfennig

Lord's Day, Lord's work.

Church was good. Music wasn't as good as last week, but better than usual. Sang with a will. Reading was okay—up-time word, I know. Not sure what it really means, but it seems to be used as the same as all right or satisfactory. Okay is shorter, faster to say. Lots of people using it now. Anyway, homily wasn't as good as Pastor Gruber's last week, but have heard worse, and recently.

Read several pages from *The City of God*. Read the story from Kings about the young men mocking Elisha and the bears coming and ripping them apart. Seemed harsh. But on the other hand, if you are faced with someone who is very close to God, it may not be wise to mock him. Even if the man doesn't take offense, God might. There's a reason why Jesus taught the Golden Rule, after all.

Was very surprised when Johann appeared at my door late in the afternoon. Immediately went to The Green Horse. Had food, some beer, talked and talked about all sorts of things, but mostly his travels and my readings. Turns out he was traveling with a wealthy companion in a great circuit around the important cities. They even went to Vienna. His friend was talking to many of the renowned teachers, and wanted someone to travel with him, so Johann went.

He was surprised at how far I have come in reading St. Augustine and in the sense I make of it. He said there are doctors teaching who have no better understanding than I do. Then he grinned and said there were a couple he could think of who didn't know as much. Unsettling thought. If a man doesn't know more than I do, why would anyone want to pay him to teach? Especially in the Grantville era. Doesn't make much sense.

Came home, lit a few candle stubs and wrote on *Portia in Tauris*. Didn't get many words down, but think I have the path for the story clearer. Hope to write more tomorrow.

Recited evening prayers, and now to bed.

From the Journal of Philip Fröhlich
17 April 1635

Tuesday
Breakfast–
1 cup morning broth 1 pfennig
1 barley roll 2 quartered pfennigs
1 mug beer 1 pfennig

Supper–
1 sausage 2 pfennigs
1 cup sauerkraut 2 quartered pfennigs
1 mug beer 1 pfennig

Very bad news at the office today. Master Schiller told us that Thomas is coming back. He didn't look very happy.

I asked why. He said that Thomas is some sort of cousin to a merchant that Master Gröning wants to do business with, but the man won't talk to him or make deals with him unless he hires Thomas back.

Told Master Schiller that we'll all be sorry if they bring Thomas back. He sighed and said it was the master's order, and that was that. Got the feeling he'd already argued with Master G about it. Just shook my head and went back to copying the new agreement that had arrived.

After work, walked with Martin to his rooming house. Told him about Thomas, told him to keep close watch on his things and not to let Thomas bully him. Suggested he mark his things some way. Told him to double check his work and then have me review it.

Nothing good will come of this.

Was so upset tonight couldn't write. Didn't read *Der Schwarze Kater* issues again. Tried to read *The City of God*, couldn't focus on that. Finally was able to read in the Bible, Psalms for the most part.

Recited evening prayers twice, then a third time. Tired, but not sure I can sleep.

From the Journal of Philip Fröhlich
18 April 1635

>Wednesday
>Breakfast–
>>*1 cup morning broth 1 pfennig*
>>*1 wheat roll 3 pfennigs*
>>*1 winter apple 1 pfennig*
>
>Supper–
>>*1 wurst 2 pfennigs*
>>*1 barley roll 2 quartered pfennigs*
>>*1 mug beer 1 pfennig*

Dreams. So many dreams last night, shifting from one to another almost like skipping pages in a book. Tossed and turned all night, never rested. Max didn't appear. Not sure what to think about that.

Made sure my clothes were clean and neat this morning. Wasn't going to face Thomas not at my best. Surprised me. He was there waiting on us when we got there this morning. Clean. Sober. More polite than usual. Did what Master Schiller told him to do. Appeared to do it right. But saw him looking around from time to time with odd little smile on his face. Nothing wrong. Still nervous about this. Really not a good idea. But it's Master Gröning's business, so he makes decisions. Just hope none of us have to regret this one.

Wrote in *Portia in Tauris* tonight. Got much done. Made breakthrough, I think, in moving story forward. Was still on edge from work, poured that into the writing. Pushed me, I think. Anyway, got more done tonight than in any three nights up until now. Felt good. Story feels good. I'm more relaxed, too.

Recited evening prayers. Now to bed.

From the Journal of Philip Fröhlich
20 April 1635

Friday
Breakfast–

1 cup morning broth 1 pfennig
1 barley roll 2 quartered pfennigs
1 mug beer 1 pfennig

Supper–

1 bowl fish stew 3 pfennigs
1 mug beer 1 pfennig

Calm night last night. No dreams I remembered upon waking, other than faint feeling Max had been around. Better rested than I have been for a week, I think. Glad.

Thomas was still behaving today. Still seems to be just coming to work and doing his job. Saw a look cross his face after Master Schiller corrected one of his entries this afternoon and made him do it over. T wasn't happy, and his face showed it for a moment, but he waited until Master S had turned away before he let it show. When he saw me looking, he turned away.

Still nervous about this.

Lots of writing tonight, just like yesterday and day before. New version of story has started flowing after working through difficult changes. Like the direction it's going. Can't let myself like it too much. Need to keep focused on telling story. Doesn't matter if I like it. Only person who counts is Master Gronow.

Tired, but good tired.

Recited evening prayers, and now to bed.

From the Journal of Philip Fröhlich
22 April 1635

Sunday
Breakfast–
Fasted

Lunch–
1 wurst 2 pfennigs
1 wheat roll 3 pfennigs

Supper–
1 sausage 2 pfennigs
1 barley roll 2 quartered pfennigs
1 mug beer 1 pfennig

Lord's Day, Lord's work.

Rained hard this morning. Church was miserable. Cold and dank. Not many people there. Music was thin and limp. Sang anyway. Reading was long, reader was dull. Managed to stay awake. Pastor Gruber did homily. Was surprised to see him, but glad. Taught on Elijah's drought, how it didn't rain for over three years, but Elijah remained faithful and prayed, and how when the king finally submitted to God, the rains came. Had to bite lip to keep from laughing as gust of harder rain beat on church roof right then. Pastor related it to how sometimes our lives are dry and seemingly barren, but if we remain faithful and pray and keep doing what we know we're supposed to do, God will send the rains of life to come and bless us and fill our heart cisterns full again. Need to think about that. Think I understand it, but want to make sure.

Johann left Magdeburg with his friend on Wednesday, headed for Hamburg. Not sure when he'll be back. So spent the afternoon reading more of *The City of God*. Latin is improving. Guess practice is useful. St.

Augustine is becoming interesting. Or I'm learning to see more in him. Guess both could be true.

Spent the evening writing. *Portia in Tauris* is nearing completion, I think. Glad. But then I need to write the good copy for Master Gronow. Not glad. But necessary. Ready for Master Gronow to see this. No tricks. No fancies. Just trying to tell the story.

Tired at the end of the day.

Recited evening prayers. Now to bed.

From the Journal of Philip Fröhlich
24 April 1635

> Tuesday
> Breakfast–
>> *1 sausage 2 pfennigs*
>> *1 barley roll 2 quartered pfennigs*
>> *1 mug beer 1 pfennig*
>
> Supper–
>> *1 wurst 2 pfennigs*
>> *1 cup sauerkraut 1 pfennig*
>> *1 mug beer 1 pfennig*

Had a dream with Max last night. Really clear. He told me to quit worrying about my dreams. Anything that he lets by isn't going to hurt me. Had a serious look on his face, and was holding his big black rifle like he meant business. I wouldn't argue with him. So, do I listen to a dream tell me about dreams?

Oh, and Max says he's really good with the rifle now.

Master Schiller says that Master Wulff is proceeding with filing the lawsuit on the Hamburg contract before a judge.

Today Martin was checking earlier entries and found a mistake in Thomas' work. I saw the look on his face and motioned him over to my desk. He showed me. I checked myself, and yes, the work was wrong, and yes, it was on one of Thomas' pages. So, I sent Martin back to his desk, and I carried the page over to Master Schiller. He looked at the page, asked me if I was sure. I said yes. He sighed, and sent me back to my desk. In a little while, he called Thomas over to his desk and showed him the error, told him to correct it. Thomas started trying to say that it wasn't wrong, but Master S showed him step by step why it was wrong. So then he tried to say that one of us had changed it. Master S told him there was no evidence of that, and told him to correct it. He took it and stomped back to his desk. Spent the rest of the day fixing it. Really mean look on his face when he looked my way.

Walked with Martin most of the way home, made sure he got home safe. Didn't see Thomas at all, but wasn't happy about it. This is not good.

Still managed to finish *Portia in Tauris* tonight. Will start working on good copy tomorrow.

Read a little out of Psalms. Read a little out of Issue 3. Sat and stared for a while at the three letters from Master Gronow pinned to the wall. Will sell a story. Want it to be this one.

Recited evening prayers. Three times. Now to bed.

From the Journal of Philip Fröhlich
26 April 1635

Thursday
Breakfast–
1 cup morning broth 1 pfennig
1 barley roll 2 quartered pfennigs
1 mug beer 1 pfennig

Supper–
1 bowl fish stew 3 pfennigs
1 cup sauerkraut 1 pfennig
1 mug beer 1 pfennig

Had very different dream last night. Dreamt that Portia—from my story—was talking to me and telling me how I hadn't gotten some things right about her and her story, and I needed to fix that right now. She said it was no wonder Master Gronow was rejecting the stories, if I couldn't do any better than that. Talked loud and fast, and her voice was high and screechy in the dream, although it's supposed to be low and furry sounding. I couldn't interrupt, but over her shoulder I could see Max standing and laughing. Think that's where I woke up. Pretty bad when your dreams laugh at you.

But wish I could remember what she told me. It might have helped.

Thomas quiet today, although he trod on my foot once. Didn't push or hit him, although was tempted. Still don't like it, but if he does nothing more than that, we—Martin and I—can put up with it. Sooner or later he had to do something stupid like before and get thrown out. I hope.

Spending more time in the contracts again. Thomas started looking at them, and at me. Think he was trying to figure out what had changed. A lot.

Did two whole pages of the clean copy of *Portia in Tauris* tonight. Looks good so far, but still have a lot to do. Not unusual, you could say.

Recited evening prayers, ready for bed.

From the Journal of Philip Fröhlich
29 April 1635

> **Sunday**
> **Breakfast–**
>> *Fasted*
>
> **Lunch-**
>> *1 sausage 2 pfennigs*
>> *1 winter apple 1 pfennig*
>> *1 wheat roll 3 pfennigs*
>> *2 mugs beer 2 pfennigs*
>
> **Supper–**
>> *1 wurst 2 pfennigs*
>> *1 cup sauerkraut 1 pfennig*
>> *1 barley roll 2 quartered pfennigs*
>> *1 mug beer 1 pfennig*

Lord's Day, Lord's work.

Sunny day this morning. Church still seemed cold and damp after all the rain the last week or so. A few more people. Music was as good or as bad as usual, however you want to think of it. Sang anyway. Pastor Gruber did the homily today. Surprised but glad. Spoke today on the Syrian woman who asked for her daughter to be healed, and how Jesus instructed her that she wasn't one of the chosen children, but she had the courage to persist and to finally say that even an unclean dog could feast on the crumbs from the children's table. And Jesus healed the daughter. The pastor spoke on the virtues of longsuffering and of persistence, and on how through them we attain both maturity and reward. Not sure that Pastor G would agree, but feel like I've been dealing with longsuffering for sure in getting my stories written. Probably not what he means at all, but still . . .

After the benediction, Pastor Gruber called to me and waved me over. Invited me to lunch with him. With Johann still traveling, no reason not to, so went with him. Think he may be a bit lonely. Smiled really big when I said I'd come. He tried to pay for me again. Told him no again. Spent a few hours talking with him, mostly about St. Augustine. Nice time. Learned a lot. Pastor has a surprising appetite for bad jokes, like "Why did the chicken cross the road?" Uggh.

Got back to rooms early, put the time to good use. Copied three more pages of *Portia in Tauris*. Over a third of the way done. Hope to submit to Master Gronow soon.

Good tired when done. Fingers cramping from holding and guiding the pen. Can't press too hard, or will break the nib of the quill.

Made note, need to get more candle stubs and left-wing quills from work this week. Master Schiller lets me take some instead of my pay.

Recited evening prayers. Now to bed.

From the Journal of Philip Fröhlich
2 May 1635

>Wednesday
>Breakfast–
>>*1 cup morning broth 1 pfennig*
>>*1 wheat roll 3 pfennigs*
>>*1 mug beer 1 pfennig*
>
>Supper–
>>*1 sausage 2 pfennigs*
>>*1 cup sauerkraut 1 pfennig*
>>*1 mug beer 1 pfennig*

Pretty sure I dreamt last night. Remember waking up at least once. But don't remember anything from them if I did.

Thomas has been quiet all week. No funny looks, no words, doing his work right. That's good. Still catch him looking at me every once in a while. He was standing by my desk one day when I came in, looking at the contracts. Didn't say anything, just looked at them. Really wonder what's going on in his mind. Can't help but worry. Haven't seen anything that proves he really has changed. Sad. I mean, to be as young as we are and to have that reputation. What's he going to be like when he's older?

Stopped in again at Syborg's Books, to stop and warm up a bit as much as anything. Glad I did. Master Johann beckoned me to their counter as soon as he saw me come in, and handed me a copy of the fourth issue of *Der Schwarze Kater*. I was very excited! Fortunately, I had started carrying the two dollars necessary for the magazine, even though I didn't expect it to come out for a few more days. So, I gave Master J the money and took the magazine. They wrapped it in a piece of extra paper, and I stuffed it inside my jacket and hurried back to my room

No writing tonight. Instead, feasted on new Poe and Lovecraft. First, Nyarlathotep, by Master Lovecraft. Shivery. Then, The Masque of the Red Death, by Master Poe. Not sure I'll sleep tonight.

Looked at the magazine submissions page. Again, I see that I am affecting the magazine, although not necessarily in the manner I wish.

Close to finishing clean copy of *Portia in Tauris*. Two pages tonight. Maybe another night or two and it will be done and ready to take to Master Gronow. Ready to be done with it.

Recited evening prayers. Three times. Now to bed.

∞ ∞ ∞

Not going to sleep. Recited evening prayers twice more, plus three Our Fathers. Now to bed—again.

From Der Schwarze Kater, *Volume 4*
Black Tomcat Magazine Submissions

1. Legibility is paramount. If we can't read your story, we won't buy it. To that end, we strongly recommend that your work be prepared with the new Goldfarb und Meier typewriting machine or something similar. If a true manuscript is presented, please use practiced penmanship and calligraphy. Standard Magdeburg and Thuringia secretary hands are acceptable.

2. Please use octavo-sized paper no larger than eight inches wide by ten inches high. All pages of a story submission should be approximately the same size. Use one side of the page only. Natural color or bleached paper only—No Dyed or Tinted Paper, please! And black ink only. Not blue, or red, or purple.

3. If the story is typed, please insert a blank line between each line of lettering. If the story is written out, please space the lines about 3/8 of an inch apart. Either way, leave a blank margin of approximately one inch on all sides of each page. This facilitates both ease of reading and making

comments or instructions on the page. Keep in mind that the easier it is for the publisher to read your work, the more likely it is to be published.

4. Whether typed or written, do not write a story in all uncials. Leading sentence character and leading noun character in uncial with the rest in minuscule is preferred. All minuscule is acceptable. Again, let us stress that legibility is critical to getting your work accepted for publication.

5. No illuminated manuscripts, please. Likewise, do not submit illustrations along with your story. If your illustrations are an integral part of your story's construction, we suggest you seek out another publisher.

6. Our manual of writing style is Martin Luther's translation of Holy Scripture. All issues of grammar and word spellings will be decided in accordance with his practice. Note that familiarity with and practice of those guidelines improve your chances of having your story published. All things being equal, the story requiring the least amount of work on our part has the advantage.

7. Format the first page such that your name, contact address, and word count of your story are in the upper left-hand corner, the story title should be in the upper edge center, and page number in the upper right corner. Subsequent pages should contain your surname and abbreviated title in the upper left corner and page number in the upper right corner. Page numbers are important. If your work gets dropped, we need to be able to put the pages back in the right order.

8. We recommend you keep a personal copy of your story. All manuscripts become the personal property of the publisher upon receipts and will not be returned, regardless of ultimate decision about publication. Allow for six months of mail and processing time before querying as to the publication decision.

From the Journal of Philip Fröhlich
4 May 1635

> Friday
> Breakfast–
>> *1 sausage 2 pfennigs*
>> *1 wheat roll 3 pfennigs*
>> *1 mug beer 1 pfennig*
>
> Supper–
>> *1 bowl fish stew 3 pfennigs*
>> *1 mug beer 1 pfennig*

To quote the up-timers, wow. Issue 4 of *Der Schwarze Kater* is intense. Relived *Masque of the Red Death* in my dreams last night. Woke up four times, even after lying awake a lot of the night. Four. Wow. Toward the end, Master Poe and Max were standing to one side commenting on the story. Tried to talk to them, but they acted like they couldn't hear me and the story kept sweeping me along. Very strange night. If Max is supposed to be my guardian angel, not sure he was doing his job last night.

Had hard day at work today. Very tired. Managed to get my work done, but was hard. Master Schiller kept looking at me, finally asked me if I was hung over. Just said I didn't sleep well last night. Didn't tell him why. Even as tired as I was, wasn't that stupid. He frowned, but didn't say anything else.

Tried to work on *Portia in Tauris* copy, but just couldn't focus, so picked up Issue 4. Had skipped over first story last night to read the important work, so went back and read it. Title was *The Brass Homunculus*, by V. I. Fuchs. Idea was a man of science created a device shaped like a man out of metal and gave it the ability to move and to reason. Things didn't go well. Man of science wasn't very smart. Have to wonder where some of these writers get their ideas. I mean, a metal man? Who could take that seriously, Master Fuchs?

Wish I had thought of it.

Can't keep eyes open. Stumbled through evening prayers. Hope I sleep better than last night. Now to bed.

From the Journal of Philip Fröhlich
6 May 1635

> **Sunday**
> **Breakfast–**
>> *Fasted*
>
> **Lunch-**
>> *1 sausage 2 pfennigs*
>> *1 wheat roll 3 pfennigs*
>
> **Supper–**
>> *1 bowl fish stew 3 pfennigs*
>> *1 barley roll 2 quartered pfennigs*
>> *1 mug beer 1 pfennig*

Lord's Day, Lord's work.

Rained this morning, just like yesterday and day before. Church was cold and dank again, not many people there. Music wasn't good because so few voices. Sang anyway. Reading and homily were dull. New young guy spoke, wasn't very good. Needs to learn to speak louder and with some feelings. Also needs to learn how to write a homily. Wasn't very good, made no sense, just rambled.

Quiet day after noon. Went back and read some of the early passages in *The City of God*. Think I understand them better now. Read some in Samuel, about David and Jonathan. Wish I had a friend like that. But not if he had a father that would throw spears at me like King Saul did at David. David was a better friend than I would be, I think.

Finished the clean copy of *Portia in Tauris* late in the afternoon. Read through it, bundled it up and addressed it and took it over to Master Gronow's office before I could get scared, pushed it through the slot in the door. Felt what was my customary panic when it left my fingers, leaned my head against the door and made my customary prayer. Went back to my room.

Reread Issue 3 of *Der Schwarze Kater* to finish the evening. Leaving Issue 4 for a treat. Got about halfway through.

Recited evening prayers. Three times. Now to bed.

From the Journal of Philip Fröhlich
16 May 1635

Wednesday
Breakfast–
1 cup morning broth 1 pfennig
1 barley roll 2 quartered pfennigs
1 mug beer 1 pfennig

Supper–
1 sausage 2 pfennigs
1 winter apple 1 pfennig
1 mug beer 1 pfennig

More dreams about Masters Poe and Lovecraft last night. They were arguing about whether stories involving demons would be more horrible and horrifying than stories that show the full depravity men are capable of. Then Max appeared and told me I was wasting my time listening to them, because they were both right and both wrong. I was trying to figure that out when I woke up.

Quiet day at work today. Thomas left early because his kinsman, the merchant that Master Gröning is cultivating, needed him for something. Okay for me. The less I see him, the happier I am.

. Realized late in the afternoon that I haven't heard anything from Master Gronow. Surprised. He usually responds to my offerings quickly. Hope nothing's wrong. Hope he's still going to publish *Der Schwarze Kater*!

Worried about that all evening.

Read another story in Issue 4. This one was *Shadow of Furies*, by Georg Hannover. Must be one of those pen names Master Matthias was telling me about. Had me looking over my shoulder before I finished it, so better than some of the down-time written stories I've read.

Recited evening prayers. Three times. So now to bed, and sleep—I hope.

From the Journal of Philip Fröhlich
19 May 1635

> **Saturday**
> **Breakfast–**
> > *1 winter apple 1 pfennig*
> > *1 wheat roll 3 pfennigs*
> > *1 mug beer 1 pfennig*
>
> **Supper–**
> > *1 sausage 2 pfennigs*
> > *1 cup sauerkraut 1 pfennig*
> > *1 mug beer 1 pfennig*

Dreams still dark. Issue 4 is almost haunting me. Woke up three times even after not reading any of the *Der Schwarze Kater* issues yesterday. Dreams ran stories together in a muddle. Max was there for a while, but tide of dreams swept me away.

Stopped in at Syborg's Books. Both Masters Syborg were there. Talked to Master Johann, told him how much I liked Issue 4 of *Der Schwarze Kater*. He asked me if the down-timer stories were as good as those by Masters Poe and Lovecraft. Told him not yet, but each issue seems to get better. Master Matthias told me I was lucky I got my copy, because they didn't get as many copies as they usually do, and a few of their regulars had been disappointed and had had to try and find copies other ways. That alarms me. Told him I want my copy no matter what, even if it means I have to pay for it ahead of time. He got a thoughtful look on his face, and said he'd think about that.

Still have not heard from Master Gronow.

Very worried. Couldn't focus on anything all day. Fortunate that work was very routine today.

Worried all evening.

Recited evening prayers. Four times. Four. Still worried, but now to bed.

From the Journal of Philip Fröhlich
21 May 1635

Monday
Breakfast–
1 cup morning broth 1 pfennig
1 barley roll 2 quartered pfennigs
1 mug beer 1 pfennig

Supper–
1 sausage 2 pfennigs
1 cup sauerkraut 1 pfennig
1 mug beer 1 pfennig

Dreams, but nothing I recall. Stupid dreams.

Messenger finally brought a letter from Master Gronow today! Late in the afternoon. Wanted to rip it open and read it right then, but both Master Schiller and Thomas were looking at me, so just stuffed it inside my shirt and carried on with work.

After a few minutes, Thomas walked over to Master Schiller's desk and said something, asked a question, I think. I couldn't hear what he said, but he looked over at me when he said it. I could hear Master Schiller tell him it wasn't any of his business and to go sit down and finish his work. Thomas didn't like that, looking at his expression, but he did go back to his desk. Caught him staring at me later on.

Finally.

21 May 1635
Master Philip Fröhlich

Your persistence is admirable, Master Fröhlich. And I will say, you have yet to make the same mistake twice. That is also admirable.

It is not, however, sufficient to achieve publication. Your work has improved, yes, but not enough.

Your latest work proves that you have mastered the art of presentation. Your manuscript was acceptable in its form and structure, with nothing of note objectionable about it. The content of your manuscript, however, is another matter entirely.

There are two things I must set out before you. First, there is a difference between noting facts and telling a story, Master Fröhlich. It is not enough to clearly state that someone is frightened or horrified or disgusted. You must describe it. You must evoke it. You must make your reader feel it along with the character.

Second, there is a movement, a progression to a story. It has a beginning, a middle, and an end. It is not enough to simply place on the page a setting where something happens, or someone has an experience. There must be reasons why the character is there, and why he has that experience. There must be a flow from scene to scene, there must be transitions. You are not scripting a play, where a character stands here and says this, then moves over there and says that. You are leading the reader through terra incognita by the hand. The reader must understand what is occurring, and you, as the author, are the only person who can give them that understanding. Progression. Transition. Beginning, middle, and end. Master these, Master Fröhlich, and you will sell your stories.

Portia in Tauris is an . . . interesting . . . title. Better than your previous titles. Nonetheless, it is not adequate. Try again.

It is now with some interest that I say when you correct the issues noted above, please resubmit your story.

Good day to you.

Johann Gronow

Editor and Publisher

Der Schwarze Kater

Episode 5

Magdeburg
From the Journal of Philip Fröhlich
22 May 1635

>Tuesday
>Breakfast–
>>*1 winter apple 1 pfennig*
>>*1 barley roll 2 quartered pfennigs*
>>*1 mug beer 1 pfennig*
>
>Supper–
>>*1 bowl fish stew 3 pfennigs*
>>*1 barley roll 2 quartered pfennigs*
>>*1 mug beer 1 pfennig*

Dreamt last night. Was mostly about the plague, everyone around me was getting sick. Woke up just as I found it on me. Was glad to do that. Think it was Master Poe's story *Masque of the Red Death* that caused it this time. Although Master Lovecraft may write more evilness in his characters, Master Poe writes the scarier stories, I think.

Master Schiller looked at me when I came in this morning and raised his eyebrows. I knew he was asking about my story, so I shook my head.

He frowned and said I'd have to do better. I knew what he meant, but both Thomas and Martin were confused. Quiet day at work, otherwise.

Pinned the fourth letter up on the wall next to the others. Reread them all. I *will* sell a story to Master Gronow.

Spent the rest of the evening rereading *Portia in Tauris*. Think I see what Master Gronow talked about. Have to tell a good story. Have to make sense. Can't just throw pretty things together. Have to build it right. Have to think about how to do that.

Meanwhile, will reread all four issues of *Der Schwarze Kater*. Need to learn from the masters.

Recited evening prayers, and so to bed.

From the Journal of Philip Fröhlich
25 May 1635

> **Friday**
> **Breakfast–**
>> *1 cup morning broth 1 pfennig*
>> *1 barley roll 2 quartered pfennigs*
>> *1 mug beer 1 pfennig*
>
> **Supper–**
>> *1 sausage 2 pfennigs*
>> *1 barley roll 2 quartered pfennigs*
>> *1 mug beer 1 pfennig*

Dreamt about Portia again last night. Is weird when character in my story starts showing up in my dreams. She yells at me, too. Or at least, I think she yelled at me last night. Don't remember very well, because Max showed up, too, and started telling me jokes even dumber than Pastor Gruber's jokes. Got me laughing so much that Portia stomped her foot and left. Woke up after that. Wish I could remember some of the jokes. Pastor Gruber might like them. Stupid dreams.

Thomas was gone most of the day. His relative needed him again. Made for easy day. Spent a lot of it working with Martin showing him more about how to check the entries. Started showing him how to work with the contract files and how to keep them organized. Catching on pretty good. I think I could trust him to work with them. Better him than Thomas.

Stopped at Syborg's Books tonight. Master Matthias was there, and greeted me. Asked me what I was doing, told him I was writing stories to submit to *Der Schwarze Kater*. He whistled at that and said good for me. He asked me how I was doing with it. Told him I hadn't sold one to Master Gronow yet, but with every try I learn something. Told him I needed some of the cheap paper to write the first copy of the next version on. He said to hang on, went in the back, and came back with a couple of what almost looked like soft-bound books like the magazine, only the binding was across the top rather than the side. He flipped the top cover up, and showed me all the pages inside were blank. Not white paper. Cheap stuff. Kind of grayish, actually. He gave them to me, told me they were a couple of samples that one of the papermaking firms had given them. Told me I could have them. Thanked him a lot. Saves me some money, which I need to do because the white paper for the final copy I give to Master Gronow is so costly. Cash is low, so no wheat bread for a while. Barley instead.

After spending three evenings thinking about it and rereading the magazine issues, think I know what to do now with the story. Fourth rewrite. Think I can keep parts of what I wrote before, but need to join them together better. Tell a story, not just word paint pictures. Think I see how to do that.

Will start tomorrow.

Recited evening prayers. Now to bed.

From the Journal of Philip Fröhlich
27 May 1635

Sunday
Breakfast–
> *Fasted*

Lunch–
> *1 barley roll 2 quartered pfennigs*
> *1 mug beer 1 pfennig*

Supper–
> *1 sausage 2 pfennigs*
> *1 barley roll 2 quartered pfennigs*
> *1 mug beer 1 pfennig*

Dreamt last night, I'm sure. Don't remember any, and don't remember waking up, but was very tired when I got up this morning, so must have. Almost didn't go to church, but Lord's Day, Lord's work, so went. Bright sunny day, so more people there than has been usual. Enough there I couldn't stand by my favorite pillar and lean against it. Music was good—loud, anyway, as everyone seemed to be glad to be there. Sang with a will. Reader was good with the reading. Homily wasn't great, but at least no one went to sleep, and it was short. If it's not going to be good, at least let it be short.

Spent the afternoon reading. Over half-way through *The City of God*. Admiration for St. Augustine as a writer continues to grow as my Latin improves. Then spent some time in Kings. Story of King Ahab and Naboth. King acted like spoiled child. Needed to be spanked. Wife murdered a man just so the king could have what he wanted. He was bad, she was worse. Is a piece of ground, any piece of ground, worth a man's life? Is anything tangible worth a man's life?

Spent the evening writing. Don't have a title for the new version. Very slow going, as I'm having to think about not only what needs to happen in the story, but if and where the story I wrote before can be made or altered to fit in the new story. Almost at the point of having to think about every single word. If I'd known writing would be this much work, might not have chosen to go into it. (Bit of a joke, there . . . but only a bit.)

Got a page and a half done before the next to last of my candle stubs guttered out. Will have to get some more from Master Schiller tomorrow.

Tired, but good tired.

Recited evening prayers, and now to bed.

From the Journal of Philip Fröhlich
28 May 1635

> Monday
> Breakfast–
>> *1 barley roll 2 quartered pfennigs*
>> *1 cup small beer 1 quartered pfennig*
>
> Supper–
>> *1 sausage 2 pfennigs*
>> *1 barley roll 2 quartered pfennigs*
>> *1 mug beer 1 pfennig*

Dreamt of *The Pit and the Pendulum* again. Funny how although Master Lovecraft's stories tend to ooze more evil, it is Master Poe's stories that seem to most haunt my dreams. Woke up at least twice, but when went back to sleep was back in the dream. Have to wonder what I could write that would affect a reader like that? Can't use the pendulum . . . that's already been done. But what could I use? Water? Think about it.

Cloudy today, cold west wind blowing. No rain, thank God, but still nasty weather.

Had big argument with Thomas today at work. Martin found more errors in his work from last week. He brought to me, I took to Master Schiller. When Master Schiller called him over to talk about it, it was like T was a gunpowder firework that exploded. He started shouting and cursing and accusing us—me more than Martin—of trying to falsify his work and get him in trouble when he's doing things right, and we're the ones who are getting it all wrong. He was standing there, hands clenched, face red, shouting at Master S's face. Suddenly realized that T has grown some, just like I have, and he is not a boy any more.

I tried to tell him that we didn't, but he just turned on me and shouted a lot of the same things in my face. He ended by pushing a stack of contract files that I was reviewing off my desk and kicking them across the office, then picked up the ledger book Martin was working in off Martin's desk and threw it on the floor hard.

Then he got scary. He stopped, pulled his jacket back into place, smoothed his hair, and said in a hard quiet tone that we'd be sorry we treated him so bad. Then he left.

Master S looked weary, almost scared. Martin was definitely frightened. Me, not sure what I looked like, but my stomach hurt, and I felt like I was about to puke.

Master S got down off his stool and told us to pick things up. He even helped us. Martin's ledger book was scuffed and bent but not broken, which was good. The contract files had been scattered around, though, and it took all three of us quite a while to get all the pages back in the right files and in the right order. When we got done, Master S got out his bottle of wine and gave each of us a small drink of it. Not sure if it was a reward or medicine, but it did help me calm down a little.

At the end of the day, after Martin left, Master S put most of our candle stubs in a paper and wrapped them up, then handed them to me. Then he handed me my full day's pay. When I told him he hadn't taken out the money for the candle stubs, he told me to consider it a small bonus after the events of the day.

When I asked him what was going to happen next, Master S just shook his head and said he didn't know. Master Gröning had already told him he couldn't discharge T again, and without that resort, and with the leverage that T's relative seems to have, Master S doesn't think anything can be done. He said he'd try to protect Martin and me. Then he pushed me toward the door.

Really scared. T was really scary today.

Don't want to leave. Might have to. But can I find another job if I do? One that pays as good as what Master G is paying?

Mind has been spinning in circles all night. No words, no writing, not able to think about the story for more than a fraction of a minute.

Recited evening prayers. Over and over again. Lost count of how many times. Need to go to bed, but mind is spinning so hard don't think I can sleep.

Help.

From the Journal of Philip Fröhlich
1 June 1635

>**Friday**
>**Breakfast–**
>>*1 barley roll 2 quartered pfennigs*
>>*1 cup morning broth 1 pfennig*
>
>**Supper–**
>>*1 barley roll 2 quartered pfennigs*
>>*1 cup small beer 1 quartered pfennig*

Dreamt last night. Was like *The Cask of Amontillado*. Thomas was in the place of Fortunato, and I was Montresor, laying the stones to seal him away. Scary how much I was enjoying listening to him scream in the dream. Just as scary that I enjoy the thought just as much when I'm awake.

Today was quiet at work. Thomas was there, but didn't say or do much. In the middle of the morning, saw Martin just stop working for a long time. Just sat there, hands on his desk, pen in his fingers above the worksheet but not moving. Finally got down from my stool and walked over. He was looking at one of T's work pages from earlier in the week. I nudged him. He looked up at me, then pointed to a number on the page with one of his left hand fingers. I looked at the numbers leading up to it. It was wrong. Very wrong. So wrong I couldn't figure out how T had got to it. Martin's hand was shaking. Didn't say anything, just took the page back to my desk, fixed it, then took it to Master Schiller and pointed to what I did. He looked at it, looked at me, then looked back at the page. After a moment he nodded slowly, then gave the page back to me. Took it back to Martin, then went back to my desk. Don't know if T saw. Don't care.

Sure the up-timers have words that describe what I've been feeling this week. They have words for everything. I think pressure is best word. Feel like what happens when something blocks one of the river channels and the water builds and builds behind it, before it finally gives way.

Have discovered you can get used to anything, even pressure. After a while, guess you start feeling numb. Not scared, much, anyway. Actually was able to write some tonight. Only half a page, but more than I've done since Sunday.

Recited evening prayers. Three times. Now to bed.

From the Journal of Philip Fröhlich
3 June 1635

    Sunday
    Breakfast–
        Fasted

    Lunch–
        1 barley roll 2 quartered pfennigs
        1 cup small beer 1 quartered pfennig

    Supper–
        1 barley roll 2 quartered pfennigs
        1 cup small beer 1 quartered pfennig

Dreamt last night. Mostly quiet dreams, Woke up once, but wasn't related to the dream. Foot got out from under the blanket and got cold. Silly foot. Kind of nice to have a quiet night.

Tired this morning. Didn't want to go to church. Hard to make myself go, but that's usually when I most need to go. Dry weather, sun was shining, kind of warm this morning, so lots of people there. Had to stand in the back. Music was kind of middle between good and awful. Still sang. Reading was good. Pastor Gruber gave the homily. Talked about turning the water into wine. That was a miracle. But what is so often overlooked was that Jesus not only turned it into wine, he turned it into good wine. Then he said that sometimes, when life hands us trouble, we need to remember that not only can Jesus help solve the trouble, he can turn it into good. That spoke to me. Needed to hear that. Day got a bit lighter after that.

Pastor Gruber asked me to lunch again today. Asked me what was going on. Told him about Thomas, asked him if I had to turn the other cheek. He thought about it, told me that most of Jesus' teachings about that dealt with situations where we are being abused because of our beliefs. He said that here, because there was no faith at issue, only truth, I was free to defend myself, and that I had a duty to defend the weak, meaning Martin.

Walked away with a bit more peace in my spirit. On the way back to my room, saw something by the side of the road, half-covered by the gravel and the road dust. Picked it up . . . was a broken bolt. Big one, big around as one of my fingers, but broken off short. Less than the width of my palm. Put it in my pocket. Finished walking back to my room.

Spent most of the evening writing. Made good progress, I think. Still need a new title for the new story.

Still tired, but good tired.

Recited evening prayers, and now to bed.

From the Journal of Philip Fröhlich
4 June 1635

> **Monday**
> **Breakfast–**
>> *1 barley roll 2 quartered pfennigs*
>> *1 cup small beer 1 quartered pfennig*
>
> **Supper–**
>> *1 barley roll 2 quartered pfennigs*
>> *1 mug beer 1 pfennig*

Dreamt about Master Poe again. Was writing away with one of the fancy metal nib pens like the really big and important offices have now. Very sloppy handwriting. He would never get past Master Gronow like that.

Quiet day at work. Martin found three errors made by Thomas last Friday. Brought them to me, I fixed them and showed them to Master Schiller, he looked at them and nodded, and I passed them back to

Martin. T didn't even look up. Hate the extra work it's causing us, but I'll put up with it just to have the peace.

Still no title for the new version of the story, even though it's starting to take some kind of shape. Still kind of slow going, but I think the pieces are starting to knit together. I think the beginning is there now. Trying to fit the middle now. Story is getting a little darker along the way.

Looked back at the Poe and Lovecraft stories in the four issues. Can see what Master Gronow means in Master Poe's stories. Can sort of see it in Master Lovecraft's stories. Master Poe made better stories, I think now. Master Lovecraft can paint a picture with his words that can make the hair bristle on your neck and give you goose flesh all over, but his stories just aren't as good as stories as Master Poe's. Master Poe shows better craftsmanship, if that word applies to writing. So, I need to reread his stories and study them harder.

Ended up copying another page tonight. Getting there.

Eating less. Saving money. May need it.

Recited evening prayers. Now to bed.

From the Journal of Philip Fröhlich
6 June 1635

> **Wednesday**
> **Breakfast–**
> > *1 barley roll 2 quartered pfennigs*
> > *1 cup small beer 1 quartered pfennig*
>
> **Supper–**
> > *1 barley roll 2 quartered pfennigs*
> > *1 mug beer 1 pfennig*

Dreams last night. Portia again. Don't remember much other than she was looking into a big mirror hanging on the wall. Woke up, think that's the title for the new story version: *Portia's Mirror*. I think it will work.

Another quiet day at work. Martin didn't find any errors in the pages he checked, which is good. Looked them over myself, quickly, didn't see anything. When Master Schiller looked at me and raised his eyebrows, I just nodded with a smile. He nodded back and went back to his own work. Martin's getting pretty good at the regular tasks, and he's learned the routine for maintaining the contracts pretty well. Not too sure the office needs three clerks. Except it's more like two and a half clerks, actually. Thomas still isn't producing more than about a half-day's work, even when he doesn't make errors.

Applied the new title to the work tonight. Decided to step back and adjust a couple of earlier passages to fit with the idea better. Took most of the evening to figure out what to do, but got it done. Think it will help pull other pieces together, too. More I think about it, more I like it.

Tired, but good tired.

Recited evening prayers. So now to bed.

From the Journal of Philip Fröhlich
8 June 1635

> Friday
> Breakfast–
>
>> *1 barley roll 2 quartered pfennigs*
>> *1 cup small beer 1 quartered pfennig*
>
> Supper–
>
>> *1 barley roll 2 quartered pfennigs*
>> *1 mug beer 1 pfennig*

Not sure I dreamt last night. Don't remember any, woke up feeling pretty good. Not even a hint of Max.

It happened today. Thomas came in late, obviously hung over. Spent most of the morning wandering around the office. He'd sit at his desk for a little while, then get up and walk around for a while, then sit back down. Just before noon he walked by my desk while I was correcting some errors that Martin had found. He frowned and asked what I thought I was doing. Told him I was fixing his mistakes. He got red in the face and shouted that he did good work. I said only if you consider four mistakes in a single day's work to be good work. He cursed at me and grabbed at the page I was correcting. It tore in two, and he threw his piece down on the floor and stomped on it. Then he picked up the ink well out of the holder in my desk and threw the ink all over the papers on the desk, which ended up splashing on me as well.

He started screaming at me, grabbed my shirt front and pulled me off my stool and hit me in the face. Still had my jacket on because I had gone out to sweep the front steps off and had gotten a bit chilled. North wind blowing today. My hands had gone to my jacket pockets when he started yelling for some reason. Right hand wrapped around the piece of broken bolt I'd found and made a fist. Brought my hands out, knocked his hand off my shirt. Was off-balance, but still hit him back. Right fist hit him in the nose, felt something crunch. He yelled more, and hit me in the ear. Brought right fist back, punched forward and caught him on the point of the chin. He went down, stayed down, moaning.

By then Master Schiller was there and got between us. Told me to go sit at my desk. Climbed back on my stool and sat there. Was surprised that I was shaking. Wasn't afraid. Mad. Master S got T up off the floor, and handed him a scrap of rag to staunch the blood coming out of his nose. May have broken it. At that moment, was glad.

You'll be sorry, T muttered. He was really woozy. I'll make you all sorry. You'll see. He stumbled out the door. Master S looked at me and Martin, had sad look on face. Just told me to clean up and do what I could to fix things. Ended up having to totally recopy two pages, the one T tore and the one that most of the ink landed on. Took most of afternoon to fix. Martin copied the torn page, fixing the mistakes. I did the other page. Was able to wipe off enough of the fresh ink that I could see the original words and numbers underneath it. Glad I was able to clear it up then, though. If it had dried, wouldn't have been able to do anything.

Late in the afternoon, after fixing the problems, just about the time I began to realize I was probably in trouble, Master Gröning came in, with another very well-dressed man and Thomas. T was smiling in a nasty way, so I knew it wasn't going to be good. Master G said he couldn't have clerks assaulting other clerks, and that I was discharged as of the end of the day. I was not to return. I tried to explain that I was defending myself from assault, but he just told me to be quiet or I'd have to leave right then and lose the day's pay.

Just closed my mouth and watched as Master G took the other man's arm, called him Master Schmidt, and said something about going to Walcha's Coffee House. They left, with T trailing along behind them.

Surprised that I felt relieved. Knot in my stomach went away. Knew that I needed to find another job immediately, but just not having to face T every day almost made it worth it.

Did feel sad. Had worked for Master S for a long time, didn't want to leave. Especially like this.

Master S and Martin looked much worse than I felt. Almost laughed. Master S told me to finish anything on my desk and put things in order. That didn't take long. Just sat there for a little while, until Master S said it was time. Gave Martin a shoulder hug, told him to be careful. He sniffled, said he would, and left. Looked at Master S and raised my eyebrows. He said he knew another office that needed a good clerk, and he was going to send Martin to them. Told me that he wasn't happy about what was happening, but he was going to stick it out a little while longer, then go back to his home village with the money he had saved and buy into a tavern there. This was just making it easier for him to decide when to leave.

He gathered up all the candle stubs plus a couple of whole candles and several of the good right wing quill feathers, made a package of them, and told me to take them. Gave me my final day's wages, and added ten dollars to it. When I tried to tell him it was too much, he said to let him worry about it. He held his hand out—first time he's ever offered to shake hands with me—told me I was a good worker, and he was proud to have worked with me. He wished me good fortune, and then I walked out the door for the last time.

Know that this puts me in a hard place. But I still feel good about not having to go back. Weird, I guess.

Didn't write any tonight. Just sat and thought, and read a little in Psalms and Proverbs.

Recited evening prayers, and now to bed.

From the Journal of Philip Fröhlich
9 June 1635

    Saturday
    Breakfast–

        1 barley roll 2 quartered pfennigs
        1 cup small beer 1 quartered pfennig

    Supper–

        1 barley roll 2 quartered pfennigs
        1 cup small beer 1 quartered pfennig

Don't recall any dreams from last night. Didn't have any trouble going to sleep, either. Felt rested in the morning.

Went out and walked around western part of Greater Magdeburg this morning. Took a while. Bigger than I realized. Made note of places to approach for work. Will start Monday. Have enough money to live over a week without losing my room. Maybe two weeks, if I'm very frugal about food. Should find work before then.

Should be worried, I know. Should be scared. Should be afraid I'm going to die. Am not. Not sure why, just not. Oh, part of it is faith, for certain, that God will preserve. But part of it is confidence, I think. Might be foolish, but I believe I will find work soon.

So after walking all over this part of the city, stopped in at Syborg's Books to rest my feet and see if they had anything new. Master Matthias was there. He smiled, asked me how I was doing in reading St. Augustine, and laughed when I told him I was actually beginning to like it. Then he frowned and asked me what I was doing there at that hour of the day. Told him I had been discharged, and if he needed a bookkeeper or clerk, I was his man. If he didn't, if he knew of anyone who did, I would appreciate hearing about them.

Master Matthias shook his head, but said he would ask around.

Right then someone tapped me on the shoulder. I turned, and it was Master Wulff, the attorney! I stepped back in surprise, and almost fell over the table I was against. He grabbed my arm and kept me on my feet until I could stand by myself. I apologized for being clumsy. He waved his hand and asked if he overheard right, that I was out of work. I must have looked funny, because he chuckled and said that was an up-time phrase. He meant, did I lose my job? I said yes. He asked me if I was the contracts clerk for Master Gröning. I said I used to be. He asked what happened, then waved his hand again and said to forget that. He pulled a card out of a pocket and handed it to me. Told me to come see him first thing Monday morning. Then he said, no wait, he was in court Monday, make it Tuesday morning. Could I make it that long? I said yes, he said good, he really wanted to see me then. He paid for the book he had in his hand, then left. I followed, kind of in a daze.

Not sure why he wants to see me. But it could be good.

Spent most of the afternoon and evening working on *Portia's Mirror*. New story is going to be longer than the originals. Has to be. Putting beginning, middle, and end structure in place takes up room. Needs more words to build structure. Words are like bricks and blocks of stone. Need them. Think it's over halfway to finish. Won't know for sure until closer to end. Hard to tell right now. Feel good about it. Can't trust that, though. Felt good about all the other versions, too, until Master Gronow read them. So will keep pushing to make it as good as it can be before I take it to him again.

Church tomorrow. Looking forward to that.

Recited evening prayers. Now to bed.

From the Journal of Philip Fröhlich
10 June 1635

> Sunday
> Breakfast–
>> *Fasted*
>
> Lunch–
>> *1 barley roll 2 quartered pfennigs*
>> *1 cup small beer 1 quartered pfennig*
>
> Supper–
>> *1 barley roll 2 quartered pfennigs*
>> *1 cup small beer 1 quartered pfennig*

Dreamt last night. Know I had more than one, but only thing I remember is one with Max. He didn't say anything. Just smiled, hefted his big black rifle, and waved a hand in a motion like he was telling me to go forward. Didn't wake up in night. Nothing disturbed me. Felt good when I finally woke up.

Lord's Day, Lord's work.

Attended church. Another sunny day. Lots of people at St. Jacob's Church this morning. Had to stand at the back. Music was good, lots of people singing, sang loudly myself. Enjoyed it. Reading was enjoyable—deacon had a strong voice. Pastor Gruber gave the homily. Was glad of that. Spoke on Joseph in Egypt, how he wasn't treated justly, but that his faith and devotion to doing what was right brought him to a high place and high renown. Obvious that it fits with what happened with my job. Kind of think it fits with my writing, too. Good to hear, though. Kind of comforting, in a way.

Spent early afternoon reading St. Augustine. Getting close to the end. Not sure what I'll do then.

Then read through Proverbs. Lots of good advice there.

Finally spent most of evening working on *Portia's Mirror*. About done with middle of story. Will start end of story tomorrow or Tuesday.

Must start looking for work tomorrow.

Recited evening prayers. So now to bed.

From the Journal of Philip Fröhlich
11 June 1635

>**Monday**
>**Breakfast–**
>> *1 rye roll 1 quartered pfennig*
>> *1 cup small beer 1 quartered pfennig*
>
>**Supper–**
>> *1 rye roll 1 quartered pfennig*
>> *1 cup small beer 1 quartered pfennig*

Dreams last night for some reason involved a giant wolf. First it was chasing me, then I was riding it. Woke up twice in the night. Both times went back to same dream. Odd. Doesn't usually work that way.

Letters From Gronow

Went to Mama Schultz's for breakfast. She said she hadn't seen me buy rye before. Told her I don't like it. Tastes bitter to me. But need to save my coins until I can find another job, so cheapest bread is all I can take. She frowned at me, told me to take two. Told her no, wasn't going to take what I didn't pay for. She kept frowning at me as she hefted her meat fork, but guess she saw I meant it. Told me to come in every day so she could see I was all right.

Put on my best and cleanest clothes. Walked around to some of the places I saw Saturday, asking if they needed a bookkeeper or clerk. Same answer everywhere. No, or maybe next week. Six or seven places, I think. Disappointing. Will continue tomorrow.

Took my shirt that Thomas got ink on to a laundress, asked her if it could be cleaned. She looked at it, scratched the stain, sniffed it, touched her tongue to it, said no, probably not. Lots of inks are just as good as dyes these days, she said. Offered me a pfennig for it, for the rag content, she said. Told her no. Not much of a shirt now, but I can wear it when I'm not working or at church and save my only other two shirts from the wear and mess.

Started working on the ending of *Portia's Mirror* tonight. Feeling good about how it's going. Have to keep reminding myself that that doesn't mean anything. Only Master Gronow's judgment counts.

Set out Master Wulff's card on the table to remind me that I'm supposed to go see him in the morning. Wonder what he wants? Doesn't matter. Someone like that calls, you go. Tried to brush off my clothes, make them look better.

Recited evening prayers. Now for bed.

David Carrico

From the Journal of Philip Fröhlich
12 June 1635

    Tuesday
    Breakfast–
        1 rye roll 1 quartered pfennig
        1 cup small beer 1 quartered pfennig
    Supper–
        1 bowl fish stew 3 pfennigs
        1 cup sauerkraut 1 pfennig
        1 wheat roll 3 pfennigs
        1 mug beer 2 pfennigs

Dreamt of the wolf again last night. Wonder if it's because I'm seeing Master Wulff this morning. Funny, if so. Despite his name, he doesn't look at all wolfish. Haven't seen him act like one, either. But I haven't seen much of him, so really don't know what he's like.

Mama Schultz tried to give me two rye rolls again this morning. Told her no. She frowned, but didn't say more.

Knew that Master Wulff said to see him first thing this morning, but doubted he meant to be there at daybreak. Waited until about an hour after dawn, then went and found the address on the card. Turns out his office is in the same building as Walcha's Coffee House, on the floor above it. Found the door to the stairs, went up. Nice wide stairs. At least three people wide—maybe four, if they're skinny like me.

Door to the office was locked, so nobody there yet. Started back down the stairs, only to see Master Wulff just a couple of steps down, coming up. Stepped back, to let him and a younger man pass me to the short hallway. Master Wulff took me by the arm and drew me to the office door as the other man stepped around us and unlocked the door. Master Wulff had a large mug of steaming liquid in his other hand, which I guessed was coffee from the shop below.

Once we were inside the office, Master Wulff released my arm and introduced me to the other man. He was named Christoph Heinichen, and Master Wulff described him as aide, assistant, and lawyer-to-be, at which Christoph grinned. Then Master Wulff took me into his inner office, telling Christoph that he wasn't to be interrupted for at least an hour.

Master Wulff closed the door, sat down behind his desk, and told me to sit in the chair in front of it. I hesitated. It was a fine chair, with embroidered cloth upholstery. Even though I had brushed my clothes, I was certain they still contained dirt, and I really didn't want to mar such a fine work as that chair. Master Wulff insisted that I sit, so I sat.

You lost your job, he said to me. Pretty blunt. But, he's an attorney, so maybe that's how they are. Tell me how that happened, he said. So I told him all about it. He sat quietly while I talked, elbows on his desk and hands laced together with his chin resting on top of them. His eyes were half-closed, like he was about to go to sleep, but I could see his nostrils flare every so often, as if he was smelling something really strong. When I mentioned Master Schmidt toward the end, his eyes opened wide and his mouth twisted, but he didn't say anything until I was finished.

When I was done, Master Wulff said he thought Master Gröning had more sense than that. I said what? He said, first, that he is wooing Georg Schmidt. I said I don't think I'd heard his first name. Mayor Gericke's half-brother, he said. Then he said Master Gröning had commissioned him to review some contracts that Schmidt had proposed, and they were filled with traps that would have hurt Master G, so he didn't see why he was seeking to tie himself to Schmidt. Plus, he continued, Master G was an absolute idiot to let go of me for any reason, much less for the reasons he did. Then he asked how much I was earning. I told him twelve dollars a day, paid daily, with occasional extra payments if I did something really good. His eyes got wide, and his mouth almost dropped open, I swear. Then his jaw firmed, and he almost bellowed for Christoph.

When Christoph opened the door from the outer office, Master W almost demanded to know if Master G's payment for the last commission they had done had arrived. Christoph said that the draft had arrived last week, and the money had been paid yesterday, so all fees due had been paid. Master W then gave a really thin-lipped smile—very hard, it was—and I think I saw what he would be like as an attorney. He told Christoph that he now had reason to doubt that Master G was going to be able to remain in business for very long, and that he would no longer accept commissions from the man. He then said something like but you don't need to tell him why. Not sure why he said that. Christoph got a serious look on his face, nodded his head, and closed the door.

Master W now turned back to me and laid his hands on the desk before him. He said he was going to offer me a job with him right then doing bookkeeping and contract file management just like I'd done for Master G, and he wasn't going to insult me. He would start me at fifteen dollars a day, and in three months, after I had learned everything about his routines and his files, I would receive a raise in pay. A significant raise in pay, he said. Then he muttered something about chiseling cheapskates. Must be up-time words. Never heard them before.

I said I wanted to ask a question. He said go ahead. I asked if I took the job, would that be all I ever did? I knew I was going to take the job, but I wanted to see if there was something better that might come from it. He got a serious expression on his face, and said that actually, if I wanted to pursue it, he saw no reason why I might not learn enough law while working there to speed my way through school if I ever thought I wanted to be an attorney someday. I already had shown him that I knew more contract law than a lot of men with fancy brass plates on their doors.

My own eyes opened wide at that. Me . . . an attorney? Boy, would Mama be surprised at that! I took a deep breath, and told him I accepted his offer. He smiled a real smile, then bellowed for Christoph again. When the door opened, Master W said meet our new bookkeeper and file clerk, Christoph. Prepare standard employment contract number 3 between Philip Fröhlich and Grubb, Wurmb and Wulff. Christoph grinned and ducked back into the outer office. He left the door open, and in a moment I heard a series of clacking noises, then a ratcheting sound. Christoph appeared in the door and carried a document over to Master W, who read it carefully. He grunted at the end, then flipped open the cap to his inkwell, dipped one of those fancy metal nib pens into it, made a couple of notes on the page and signed it at the bottom. He spun the document around on the desk and offered me the pen. I read through the contract, which just said that I agreed to work for Grubb, Wurmb, and Wulff, a partnership, to do any work for which I was capable, and to keep all matters I learned about in the course of my employment there confidential. And it stated that my starting pay was fifteen dollars a day. I kind of shook my head at my good fortune, but I took the pen, dipped it, and carefully signed my name where his finger was pointing.

When I laid the pen back down on its rest, Master W walked around the desk, reached out to take my hand and shake it. He shook my hand. Master G never shook my hand. Wow. He passed the contract to Christoph, who took it back into the outer office. Then he reached into his pants pocket and pulled out something that when he undid a clip and unfolded it turned out to be a lot of money. He peeled off four five-dollar bills and handed them to me. He told me that was my signing bonus—more up-time words, I guess—that I should go have a good meal, and be here tomorrow morning at 9 A.M.

With that, he ushered me to the front door. Moments later I was down on the street with my head spinning. Wandered around for a while, then ended up in Syborg's Books, where Master Matthias greeted me and told me he had been asking around about jobs but hadn't found anything. Told him he didn't need to bother as I start work tomorrow for Master Wulff. He smiled and seemed really pleased by that. Spent most of the afternoon browsing through all the books in the store, talking to Master Matthias about some of them. I may try some of them.

Had an early supper. Was hungry. Ate better than I have in a while, secure in knowledge that I can afford it again.

Spent the rest of the evening working on *Portia's Mirror*. Everything flowed. Three pages of story told tonight. Getting close to end. Got the job just in time to start thinking about getting the good paper for the copy to give Master Gronow.

Not really tired now, but need to try and sleep. Tomorrow will be busy day.

Recited evening prayers, twice, and now to bed.

From the Journal of Philip Fröhlich
15 June 1635

Friday
Breakfast–
>*1 wheat roll 3 pfennigs*
>*1 cup morning broth 1 pfennig*
>*1 mug beer 2 pfennigs*

Supper–
>*1 bowl fish stew 3 pfennigs*
>*1 wheat roll 3 pfennigs*
>*1 mug beer 2 pfennigs*

Dreams were mostly quiet last night. Max floated in and out, waved at me once. Don't think I woke up. If I did, went right back to sleep and don't remember it.

Mama Schultz smiled at me this morning when she saw what I was getting for breakfast. Almost dropped my roll. Wasn't sure her face could bend that direction without cracking or breaking. Surprised me when it did. She put her meat fork down and reached over and patted me on the cheek, told me I was a good boy.

Third day at new job. Didn't feel as lost as I did the first two days. Kind of know where things are, starting to understand how things are organized. Was actually able to do a few things without looking to Christoph first.

Like Christoph. Very good-natured, good at explaining, very patient. Likes to laugh. I think I'll enjoy working with him.

According to C, Master Wulff is good to work for. Gives good clear directions. Tolerates honest mistakes. On the other hand, has no tolerance for willful stupidity and is sudden death on dishonesty. Thought to myself that Thomas would never make it here, then.

C says Master W demands a lot, but of himself most of all. Says he's scary smart, and picks things up very fast, which is why it's stupid to try and lie to him or mislead him. He never forgets anything and puts things together in ways no one expects. If I don't know something for sure, just say so. He wants truth above all. I think I'll like that in my master.

C did say that as long as Master W is being loud and bouncing around like a child's toy, things are okay. But if he gets still, and quiet, and his voice goes to a smooth even tone, those are storm warnings, we need to find cover, and God help me if I'm the cause. Still think I'll like it here.

Really like the paper they use in the office. Really smooth, really white, and about the right size. Finally asked today if I could buy some. Christoph shrugged, said probably, went to ask Master W, who came out of the back office and said I could, but wanted to know why. Told him I'm a writer and need some to finish a story I'm working on. His eyebrows raised, and he smiled, then told C to sell it to me for what he paid for it. So I brought home twelve pages of it. All I could afford today. Looking forward to writing the clean copy of *Portia's Mirror* on it.

Which will begin really soon, because after tonight's writing, I think I only have about one more night's work, and the new story will be done.

Recited evening prayers. Now to bed.

From the Journal of Philip Fröhlich
17 June 1635

>Sunday
>Breakfast–
>>*Fasted*
>
>Lunch–
>>*1 wheat roll 3 pfennigs*
>>*1 chunk cheese 2 pfennigs*
>>*1 mug beer 1 pfennig*
>
>Supper–
>>*1 wheat roll 3 pfennigs*
>>*1 sausage 2 pfennigs*
>>*1 mug beer 1 pfennig*

Dreamt last night. Max showed up early, talked for a long time. Don't remember a lot of it, except I think he was talking about how much fun it is to be a guardian angel. Well, maybe not fun, but how much he enjoys it. Said something about doing what you love and loving what you do. Took me a moment to understand what he was saying. Not sure everyone would agree with it, but makes some sense to me. He told me some more old bad jokes and bad old jokes, too. Wish I could remember some of them.

Lord's Day, Lord's work.

Church was pleasant. Not as many people as the last couple of Sundays, but still full enough that the singing of the music was good. Sang with a will. Reading was okay. Homily was a bit dull. Not by Pastor Gruber, unfortunately. Preacher got St. John the Baptist confused with St. John the Evangelist. Not the first time I've heard that. Happens with Saints Jacob, Jacob, and Jacob as well. I can understand how lay people can do that, but preachers and pastors are supposed to know. I mean, really.

After lunch, spent part of the afternoon reading *The City of God*. Almost done. Don't know if I'll start over again when I'm done or if I'll read another book by St. Augustine. Actually want to do both. Torn between seeing if I can make more sense of it the second time or if I want to read something new. We'll see. Probably a few weeks from that decision.

Finished *Portia's Mirror* tonight. Good. Ready to start the clean copy tomorrow. Have enough paper to get started, have quills and candles, have a fresh supply of ink. Ready to go.

Feeling good about that.

Recited evening prayers. So now to bed.

From the Journal of Philip Fröhlich
21 June 1635

Thursday
Breakfast–
1 wheat roll 3 pfennigs
1 sausage 2 pfennigs
1 mug beer 2 pfennigs

Supper–
1 wurst 2 pfennigs
1 wheat roll 3 pfennigs
1 mug beer 2 pfennigs

Dreamt of water last night. River, I think. Seemed to be a current, anyway. No idea which river, though. Pretty big . . . bigger than the Elbe, anyway. Of course, I've never seen another river than the Elbe, so I couldn't tell by looking at it what it was. And Max wasn't there to ask. Just me. No Max, no Portia, nobody. Strange dream, I guess.

CoC broadside sellers all out in full voice today. Heard several of them calling out about a battle at someplace named Güstrow. CoC soldiers apparently fought a battle with some troops of some of the *Niederadel* over Jews. Don't understand that. But CoC won. Guess that's good.

Work has been smooth. Routine, guess you could say. Master Wulff sees a lot of people every day. Some of them he decides he can't do anything for, so he turns them away. But the ones he decides to try and help, they get at least two folders set up—one for his work notes on whatever the situation is, and one for any agreement he sets up with them. A couple of people there was a third folder set up, but not sure why. Christoph set those up. Anyway, I set up the folders, file the papers, and put the folders where they need to go. Kind of like what I was doing for Master Gröning toward the end, only using the system C showed me, which is way better than what I had worked out for Master G.

Funny . . . Master W isn't very tall, and is not fat—trying to say he's not a big man—but after you're around him for a little bit you forget that. He seems as big or bigger than anyone else in the room.

He looked over my shoulder today as I was copying a statement, and said that my hand was good. First time anyone's complimented my penmanship. Guess all the copies I've done for Master Gronow have helped there, too.

Copying about a page per night, maybe a bit more. Not rushing it. Wanting it to be as clean as possible. Plus, this new paper is a little different than what I've used before, so making sure I know how it takes pen work and ink before I start trying to hurry with it. Anyway, several pages done, quarter done, maybe. Should have it done by the first of next month, or maybe a day or so later.

Reread parts of *Der Schwarze Kater* Issue 3 tonight. Not sure which issue I like best. They're all good.

Recited evening prayers, and now for bed.

From the Journal of Philip Fröhlich
27 June 1635

>Wednesday
>Breakfast–
>>*1 wheat roll 3 pfennigs*
>>*1 cup sauerkraut 1 pfennig*
>>*1 mug beer 2 pfennigs*
>
>Supper–
>>*1 sausage 2 pfennigs*
>>*1 wheat roll 3 pfennigs*
>>*1 mug beer 2 pfennigs*

Dreamt Masters Poe and Lovecraft were walking down Kristinstrasse in Magdeburg. Everyone they met knew who they were, even the pastor they passed, and everyone smiled and said hello. Then they turned into the Magdeburg *Polizei* headquarters and went in the front door. I kept walking, and after a while woke up. Have to wonder what that was about. Really curious about who they were going to see and what they were going to talk about. Stupid dreams.

Since the last couple of days were really busy, was nice that today was quiet. I mean, not so good because no new clients means not as much money, but it was nice to get caught up on the other papers and get them filed. Christoph is still showing me some new things almost every day. Lot more to think about here than at Master Gröning's.

Speaking of Master G, ran into Martin after leaving work in the evening. He was on the other side of the street going the other way. Called out to him and crossed over. Almost got stepped on by a mule team. Drover had some not nice things to say about how stupid I was. Couldn't argue with him. Was stupid to try to cross right in front of the mule team. Anyway, made it to other side, embarrassed, talked to Martin for a little bit. He said that Master Schiller had gotten him another position at another office near where we were. He's getting the same money, but having to work a little harder, but he said that was okay because the people were nice and fair and he'd have done anything to get away from Thomas. He said he almost wept when he left, because Master Schiller looked so weary and alone. Told him what Master S had told me about going back home and buying a share in a tavern. That perked him up a little. We agreed to try and meet like this every Wednesday just to keep in touch.

Making good progress on the final copy of *Portia's Mirror*. Over halfway done. Two-thirds done, maybe. Won't be long. Moving a little faster now that I'm more used to the paper. Did have to buy some more paper, though, but I knew I was going to have to do that.

Recited evening prayers. Now to bed.

From the Journal of Philip Fröhlich
1 July 1635

> **Monday**
> **Breakfast–**
>> *1 wheat roll 3 pfennigs*
>> *1 cup morning broth 1 pfennig*
>> *1 mug beer 2 pfennigs*
>
> **Supper–**
>> *1 sausage 2 pfennigs*
>> *1 wheat roll 3 pfennigs*
>> *1 mug beer 2 pfennigs*

Dreamt that Master Wulff turned into a wolf in the office. Funny thing was, he could still talk, so we kept on doing business. Just that he was sitting in the chair like a dog would, instead of like a person.

Remember thinking in the dream that Christoph was sure taking it calmly. Woke up with a giggle after that.

Mama Schultz tried to get me to eat something different for breakfast. Told her I was tired of the winter apples and sauerkraut, and the new plums were just now starting to show up. She pointed her meat fork at me and told me to eat turnips and cabbage. I stuck my tongue out at her. She smiled a little bit. Second time I've made her smile. Need to figure out how to do that more often.

Frau Grubb, Master W's wife, came by the office right before lunch to go to lunch with Master W at Walcha's Coffee House. Master W introduced us. Her name is Portia! I was so astounded by that. I must have looked stupid or something, because she laughed and asked me if I knew another Portia. Before I could think, I blurted out only in the story I was writing. Her eyebrows went up, and she got a surprised expression on her face. That's when Master W said yes, he's a writer, didn't I tell you that? She slapped him on his arm and said no. Then she looked back at me and asked me if I had anything published yet. I said no, but I'm submitting to a magazine, and with each submission I get closer. She said which magazine? I said *Der Schwarze Kater*. She got that surprised look on her face again, then grinned and said, Really? It was her favorite magazine.

Master W broke out laughing, and said that we would obviously become close acquaintances, and no, she couldn't spend all my afternoon talking about stories and writing. She slapped him on the arm again, then said to me, another time she wants to talk to me about stories, and did I know the writing of Stephen King? I said no. She smiled and said I would.

Then she tucked her arm in Master W's arm, and they went to lunch. I asked C if Frau G was always like that. He said yes, and sometimes even more so. She was a good match for Master W because of that.

So, head was still spinning when I left work today. Master W and wife are interesting people, but I think keeping up with them all the time could wear a person out.

Finished the final copy of *Portia's Mirror* tonight. Looked everything over carefully, made sure I had the address for Master W's office down for my contact rather than Master Gröning's office. Wouldn't want the response to go to the wrong place.

Will take it by tomorrow after work.

Recited evening prayers, so now for bed.

From the Journal of Philip Fröhlich
2 July 1635

Tuesday
Breakfast–
1 wheat roll 3 pfennigs
1 cup morning broth 1 pfennig
1 mug beer 2 pfennigs

Supper–
1 sausage 2 pfennigs
1 wheat roll 3 pfennigs
1 mug beer 2 pfennigs

Dreams were dark last night. Woke up twice. But don't remember any of them.

Nervous all day. Good thing nothing new or unusual happened at work today. Not sure I would have been any good. Looked forward all day to getting *Portia's Mirror* to Master Gronow's office.

End of day arrived, headed straight for his office. Door was closed as usual. Dropped the story through the slot like usual, with usual flash of panic, followed by usual prayer.

Stopped by Syborg's Books on the way home, browsed a little bit. Georg was minding the store, talked to him a little bit.

Went home. Tried to read the issues of *Der Schwarze Kater*. Couldn't connect. Tried to read St. Augustine. Couldn't focus. Tried to read the Bible. Even that couldn't focus me.

So said evening prayers . . . over and over again until I calmed down. Think maybe I can sleep now, so now to bed.

I hope.

From the Journal of Philip Fröhlich
5 July 1635

> **Friday**
> **Breakfast–**
> > *1 wheat roll 3 pfennigs*
> > *1 cup sauerkraut 1 pfennig*
> > *1 mug beer 2 pfennigs*
>
> **Supper–**
> > *1 bowl fish stew 3 pfennigs*
> > *1 wheat roll 3 pfennigs*
> > *1 mug beer 2 pfennigs*

Don't remember any dreams at all, but woke up three times, so must have been something.

Was really hoping the messenger didn't try to deliver yesterday. Didn't realize we were going to be closed for the up-timer holiday of July 4th when I put the story in the slot, or I would have put a note with it. Need to remember that in the future.

Didn't need to worry. He showed up late afternoon. Usual guy, guess Master Gronow uses him for all that work. He stepped in the door, looked around, saw me, brought me the message, touched a finger to the brim of his cap, and left.

Master Wulff had come to the door of the inner office. He looked at me with one raised eyebrow. I held up the message, told him I had submitted a story early in the week, and this was word from the publisher. I went to put it in my shirt, and Master W told me to go ahead and open it. He wanted to know, too, so he could tell Portia. He was smiling as he said that. Felt weird, but I opened the message.

5 July 1635
Master Philip Fröhlich

I see that your contact address has changed. I hope that represents an improvement in your situation and not a downturn.

Once again you have delivered a clean manuscript. Well-crafted, well-written as to your hand, nice paper. Congratulations. I believe this is the nicest manuscript I have ever seen, including my very own. I could almost be jealous.

You prove yourself to be an apt pupil, Master Fröhlich. With each successive cycle of give and take, of offering and rebuttal, your work improves. I wish I could say that it has improved enough for me to buy this story, I really do.

Portia's Mirror is far and away your best effort so far. The story has structure, and things happen, and the characters do things. These are all good. There is a beginning, a middle, and an end. But it needs still more. You need to continue to improve your skills at describing things. It's not enough to say that someone is horrified and show us their actions. You must describe the thing that is causing the fear. You must make the reader just as horrified of the thing as the character is. You made strides in this direction with *Portia's Mirror*, but not enough. When you can make the hair on my neck stand up, you will have achieved it, and the readers will love to hate you for it.

Second, it's not enough to have structure. If there is more than one character, there needs to be dialogue. In short, they need to talk to each other. And frankly, your dialogue in the story sounded as if it was written by a drunken Roman, trying to be serious and pompous. It wasn't natural. When you write your stories, read them out loud, especially the dialogue. Your ear will tell you when something isn't right.

Portia's Mirror is a good title. I could probably publish that title. But see if you can find a better one. Your first story, when it's finally published, needs to be memorable in every respect.

Yes, I begin to think that you will achieve your goal, and have a story published in *Der Schwarze Kater*. It is now with anticipation that I say when you correct the issues noted above, please resubmit your story.

Good day to you.

Johann Gronow

Editor and Publisher

Der Schwarze Kater

Episode 6

Magdeburg
From the Journal of Philip Fröhlich
6 July 1635

> Saturday
> Breakfast–
> > *1 wheat roll 3 pfennigs*
> > *1 sausage 2 pfennigs*
> > *1 mug beer 2 pfennigs*
>
> Supper–
> > *1 wurst 2 pfennigs*
> > *1 wheat roll 3 pfennigs*
> > *1 mug beer 2 pfennigs*

Dreams were almost riotous last night. I remember them being colorful, which I don't do very often. Usually dream in shades of gray or sepia. Don't remember any one dream well, but some were stories, and some were conversations, and a few were Max laughing, either at the other dreams or at me. Didn't care. Was pretty happy myself.

Master Wulff closed the office today. The up-timer July 4th holiday lasted three days this year. Shows, concerts, baseball games. He told us to have fun over the weekend and come to work tired on Monday morning.

Wasn't sure if he was serious, but he's the master over the office, so Christoph and I could not argue with him over something like that.

So wandered around today, looking at some of the things. There was an outdoor dance thing that I saw part of. Pretty girls, anyway. Wandered over to where the baseball game was being played. Didn't make any sense to me: bunch of guys standing around while one guy throws a ball past a guy with a stick who tries to hit it. Up-timers supposedly like it . . . but up-timers are different. If they like baseball, they're really different.

Master W asked to see Master Gronow's letter yesterday after I read it. No great surprise to me that Master G didn't buy the story. Getting better, though . . . Master G said as much. So maybe next time. Anyway, Master W read the letter and handed it back to me. He said it sounded promising and that his wife would be interested in hearing about it.

So, thinking about what Master G said, think I see what he means. Didn't go far enough in last rewrite to show how the characters were touched. Need to show, not just tell. That's not what he said, but think that's what he meant.

And need another title. Titles are hard. Would rather rewrite whole story than to try to find new title. But Master G asked for one, so need to think of one.

Long day. Church tomorrow. Need to go to bed.

Recited evening prayers. Now for bed.

Letters From Gronow

From the Journal of Philip Fröhlich
9 July 1635

>Tuesday
>Breakfast–
>> *1 wheat roll 3 pfennigs*
>> *1 cup morning broth 1 pfennig*
>> *1 mug beer 2 pfennigs*
>
>Supper–
>> *1 sausage 2 pfennigs*
>> *1 bunch raisins 1 pfennig*
>> *1 wheat roll 3 pfennigs*
>> *1 mug beer 2 pfennigs*

Dreamt of home last night. Don't do that very often. Dreamt I was cold. Woke up shivering, although it was actually warm in the room. Not sure what that was about.

Quiet day at work today. No problems, just regular business. Quiet until Frau Grubb came in, I should say. She teased Christoph and me, then went into Master Wulff's office. I heard him laughing a few minutes later.

Frau G came out of the inner office on Master W's arm and stopped in front of my desk. She said she wanted to read my story. After a moment, she reached out with a finger and pushed up on my chin to close my mouth. Told her it wasn't good. It wasn't ready for anyone to read yet. She told me that since she was Portia, she was entitled to read anything that had Portia for a character. And besides, she might be able to help me make it better. All I could do then was stutter. She beckoned with her fingers. Finally said it wasn't here and I'd have to bring it in tomorrow. She smiled and said, see, that wasn't so hard. Then I said, but you're going to find it hard to read. It's my original copy, not a clean submission copy. She laughed and said if she could read her father's hand, she could read anything. So gave up and said I'd bring it in. She said she'd be here after lunch tomorrow, told Master W goodbye, and swirled out the door.

Realized then that I hadn't seen a companion for Frau G in the two times I've seen her. Asked Christoph about that. He said she seldom takes one. He said she appears to have no fear, but that she also has a small Hockenjoss & Klott revolver in the little bag she carries, and according to Master W she knows how to use it.

Wow. Never thought of a woman I know carrying a pistol. I mean, I can understand it, especially in parts of Greater Magdeburg, but still . . . On the other hand, Julie Sims and Gretchen Richterin both handle guns, and the CoC thinks the world of them. The world is changing. Why not?

Started making notes on what to do to make the story better, where and how to make the reader feel what's going on. Not done, but good start.

Good tired tonight.

Recited evening prayers, and now to bed.

From the Journal of Philip Fröhlich
10 July 1635

Wednesday
Breakfast–
1 wheat roll 3 pfennigs
1 bunch raisins 1 pfennig
1 mug beer 2 pfennigs

Supper–
1 wurst 2 pfennigs
1 cup strawberries 1 pfennig
1 wheat roll 3 pfennigs
1 mug beer 2 pfennigs

Dreamt about Portia—my character, not Frau Grubb—who was yelling at me again about how I couldn't get anything right, and she was getting tired of my taking so long to tell her story. Didn't look like Frau G, didn't sound anything like her. Probably a good thing. Not sure I want my master's wife in my dreams. Max floated in and out while she was yelling, smirking at me over her shoulders. Not fair. Max needed a good smack, and I couldn't reach him. Dream, though . . . probably wouldn't have been able to smack him anyway. Not fair.

Interesting day. Sergeant Brendan Murphy came in the office in the morning. Up-timer, client of Master Wulff. Came in to tell Master W something that had happened about a matter that Master W had handled for him not long ago and to pay on his account. He started telling jokes, and even with his up-time English and his use of what's started to be called Amideutsch, he can make you laugh. My ribs were hurting and I was out of breath when he left. He says he tells jokes some nights at The Green Horse, one of the nights when Marla Linder and her friends aren't singing and playing. Heard them once. Really good. Need to go hear him, just to see what a 'comedy routine' is like. Think that's what he called it.

Frau G came in after lunch just like she said she would. Not used to someone like that keeping a simple promise like that. Guess not all people of rank are that casual about their word, even to a clerk like me. Reluctantly handed her the story copy. She took it with more of a grin than a smile, moved over to a work table beyond Christoph's desk, and settled down to read.

Worked on the files I was supposed to be preparing, but was hard to do . . . especially when she giggled. Giggled! Not supposed to giggle at a horror story. What could she be giggling at? And do I really want to know?

When she got done she came back and asked if I had the latest letter from Master Gronow with me. Actually did. Hadn't gotten around to pinning it up on the wall in the room. So took it out of my pocket and passed it to her. She took that back to the table and spent more time reading it than I think it deserved. Then she brought the papers back over to me and said she wanted to think about it, but she would see me tomorrow, and she would clear it with Master W so I wouldn't get in trouble. Not sure what she meant by that. Sounds ominous.

Went back to rooms at end of day. Pinned the letter up on the wall next to the others. Spent rest of evening thinking over story and wondering what Frau G was going to say.

Finally recited evening prayers, and now for bed.

From the Journal of Philip Fröhlich
11 July 1635

    Thursday
    Breakfast–

1 cup morning broth 1 pfennig
1 cup berries 1 pfennig
1 mug beer 2 pfennigs

    Supper–

1 bowl fish stew 3 pfennigs
1 cup sauerkraut 1 pfennig
1 wheat roll 3 pfennigs
1 mug beer 2 pfennigs

Dreamt about Master Wulff as a wolf again. He was walking around on his hind legs and dressed as a man working in the office. Weird. Was even wearing his regular clothes. Looked like they fit, too. Weird. Max was with me, didn't say much, just had his rifle ready and kept his eyes on Master W. Did say that Master W was a very hard man, and I should be careful with him, not be stupid. Asked him if he was evil. He said no, just partook more of the nature of the judge than he did of an intercessor. Not sure I understand that, but maybe it will become clearer.

Mama Schultz told me she was glad I was eating more than bread and meat. Told her I don't like most other stuff. She said it was good for me. I laughed.

Really like working for Master W. Instructions are clear, materials are available, know what to expect from him. Makes sure I know what I'm doing before he gives me responsibility for something. Like Christoph, too. He is a big help. So much calmer than back in Master Gröning's office. Didn't see Martin last night. Wonder what's going on.

Frau G came in after lunch. No clients were here, so she went into the inner office, and came back out a few minutes later. Told me that she would be by at 3 o'clock and that I was going to go down to Walcha's Coffee House with her for an hour to talk about my story. She said Master W said it was okay. Behind her I could see Christoph nodding his head and mouthing the words Say Yes. So I did. She smiled and left. Looked over at Christoph. He grinned and said that if she said Master W had said so, he had. She never said anything like that if it wasn't true. I said I wasn't sure I'd have my assigned work done by then. He said he'd help me.

And he did. We finished the last of my projects right before 3 o'clock. Frau G walked in the door just as I wiped my pen nib clean and placed my pen on its rest. Did I mention I got my own metal nib pen here at Grubb, Wurmb, and Wulff? I did, I do, and it is very nice. Again, I really like working for Master W.

Anyway, Frau G told me to come with her. I looked at Christoph just to make sure. He nodded, so I followed her down the stairs and out through the door, then into the adjacent door to Walcha's Coffee House. The place was a little larger than The Green Horse on the inside, with I think more chairs and tables, but only because the tables were smaller.

She led me to a small table to one side with only two chairs. She sat in one and pointed to the other. I sat. She asked me if I have ever had coffee or chocolate or Indian or Chinese tea. Said no, no, and no. She laughed. Woman came over, said Good afternoon, Frau Grubb, will you have your usual. Frau G said yes, and bring Philip a small Dutch chocolate. The woman nodded and left. Frau G leaned over the table and said, what I ordered you isn't coffee. It's a drink made from chocolate. The taste isn't as strong as coffee, and it's a bit rich. If I'd ordered the American style, it would have had so much sugar in it that it probably would have made you sick. Up-timers put sugar in almost everything. Or at least, they used to. Then she leaned back.

The woman came back about that time with two cups on a tray. One she set before Frau G and one she set before me. Frau G lifted hers, took a sip, and smiled. Perfect, she said. Tell Georg I said so. The woman smiled and looked at me. After a moment, realized she was waiting on me to taste mine. Took up my cup and took a sip. It was hot, and the flavor was a bit bitter, and dark, if that makes sense, but after a moment, realized I liked it. Told Frau G. She smiled.

Wasn't sure why we were there or what to do, so said nothing. Watched Frau G . . . when she took a sip, I took a sip. Cups weren't very big, before long they were empty. She pushed hers to one side, and got a thin book out of her bag and put it on the table.

You don't know much about girls, she said. Wasn't a question. Definite statement, almost declaration. Said no, had two brothers, but only sister I had died as a baby. She closed her eyes for a moment and nodded.

It shows in your story, she said. Portia sounds like a boy or young man. She doesn't talk like a girl. She doesn't think like a girl. She doesn't act or walk like a girl. That's a big part of what your editor is trying to tell you, but I'm not sure he even understands it. That's something the up-time authors were better at than most of our writers today and historically. Even the men up-time writers could usually portray a woman more realistically than the writers of today. You need to read some of the up-time writers.

Said I was reading Masters Poe and Lovecraft. She snorted. Surprised me. Big sound out of little woman, little lady. She said that by late up-timer standards, both were second-rate writers. Poe was, Lovecraft not even that good. Both could work the ideas, but they weren't very good at description or at characterization. Think that's the word she used. Making the character seem real and alive. She said one writer made his characters so real to her she found herself praying for them one day.

Sat back, surprised. Don't look at me like I'm a heretic, she said. Shook my head, said I'd never thought of it like that. She quirked a corner of her mouth, said if I learned it, I'd be the first seventeenth-century bestseller. Really confused by that, but pushed it back to think about later. How does a girl think, I asked. She smiled and said I'm glad you asked that. Spent the rest of the hour talking about boys and girls, how they were the same and how they were different and how they needed to be described to come alive. She made lots of notes in her book, and when we were done she handed it to me. Told her I would have the notes copied tonight and get the book back to her tomorrow. She said to keep it . . . she had others.

This is a bound volume, in very nice calfskin, of very fine paper. This book probably costs more than everything I own put together. And she gave it to me. Surprised. Confused. Wondering.

Made it through rest of work.

Spent evening reviewing her notes.

Tired.

Recited evening prayers. Now to bed.

From the Journal of Philip Fröhlich
15 July 1635

Monday
Breakfast–

1 cup morning broth 1 pfennig
1 cup berries 1 pfennig
1 mug beer 2 pfennigs

Supper–

1 sausage 2 pfennigs
1 bunch raisins 1 pfennig
1 wheat roll 3 pfennigs
1 mug beer 2 pfennigs

Dreamt a little bit last night. Didn't wake up, don't remember much other than knowing I was dreaming. Funny how you can be in a dream and know you are dreaming, but still have the dream.

Busy day at work today. Several new consultations, lots of action for some existing clients. Lots of paper generated. Christoph was typing almost all day long and was using something called carbon paper to make more than one copy at a time while he typed. Didn't know that was possible. Really neat. Makes me wish I had a Goldfarb und Meier machine of my own. But it costs way more money that I have, or will probably ever have. I should be content with my new pen nibs.

Stopped by Syborg's Books after supper. Master Johann says the next issue of *Der Schwarze Kater* will be out early next month. Really looking forward to it. Saving my pfennigs.

Meanwhile, still need a new title for the new version of my story. Thinking about *The Apotheosis of Portia*. Will have to think about that.

Started writing the new version tonight. Have a strong idea of where this one is going as a story. Will keep that in mind as try to put the words down.

Tablets that Master Matthias gave me are not great paper. Not the same. Some pages take the ink fine, some pages the ink spreads a bit, almost blots. Have to keep the touch very light and not put much ink down. May have to go to pencil. Not cheap there.

Got opening of story done. Trying to keep in mind everything Frau Grubb told me about writing girl characters. Never occurred to me that have to write them differently. But after thinking about it, makes some sense. Never had a sister, never had a betrothed, but the guys I knew who did sure talked like girls are a mystery. Have to take their witness for it.

Spent some time rereading Issue 2 of *Der Schwarze Kater*. The story *Legion* . . . didn't like it at first. But tonight when I read it, it really seemed to connect somehow. The idea of a demon possession happening seemed farfetched at first. Despite the Inquisition and the witch finders active over by the Rhine, had trouble accepting that. But they did happen in the time of Our Lord. Scripture says so. So what if they could happen today? What would be the effect if there was a modern-day Legion possession? And would people be scared about what could happen, remembering what happened when the Lord exorcised the Legion of his day? Guess sometimes you have to read stories more than once to understand them. Definitely do with this one. Wow.

Recited evening prayers, twice. Now for bed.

∞ ∞ ∞

Not sleeping. Recited evening prayers again—twice. Try again.

From the Journal of Philip Fröhlich
17 July 1635

> *Wednesday*
> *Breakfast–*
> *1 cup morning broth 1 pfennig*
> *1 barley roll 2 quartered pfennigs*
> *1 mug beer 2 pfennigs*
> *Supper–*
> *1 sausage 2 pfennigs*
> *1 cup sauerkraut 1 pfennig*
> *1 wheat roll 3 pfennigs*
> *1 mug beer 2 pfennigs*

Dreamt I was back in Master Gröning's office, only Thomas was in charge and was sitting at Master Schiller's desk. Was working very hard, and every few minutes he'd pick up the page I was working on, tell me it was all wrong, tear it up, and make me start over again. Felt hopeless in dream. Very glad when I woke up from that one. Rest of night was quiet. Where was Max when I needed him?

Regular day at the office. Did lots of filing, finally got caught up from Monday.

Christoph started showing me how to use the typewriting machine. Letters don't make any sense, why they are arranged the way they are. Why would QWERTZ be put next to each other? He says the arrangement is something that came down from the up-time, and that all their typewriters and keyboards, whatever they are, use it, except that the Z and Y keys are in different places. Guess it becomes normal. C can sure type fast. And he says the woman in Grantville who taught him could type twice as fast as he does, and that she says she knew people who could type a lot faster than she does. Wow.

Even typing slowly, really like how nice the letters look, and how they look the same every time they're used. See now why Master Gronow said that he lusted for one of the typewriting machines. Afraid I do too, now.

Wednesday. Managed to speak with Martin after work. Saw him at the corner where we had talked before. He told me that he was doing good at his new job, and that they had even increased his pay a little. Told him I was glad. We talked about what I'm doing for a bit, then he asked me if I had heard about Master Schiller. I said no. He said that one day last week Thomas had apparently started shouting at Master S and then physically assaulted him, hitting him and kicking him and actually knocked him down. Said that Master S was bruised and cut and had a black eye and a big lump on the back of his head. Said that what he heard was that when Master Gröning came to the office the next day he blamed Master S for the trouble, although Master S was the one who had been hurt. Master S told Master G that if he was so concerned with preserving his relationship with Master Schmidt over taking care of his long-time employees, he wished him well of it, and he quit and left right then. Supposedly Master G stood in the doorway of the office and shouted after him that he would make sure that Master S never worked in Magdeburg again. M said that the story is making the rounds of all of the offices, and Master G is losing respect everywhere.

Angry. Really angry. Never thought Master G was a fool, but he acts the fool now. Master S may not have been the best manager in Magdeburg, but he was fair and tried hard. Did not deserve that.

Took a while to calm down after got back to the room. Finally started working on new Portia story. Wrote enough to make a stopping place. Hard to write a girl. Guess it makes sense. I'm a boy . . . man, I guess. Not a girl. Hard to think like one. Frau Grubb's notes really help.

Ended in Scripture tonight. Found one of the Psalms that speaks to what I feel tonight:

*When he shall be judged, let him be condemned: and let his
prayer become sin.
Let his days be few; and let another take his office.
Let his children be fatherless, and his wife a widow.*

David knew. David understood.

Recited evening prayers—three times. So now to bed.

From the Journal of Philip Fröhlich
18 July 1635

Thursday
Breakfast–
*1 barley roll 2 quartered pfennigs
1 mug beer 2 pfennigs*

Supper–
*1 wheat roll 3 pfennigs
1 mug beer 2 pfennigs*

Dreamt last night, but only thing I remember is being cold. Was warm when woke up in the morning, though.

Wasn't hungry today.

Told Master Wulff about what I'd heard from Martin. He frowned, shook his head, and said there's no fool like an old fool. I guess I looked surprised, because then he said that was a saying from Grantville, one that he thought was really fitting to what Master Gröning was doing. Then he looked over at Christoph and asked if Master G had paid everything he owed to the firm. C said yes. Then Master W asked if we had any open matters with Master G. C said only that one contract that had come in for review two days ago. Master W said to return it to Master G with a note that due to the press of business we would be unable to take on that task. And that any other requests for service or representation were to be declined for the same reason unless he, Master

W, personally said otherwise. Then he muttered something about rather trusting a marsh rat than a man who treated his own so poorly. After he went in his office and closed the door, C and I looked at each other. Said wow. Indeed, C said. He let me do the typewriting of the note going back to Master G. Giggled while I was doing it. Serves Master G right.

Think I'm beginning to understand Max's comment about Master W having the nature of a judge.

Weary tonight. Got a few words written, but couldn't think clearly, so gave up after a while.

Recited evening prayers, and now to bed.

From the Journal of Philip Fröhlich
21 July 1635

> **Sunday**
> **Breakfast–**
>> *Fasted*
>
> **Lunch–**
>> *1 wurst 2 pfennigs*
>> *1 bunch raisins 1 pfennig*
>> *1 mug beer 2 pfennigs*
>
> **Supper–**
>> *1 sausage 2 pfennigs*
>> *1 cup sauerkraut 1 pfennig*
>> *1 wheat roll 3 pfennigs*
>> *1 mug beer 2 pfennigs*

Dreamt of Thomas last night. Dreamt that we were fighting again. Dreamt that I punched him in the face, over and over again, then kicked him where it hurts most, and again, then kicked him in the back again and again and again after he fell down. Felt good doing it. Was really angry at him, shouting and cursing him. But in a weird way, I was watching myself do it, surprised, not happy, upset even. Then Max showed up, and took my arm and turned me away. Told me that that was not me. That I was not to be confused by that temptation, and to take no joy from seeing someone hurt. Woke up after that, really had trouble going back to sleep, but finally did. No dreams the rest of the night, thanking God for that.

Lord's Day, Lord's work. Music was good at church today. Lots of people there, so singing was loud. Sang along with them. Enjoyed the reading. Deacon had a good clear voice. Other pastor spoke the homily, not Pastor Gruber, but he did better than usual. Enjoyed that as well.

Almost done with reading *The City of God*. St. Augustine continues to feed me.

Spent time in Scripture today, book of Esther. Interesting story. Interesting description of the emperor's court. Interesting how Mordecai managed to set Haman's plans to ruin, by simply being a bit smarter and understanding people so much better. Wonder if I can make a story from that someday. Think Master Wulff is smart like that. Need to watch and see if I can learn from him.

More words on the new Portia story. Too long to write full title. Maybe *A of P*. Anyway, starting to get a little easier to tell the story. Little easier to move the story and the characters along. Hope that means I'm getting used to telling it right, and not that I'm just putting words together.

One of these days Johann will come back through Magdeburg, and we'll be able to sit and talk about everything that has happened here and my writing. Hope that happens soon.

Recited evening prayers. Now to bed.

From the Journal of Philip Fröhlich
22 July 1635

>Monday
>Breakfast–
>>*1 cup morning broth 1 pfennig*
>>*1 barley roll 2 quartered pfennigs*
>>*1 mug beer 2 pfennigs*
>
>Supper–
>>*1 sausage 2 pfennigs*
>>*1 cup strawberries 1 pfennig*
>>*1 wheat roll 3 pfennigs*
>>*1 mug beer 2 pfennigs*

Dreamt of storm clouds. Stood on Gustavstrasse and watched them roll in from the north. Tall, black, ominous, removing the light of day as they came. Air grew colder. Advanced like a moving wall. Grew dark around me until Max arrived. Took a position in front of me. Held his rifle across his chest. After a few moments, gave a shrill whistle, suddenly there were a myriad of angels facing the clouds. Clouds kept advancing, angels started shining, then they all gave a shout, and the clouds turned to wisps and faded away. Angels faded away as well, except Max, who gave me a big grin and told me everything was fine. Woke up then. Not sure that was a regular dream. Not sure what it was. Hope I don't have another one like it.

Regular day at work. Nothing exciting, except Frau Grubb came in right before noon to take Master Wulff to lunch. Asked me if I was writing, said yes. Asked how much, told her maybe a fourth done, bit more. She said she wanted to read it, I said it wasn't ready. She said piffle, and told me to bring it in tomorrow.

Asked Christoph what piffle means after Frau G left. He doesn't know either. Must be something from the up-time.

Stopped at Syborg's Books after work. Talked to Master Matthias. Told him I was about done with *The City of God*, and wasn't sure if I should start over or read something else. He got a serious look on his face and said he would think about that and have a recommendation for me the next time I come in. Kind of nice having my own book recommender.

Made good strides on the story tonight. Portia seemed to stand up and stand forward and do what she wanted, just leaving me to write it down. Felt kind of funny, but got a lot of words down tonight. Need to get some more candles, yes. Down to two, and that won't make it through a long night of writing.

Recited evening prayers, so now to bed.

From the Journal of Philip Fröhlich
23 July 1635

> **Tuesday**
> **Breakfast–**
>> *1 cup morning broth 1 pfennig*
>> *1 wheat roll 3 pfennigs*
>> *1 mug beer 2 pfennigs*
>
> **Supper–**
>> *1 wurst 2 pfennigs*
>> *1 cup sauerkraut 1 pfennig*
>> *1 wheat roll 3 pfennigs*
>> *1 mug beer 2 pfennigs*

Dreams were quiet last night. Don't remember much, kind of think Max was nearby, but nothing stirred me or woke me. After the last few nights, don't mind a quiet night.

Another regular day at work. Ended up doing more filing than I expected, as Master Wulff spent a lot of the day dictating letters and reports to Christoph, who then started typewriting them up. Carbon paper made copies as he worked, so had to file those as he finished them. He is so fast with the machine that he produced a lot of them.

Frau Grubb came in right before noon again, talking about the big CoC parade happening in Magdeburg. Apparently, now that their campaign against the *Niederadel* who rejected the freedom of religion rule is over, especially after the battle at Güstrow, the men involved came to Magdeburg to assemble. She said that some of them marched in from the south along the river road, some marched in from the west along Kristinstrasse, and some from the north along Gustavstrasse. They are assembling in Hans Richter Square. Think I'm glad I wasn't there. Would have been very crowded.

Frau Grubb and Master Wulff talked about that some, but eventually he had to meet with an appointment. When the door to the inner office closed, Frau Grubb looked at me and raised her eyebrows. Was busy, so just gave her the pages I had written and carried on with my work. She took them over to the table she had used the last time and read through what I had done. Didn't take her long. At least she didn't giggle this time.

Brought the pages back to me and told me it was a better story than the last one, and it seemed to flow well, especially the last part of it, but that I still needed to work at making Portia sound like a woman. Then Master Wulff came out of the inner office and they went to lunch. Sighed after they left. C laughed. Told him writing stories was hard work, especially when you've never done it before. He said he could see that. Told him he should try it. He laughed again, said no, his betrothed was enough of a burden to bear, he didn't see any need to inflict additional labor and woe on himself. Said I wouldn't know. He laughed yet again, said I would, sooner or later. Could be, I guess, but not happening right now.

Got more writing done tonight. Story seems to be going well. Which makes me suspect it's not, really. Every time I thought that before, turns out Master Gronow didn't agree. But Frau G says this is better, so maybe it is. Have to keep trying, I guess.

Recited evening prayers, and now to bed.

From the Journal of Philip Fröhlich
29 July 1635

Monday
Breakfast–
>*1 cup morning broth 1 pfennig*
>*1 barley roll 2 quartered pfennigs*
>*1 mug beer 2 pfennigs*

Supper–
>*1 bowl fish stew 3 pfennigs*
>*1 cup sauerkraut 1 pfennig*
>*1 wheat roll 3 pfennigs*
>*1 mug beer 2 pfennigs*

Dreamt of Portia last night—the character, not Frau Grubb. She was calmer than in last dreams, but still wants me to hurry and finish her story. Told her I was working on it as fast as I could. She crossed her arms and stared at me, and after a bit said to get it done. Then she faded away just as Max showed up. Asked him why he didn't keep her out of my dreams. He laughed and said I was a writer, she was only the first of the characters I'd write that will visit my dreams, and I'd better get used to it, because they weren't really other people, they were all going to be me, or part of me. Not sure I understand that, but he's the angel, not me.

Got to do more typewriting today. Not as good at it as Christoph is. Make more mistakes, harder to fix, but think I'm getting better. C didn't laugh at me, anyway.

More words tonight on *AofP*. Read a little more in *The City of God*, too. Almost done.

Recited evening prayers. Now to bed.

From the Journal of Philip Fröhlich
31 July 1635

Wednesday
Breakfast–
1 cup morning broth 1 pfennig
1 cup berries 1 pfennig
1 mug beer 2 pfennigs

Supper–
1 wurst 2 pfennigs
1 wheat roll 3 pfennigs
1 mug beer 2 pfennigs

Dreamt of Master Wulff as wolf again. He was facing Master Gröning and Thomas and had them backed into a corner. Wasn't growling or snapping, but wouldn't let them leave. Woke up from that, went back to sleep, don't remember any others.

Frau Grubb came in today, asked me how the story was going, told her it was almost finished. She said how long, I said maybe by Friday. She said to bring it in then, she wanted to read it. Christoph shook his head when I opened my mouth, so didn't even try to argue with her.

Wrote late tonight because was so close to end. Finished *AofP* with just a bit of candle stub left. Will read it again tomorrow and see if it's good.

Tired, but good tired. Not even going to read anything else tonight.

Recited evening prayers, and now to bed.

Letters From Gronow

From the Journal of Philip Fröhlich
2 August 1635

Friday
Breakfast—
1 sausage 2 pfennigs
1 cup berries 1 pfennig
1 mug beer 2 pfennigs

Supper—
1 bowl fish stew 3 pfennigs
1 wheat roll 3 pfennigs
1 mug beer 2 pfennigs

Dreamt about sitting in Walcha's Coffee House at a table with other writers. All men, didn't know any of them, they were all dressed in down-time-style clothes, so must have been down-time writers. Talking about writing, and characters. Told them what I learned from Frau Grubb about women characters. Couple of them laughed, most listened. Seemed to be respectful. Was very weird. Getting respect from other writers, I mean.

Took the finished story to work today. Frau Grubb came in, just as she said she would. Didn't say anything, just held out her hand. Put the story in it. She went to her table and sat down to read it. Was busy in making a copy of an agreement, didn't think about her or the story until I was done. When I looked up, she stood and came back to my desk and handed me the story. Said she thought it was good, and to submit it to *Der Schwarze Kater*. Told her I would as soon as I finished making a clean copy. She grinned and said good luck.

Got some of the good paper from Christoph before I left work. Only had three pages left in the room. Not near enough to finish a clean copy of *AofP*.

Stopped by Syborg's Books. Master Johann was there, waved at me as soon as I walked in the door and held up Issue 5 of *Der Schwarze Kater*. Had been carrying the money for it the last couple of days, immediately dug it out of my pocket and handed it to Master Johann and took possession of Issue 5. At last! Turned without saying goodbye or farewell, hurried out of store and almost ran back to the room. No words tonight. Was reading instead, naturally.

Two up-time translated stories in this issue, one by Master Poe, *The Tell-Tale Heart*. Big change—other not by Master Lovecraft, but by a different up-time writer named Master Robert E. Howard. Title is *Pigeons from Hell*. So naturally had to read it first. Wow, wow, and wow again. May not sleep for a week. Very powerful story. Now see what Frau Grubb meant when she said that Masters Poe and Lovecraft were second-rank writers. Master Howard's story turned my guts into not a knot, but knots. Like he took some of the ideas from Master Lovecraft, but made them his own. Reshaped them. Reforged them. Something. Wow.

Recited evening prayers. Lost count of how many times. Need to go to bed, but eyes won't close. Will lie down and try to sleep.

∞ ∞ ∞

Later. Much later. Not sleeping. Not sleepy. Lit candle, read through the end of *The City of God*. Think now I'm calm enough, so now to bed.

From the Journal of Philip Fröhlich
4 August 1635

Sunday
Breakfast–
> *Fasted*

Lunch–
> *1 sausage 2 pfennigs*
> *1 cup berries 1 pfennig*
> *1 mug beer 2 pfennigs*

Supper–
> *1 bowl fish stew 3 pfennigs*
> *1 bunch raisins 1 pfennig*
> *1 wheat roll 3 pfennigs*
> *1 mug beer 2 pfennigs*

Dreamt I was on a boat floating down a river. That was all. Just floating. Eventually woke for a moment, then went back to sleep with no dreams. Not sure why I got that. Not connected to anything in life or writing, don't think. Weird. But after night before, welcome.

Lord's Day, Lord's work.

Not quite as many people at church, but still plenty of voices to sing the music. Sang loudly. Reading was not as good as last week. Another deacon, with a mush mouth. Could only understand about one word in four or five. Disappointed. Homily wasn't as good either. Same pastor, just not as good a word. Need to get Pastor Gruber back at the lectern.

Quiet day, otherwise. Much writing as copied *AofP* to clean copy. Making good progress.

Much reading as read through rest of Issue 5 of *Der Schwarze Kater*. In comparison to the previous issues, *The Tell-Tale Heart* was effective. In comparison to *Pigeons from Hell*, no, not nearly as powerful. Have to wonder. Surely Master Gronow knows this, sees this, can read and know the difference. I can. Confused. Wondering.

More evidence that I'm affecting the magazine in the submissions guideline page. I should be paid for that.

Think I'll be able to sleep tonight. Need to. Still feeling lack of sleep from Friday night.

Recited evening prayers. Now to bed.

Black Tomcat Magazine Submission Requirements

Legibility is paramount. If we can't read your story, we won't buy it. To that end, we strongly recommend that your work be prepared with the new Goldfarb und Meier typewriting machine or something similar. If a true manuscript is presented, please use practiced penmanship and calligraphy.

Please use octavo-sized paper no larger than eight inches wide by ten inches high. All pages of a story submission should be approximately the same size. Use one side of the page only. Natural color or bleached paper only—No Dyed Or Tinted Paper, please! And black ink only. Not blue, or red, or purple.

If the story is typed, please insert a blank line between each line of lettering. If the story is written out, please space the lines about 3/8 of an inch apart. Either way, leave a blank margin of approximately one inch on all sides of each page.

Whether typed or written, do not write a story in all uncials. Leading sentence character in uncial with the rest in minuscule is preferred. All minuscule is acceptable. Again, let us stress that legibility is critical to getting your work accepted for publication.

No illuminated manuscripts, please. Likewise, do not submit illustrations along with your story. If your illustrations are an integral part of your story's construction, we suggest you seek out another publisher.

Our manual of writing style is Martin Luther's translation of Holy Scripture. All issues of grammar and word spellings will be decided in accordance with his practice. Note that familiarity with and practice of those guidelines improve your chances of having your story published. All things being equal, the story requiring the least amount of work on our part has the advantage.

Keep in mind that your purpose is to tell a story, not provide a learned tome of erudition and rhetoric. A story should have a beginning, a middle, and an end. Write accordingly.

Format the first page such that your name, contact address, and word count of your story are in the upper left hand corner, the story title should be in the upper edge center, and page number in the upper right corner. Subsequent pages should contain your surname and abbreviated title in the upper left corner and page number in upper right corner.

Keep a personal copy of your story. All submissions become the personal property of the publisher upon receipt, and will not be returned, regardless of ultimate decision about publication. Allow for six months of mail and processing time before querying as to the publication decision.

All things considered, the shorter a story is, the better its chances of being published.

Finally, remember Rule 1 above—Legibility is paramount.

Good luck!

Johann Gronow, Publisher and Editor, Black Tomcat Magazine

From the Journal of Philip Fröhlich
5 August 1635

Monday
Breakfast–
> *1 cup morning broth 1 pfennig*
> *1 cup berries 1 pfennig*
> *1 mug beer 2 pfennigs*

Supper–
> *1 sausage 2 pfennigs*
> *1 wheat roll 3 pfennigs*
> *1 mug beer 2 pfennigs*

Dreams very quiet last night. Don't remember anything, even Max. Don't mind. Just a bit odd to have nothing.

Frau Grubb came to the office today. Still getting used to that. Master Gröning's wife never appeared at his offices. Don't think I ever saw her. Or at least, if I did, no one told me that was her. Frau G shows up at least once a week, if for nothing else than to have lunch or coffee with Master Wulff. But she seems to enjoy being here. Talks to Christoph and me, seems to understand our work. Christoph told me that her father is an attorney, so unless her father sent her away, she probably grew up around attorney stuff. Hard to do that, I guess, and not learn something about it. Then she married Master Wulff, who is scary smart and doesn't seem to mind talking to her about anything. More I see of them, the more I wonder what it would be like to be married to someone like that . . . either one of them. Not like Mutti and Vater, not like any married couple I know. Of course, since I'm not betrothed, not a practical consideration at the moment.

Anyway, Frau G's reason for coming in today was a shock to me. She stopped in front of Christoph's desk, and said that she wants both of us to attend one of Frau Mary Simpson's salons this Friday in company with her and Master Wulff. Surprised me. Shocked me. Felt like I'd been punched in the belly. Couldn't breathe. Opened mouth, couldn't talk. Closed it. Opened it again. Couldn't talk. Closed it. Did that several more times. Felt cold, clammy. Must have gone pale. She stepped over and patted my hand and said it would be okay. She used the up-time word so naturally. Okay. How can it be okay? How can my being in the middle of the highest and most important folk in Magdeburg be okay? How can I not be the pile of horse dung in the middle of the assemblage? How can I not be a discredit to them, to the firm, to me? I'm not one of those folk.

Somehow I managed to say enough of that that she realized my concern. She leaned over and placed her hand under my chin and closed my mouth. When I tried to keep talking, she did it again. When I opened my mouth a third time, she pointed at me and I closed it. She told me that Christoph had gone to a salon a couple of months ago, and had survived it. He nodded. She told me that Frau Simpson's salons were very likely to have all kinds of different people from all over Magdeburg and Grantville. It was not the patricians and *Adel* only; it was anyone that Mary found interesting. And she, Frau G, thought that Mary might find me of interest. I shook my head, she tapped my cheek to make me stop.

Clothes, I said. I patted my chest. Best I have. Not good. Not good enough. Frau G tilted her head and drew her eyebrows down. Hmm, she said. Stand up. She walked to the inner office door and asked Master W to step out. He appeared in the doorway, she looked from him to me and back again. She said we were close to the same size, Master W being just a little bit taller. There would be something I could wear, and I shouldn't worry about it. And after that, they went to lunch.

Not worry? NOT WORRY? How am I to not worry about this? I have no business attracting Frau Simpson's attention!

Christoph told me it would be fine, it would just be a lot of different kinds of people walking around and talking and drinking wine and spirits.

As long as I didn't puke on someone or knock them over, no one would think anything of me one way or another.

Great. My stomach is back in knots. Not a knot—knots. I may not eat for the rest of my life . . . which I don't expect to be very much longer.

No writing tonight.

Recited evening prayers—many times. Not very calm, but going to try and go to bed.

From the Journal of Philip Fröhlich
6 August 1635

> **Tuesday**
> **Breakfast–**
> > *1 barley roll 2 quartered pfennigs*
> > *1 mug beer 2 pfennigs*
>
> **Supper–**
> > *1 wheat roll 3 pfennigs*
> > *1 mug beer 2 pfennigs*

Dreamt I was drowning last night. Someone had pushed me in the river, and it was deep and fast and cold, and I couldn't swim, could barely keep my face out of the water enough to breathe some. Was getting tired, kept slipping down. Tried to yell for help, kept getting water in my mouth, no one heard me. Woke up just as was about to go under the water. Lay awake for long time, finally went back to sleep. Same dream. Same result. Woke up. Eventually went back to sleep. Same dream. Same result. Woke up. Stayed awake at that point. Was very tired of that dream.

Not hungry today. Was almost useless at work. Kept dropping things, kept putting things in wrong places. Spent most of afternoon undoing and redoing things I did in the morning. Frustrated with myself. Angry. Shouldn't be that way. But I was. So then got angry with Frau Grubb for doing this to me. That lasted most of the day. By evening, Christoph was tired of it, I think. He asked me if I was still bothered by the salon. Said yes. He told me not to be. There would be a few upper rank people there, but mostly there would be people like us, people who make Magdeburg happen, who make the businesses thrive, who have the ideas and make them work. And most of them are nice people who will talk to us just like they talk to each other.

Master Wulff appeared in the door to the inner office. Christoph is right, he said. None of these people are inherently better than you. None of them are any more desirable in the sight of God than you are. All of them eat and drink and piss and shit and sleep just like you do. Under their clothes, they're all human beings, just like you are. They may have more of the world's possessions than you do, they may have more rank in the world than you do, but when their lives are over, what they had won't matter and they're going to stand before the same God, and they're going to be judged by the same standard. So don't be rude, don't be aggressive, but don't be timid. He promised me that when some of them find out I'm a writer, they would be impressed.

Wow.

Spent the rest of the evening thinking about what Master W said. Decided he's right. Doesn't mean it will be easy. But knowing what he said, remembering that, calms my mind.

No writing tonight, either. But writing tomorrow.

Recited evening prayers. Now to bed.

From the Journal of Philip Fröhlich
7 August 1635

>Wednesday
>Breakfast–
>>*1 cup morning broth 1 pfennig*
>>*1 cup berries 1 pfennig*
>>*1 mug beer 2 pfennigs*
>
>Supper–
>>*1 wurst 2 pfennigs*
>>*1 cup sauerkraut 1 pfennig*
>>*1 wheat roll 3 pfennigs*
>>*1 mug beer 2 pfennigs*

Dreamt of the judgment throne last night. Christ on it and surrounded by a host of people. Saw Master Schiller, Master Wulff, Master Gröning, others. Master S, Master W were given a Well done, my good and faithful servant. Master G got a What you did to the least of these you did to me. Which made me feel good. Was suddenly my turn, and then Max showed up and made me wake up. Told me I couldn't see my own future. Big grin on his face, too.

Back to normal at work. Good thing, had a lot of work today.

Frau Grubb arrived just before lunch with an older woman not dressed quite as well. Told me to come out from behind my desk and take off my jacket. Did so, even though my shirt wasn't my best one. She handed me a jacket to put on. Did. Fitted a little funny. Didn't come past my waist. She checked the shoulders and the chest. Fit okay there. Sleeves were a bit long. Older woman measured sleeves and where my wrist was. Said it would be simple fix. Held a pair of pants up to my waist. Couldn't see where they hit my feet, but no indication of needing adjustment. Rolled them up. Frau G said they would be back tomorrow to try them on me. They left. Put my jacket back on, looked at Christoph. He shrugged. We got back to work.

Lots of writing tonight, copying *AofP*. Getting very practiced at copying. Seems to be going very smoothly. Which, of course, makes me worry that there's something wrong, or going to go wrong, or something. Over half-way done, even so.

Two days to the salon. Will really really really be glad when that's over. Recited evening prayers. Now to bed.

From the Journal of Philip Fröhlich
8 August 1635

> Thursday
> Breakfast–
>> *1 cup morning broth 1 pfennig*
>> *1 mug beer 2 pfennigs*
>
> Supper–
>> *1 sausage 2 pfennigs*
>> *1 wheat roll 3 pfennigs*
>> *1 mug beer 2 pfennigs*

Dreams were very muddled last night. Had some, but they flickered like the embers of a fire, flaring up for just a moment, just a single picture, then dropped back down to darkness. Not sure what was going on. Didn't see Max, so couldn't even ask him what it was.

Older woman brought clothes by today. Had to go into the inner office to put them on, she checked fit, said they were good. Put regular clothes back on. Finished work. Stopped at bathhouse tonight after work, had hair and beard trimmed after bathing. Beard very short.

More copying tonight. Good progress. Will have new copy done before long.

Tired. Good tired, though.

Recited evening prayers, and now to bed.

From the Journal of Philip Fröhlich
9 August 1635

Friday
Breakfast–
1 cup morning broth 1 pfennig
1 cup berries 1 pfennig
1 mug beer 2 pfennigs

Dreamt I was watching a riot. Apprentices and journeymen were yelling at troops wearing the colors of Gustavus Adolphus, and throwing rocks and dung and whatever else they could find at them. Troops took it until a stone hit an officer and cut his face. He shouted, the troops faced forward and started moving toward us with their bayonets mounted. Woke up just as they reached the apprentices and journeymen. Sweating. Panting. Was really glad not to see more of that one. Didn't go back to sleep for a long time. Didn't want to start that one up again.

Wore the fancy clothes to work today. Christoph raised his eyebrows and grinned at me. Went out at lunch, found a cobbler, had him clean and oil my boots. Don't look new or fancy, but look better than they did.

When asked if I would have time for supper, Christoph told me that there would be food at the salon that I could eat. Told me there would be wine and spirits, but if I wasn't used to that I could ask for beer. Said that was what I would do. Made up mind not to have a lot of even that.

Toward the end of work, Frau Grubb arrived. She looked . . . different . . . somehow. Same woman. Hair was a little different. Was wearing a black dress, I think, with a black cloak over it. But something different. Master Wulff came out of the inner office. He was also wearing something different, like what he usually wore to the office, only a bit nicer, maybe. He said shall we go, led us out of the office, then turned and locked the door. Frau G took his arm, and they led the way down the stairs and out onto the street. We walked back east along the street until we reached where it crossed the Big Ditch and through the city walls into Old Magdeburg. It was but a few more minutes until we arrived at the Brewer's Guild guildhall. Dragged along behind. Sudden surge of I don't belong here. Frau G must have sensed it. She looked back at me, grinned, and beckoned with her head. Sighed, caught up with them just as they entered.

Stopped inside just long enough for Master W to hand his hat to an attendant, then he turned and removed Frau G's cloak from her shoulders and handed that off as well. Heard Christoph suck air, looked at him, whispered What. He leaned over and murmured that every down-time woman there was going to hate Frau G by the time the evening was over. Looked at her, understood. Full skirt, tight bodice that rose to her neck, no patterns or colored patterns. Pure black, which means horribly expensive. Golden collar around her neck, almost as tall as my hand is wide. Stark contrast. But her arms were bare. Very slender, and nothing on them from her fingertips to past her shoulder joint. An up-time style, I'd wager, C murmured again. And after seeing her, no man here is going to look at any woman but her tonight.

Master W held his arm out and Frau G tucked her hand into it. They walked toward two women standing together a few steps into the foyer. Mary, Lady Beth, said Frau G. The two women smiled, and the shorter dark-haired one said, Andy, Portia, so good of you to come. And who are these young men with you?

Christoph Heinichen, my assistant and lawyer-to-be, said Master W, and Philip Fröhlich, of my staff. Be known to Frau Mary Simpson and Frau Lady Beth Haygood. Christoph bowed, I tried to copy. Welcome, gentlemen, she said.

Philip is a writer, Frau G said. I gulped. Frau Simpson, for so the older woman had to be, smiled and said, then we shall have to find time to talk tonight, young man. Great, I thought. Frau Simpson wants to talk to me. Can I run away? She said, For now, welcome again. With that, Master W and Frau G led the way into the guild hall. Once inside, Frau G looked around and said, walk around, talk to folks, have fun. We'll find you later.

Christoph took me to a table in one room where they had had wines and such. He looked at me. Beer? I nodded. He told the attendant, one beer for him, one red wine for me. A moment later, cups in our hands, we wandered on.

There were a few musicians in one room, playing violins and flutes. In another room, there was a card game being played with people standing around and laughing about the play. In other rooms there were people sitting and talking, or standing in groups and talking. In the fourth room, Christoph stopped and began talking to a couple of women. Down-timers by their dress and speech. Pretty, I guess. He looked at me from the corner of his eye, and made a slight movement of his head. So I moved on.

Walked around the rooms again. Found some things to eat. Lots of cheeses and little hard crackers. Tasty, but takes more than a few to fill up.

Interesting to watch the people. Made me think of them all as characters. Guess they were, in a way. Characters in their own stories.

Characters, someone said. Looked around to see Frau Simpson. Gulped. Do you see them that way, she said. Stuttered, then managed to say yes, at least some. She laughed, said you're a writer all right. What do you write? Told her trying to write up-time style horror. She laughed again, said she should have guessed since Portia had introduced me. Asked me if I knew *Der Schwarze Kater*, told her it was my favorite and I was trying to get them to publish a story. She said if she had known that, she would have made sure that Johann Gronow had come tonight, but she didn't think he was here. Hadn't even thought about that, but was disappointed.

She led me to another room, where there were a few younger folk. Ella, she called out. A girl turned and came to her. This is Philip, and he's going to be a writer. Her eyes lit up. We talked, I don't know, for a long time. Until Christoph appeared and an older man appeared beside Ella and said it was time to leave. She grimaced, said good-bye, and left. Christoph said Frau G had sent him. Followed him to the foyer, where Master W and Frau G stood waiting, he holding his hat and she wearing her cloak. She looked at me closely, and smiled. Bade farewell to Frau Simpson and Frau Haygood.

Walked back to my room.

Not sure what to think. Wasn't what I thought it would be. But Frau Simpson knows who I am. What will that mean?

Weary. Didn't do anything, but weary.

Folded up nice clothes.

Recited evening prayers. Now to bed.

From the Journal of Philip Fröhlich
10 August 1635

Saturday
Breakfast–
> 1 cup morning broth 1 pfennig
> 1 early apple 1 pfennig
> 1 mug beer 2 pfennigs

Supper–
> 1 sausage 2 pfennigs
> 1 wheat roll 3 pfennigs
> 1 mug beer 2 pfennigs

Dreams last night were . . . different. Dreamt of Ella. Not sure I even heard her surname. Talked for the longest time last night. Mostly me talking. Weird. Don't normally do that, especially with someone I don't know. But she started asking questions about the writing, and somehow that opened the weir to let the words flow. Dreams were more of the same. Couldn't have told you last night what she looked like, but in dreams she had blue eyes, dark blonde hair. Face not long, not round. More heart-shaped, maybe. Straight nose. Small chin. How do I know that about her? Swear I didn't look directly at her that much last night. Wonder if she really looks like that, or if that was just dreams. Didn't wake up, but dreams would fade in and out, but always back to her. Really confused.

Mama Schultz had a few apples today. Early for them, but took one as soon as she offered it to me. Bit small, bit tart, but juicy. Savored it. Favorite fruit, but prefer early ones to late or winter ones.

Took nice clothes back to the office today. Was working on agreement copy when Frau Grubb came in. Picked up clothes to hand back to her. She wouldn't take them. Said they were older things of Master Wulff's that he either wouldn't or couldn't wear any more, and she would rather someone she knew got some use out of them than to sell them to a rag picker. I tried again, she insisted I keep them. Tone of voice was starting to get sharp. Didn't want to see her angry. Suspect like her husband, not a good experience. Shrugged, told her many thanks, put back on my desk. She turned to Christoph, asked who the young woman was he had spent the evening talking to. He said it was his betrothed's cousin, who works as an assistant at the Duchess Elisabeth Sofie Secondary School for Girls. Think I got that right. She is married. He was getting to know her a little better, and was, he said, picking her brain for information about his betrothed. They haven't spent much time together yet, and he just wants to know her better so he can avoid mistakes and set their foundation as a couple squarely. Or so he says. Myself, the girl was pretty. Have to wonder if that affected his desire to talk to her.

Then Frau G asked me who the girl was I had been talking to. Stammered a bit, said her name was Ella, but that was all I knew. Frau Simpson had introduced us. Ella, she said. Ella. Who would Ella be? Then she grinned. Okay, she said, almost has to be Ella Kamererin. Daughter of Peter Kamerer. Businessman from Nürnberg who moved to Magdeburg when he inherited property as a result of the Sack in 1631. Said I didn't know him. She said she thought he was in metals. Said she didn't know much more than that about her.

So, I know a bit about Ella now. I think.

More pages done on the copy tonight. Close to halfway done.

Recited evening prayers. Now to bed.

From the Journal of Philip Fröhlich
11 August 1635

Sunday
Breakfast—
> *Fasted*

Lunch—
> *1 sausage 2 pfennigs*
> *1 bunch raisins 1 pfennig*
> *1 mug beer 2 pfennigs*

Supper—
> *1 bowl fish stew 3 pfennigs*
> *1 wheat roll 3 pfennigs*
> *1 mug beer 2 pfennigs*

No dreams to speak of last night. Quiet. Didn't wake up at all. No Max. Disappointed in the morning. Boring.

Lord's Day, Lord's work.

St. Jacob's wasn't as full today as the last few weeks. Quieter. Not as loud singing. Music was still good, so sang loudly. Reading was good. One of the better deacons there this morning. Homily from Pastor Gruber. Was glad at that. Spoke about the exorcising of the Legion demoniac. Weird after thinking about that not too long ago from the story in *Der Schwarze Kater*. Talked about the miracle of the cleansing, talked about the release and destruction of the demons into the swine. Talked about how everyone stops there, and never talks about the impact on the community, on what it cost the community to lose the herd of swine in order to regain the possessed man. Always a cost, he said. Always a cost to heal, to cleanse, to restore. Sometimes God pays the price, as with Christ on the cross, sometimes we pay the price, but always a price. We need to understand and not be surprised. Pastor G always makes me think with his homilies.

Pastor G invited me to lunch today. Didn't even try to buy my lunch. Good. We talked for quite a while. He asked me all kinds of questions about my new job, and Master Wulff, and the work I do. Then he asked me what I was reading. Told him I had finished *The City of God*. Asked him if he had something to suggest for what I should pick up next. He thought for a while, and said I should consider Martin Luther's *Divine Discourses* writings. Hadn't thought of that. Said I would look for a copy.

Still no word from Johann. We will surely have a lot to talk about when he next gets back to Magdeburg.

Spent part of the evening in Scripture. Book of Ruth this time. Amazing how a woman of one of Israel's greatest enemies became part of the lineage of the Savior. Nice story. Can learn from it as a writer as well as the spiritual lessons.

Spent rest of the evening working on the clean copy of *AofP*. Two complete pages done. Good progress.

Good day.

Recited evening prayers, and now for bed.

From the Journal of Philip Fröhlich
12 August 1635

Monday
Breakfast—
1 cup morning broth 1 pfennig
1 cup berries 1 pfennig
1 mug beer 2 pfennigs

Supper—
1 wurst 2 pfennigs
1 wheat roll 3 pfennigs
1 mug beer 2 pfennigs

Dreams mostly about weather. Windy. Rainy. Trying to get to work and the rain was pouring. Cold. Wet, of course. Took forever. Finally got to work, and it was Master Gröning's office, and Thomas was there yelling at Ella. Put myself between them. Thomas took one look at me, and faded away. Turned and took Ella's hand. She smiled, and faded away. Woke up then, feeling chilled from the dream. Went back to sleep, no dreams remembered.

Interesting day at work. Master Kamerer sent a message in the morning, asking for an appointment in the afternoon. When he arrived, Ella was with him. Surprised me. Think it surprised her. She looks much like my dream pictures of her, so even though I didn't look at her much Friday night, must have looked well. Master Wulff ushered both into the inner office and closed the door. Kept working on my files, but really curious about what was going on. After a while, door opened and Ella came out. Master Kamerer remained inside and closed door. Looked at door with what must have been weird expression. She smiled and said, they are talking money now. Father wants to settle a trust on me, but will not tell me how much money. And he won't tell me about how much he's paying to do this, either. Kind of old-fashioned about that kind of thing. Not like I won't find out somehow someday.

Shrugged. Told her I hoped it worked out. She laughed, said her father understood money very well. People, not so well, especially women people. Told her that I had seen that in other people and not just men of business. Sometimes people just aren't either understanding or nice. She agreed. She asked me where I bought my books. Told her mostly Syborg's Books just down the street. She said she goes in there sometimes. Told her I was going after work to see if they had a book my pastor had recommended. She said nothing, but looked thoughtful. Door opened then and Master Kamerer came out, nodded to Master Wulff, collected Ella, and left.

After work went to Syborg's Books. Master Matthias was there. He smiled, asked if I had sold a story yet. Told him not yet, but was about to submit latest effort. He said good. Asked what else was happening. Told him Pastor Gruber recommended I read Luther's *Divine Discourses*. His expression turned serious, said it was now more often called *Table Talk*. Then said, of course, and led me over to one particular shelf. Pointed me to one copy, said that was the newest edition. Gulped at the price. Pointed to a copy on the next lower shelf, said that was a really clean previously-owned copy of an earlier edition. Picked it up. Nice. Very good shape. Could almost afford price. Pointed to a copy on the next lower shelf, said it was an older copy, not in as good a shape, but all the pages were there. Picked it up. Felt loose in my grip, shifted, but nothing fell out. Could pay the price, but Master Matthias said he would take a dollar off the price, because it really was not in good shape. Said sold.

Turned around and there was Ella with her father. I said good evening. She responded, and formally introduced me to her father, telling him that Frau Simpson had introduced us on the night of the salon and that I worked for Master Wulff. That eased the frown forming on his face like a storm cloud. He nodded, but remained at her side. Showed her—and him—what I was getting ready to buy. She took it in her hands to leaf through it. His face relaxed a bit more. Noticed that her hand holding the book was gloved in a very thin glove, but her hand turning the pages was bare, holding its glove. She read parts of a couple of pages, handed it back, said it looked good. Looked to her father and raised her eyebrows. He got this pained expression and looked at Master Matthias and asked if there were any other copies. Master Matthias' mouth tried to smile, but he held it straight, barely, as he picked up the new copy and handed it to Master Kamerer. Had to turn away to hide my own smile. She waved at me as they left.

More pages copied. Getting close to having the clean copy completed. Recited evening prayers. Now for bed.

From the Journal of Philip Fröhlich
15 August 1635

Thursday
Breakfast–
1 sausage 2 pfennigs
1 cup berries 1 pfennig
1 mug beer 2 pfennigs

Supper–
1 bowl fish stew 3 pfennigs
1 wheat roll 3 pfennigs
1 mug beer 2 pfennigs

Dreamt of being at a salon, talking with Frau Simpson and Ella and walking around. Master Poe was there, Master Lovecraft was there, and other writers that Frau Simpson knew. She pointed them out as we walked around. Master Howard wasn't there, though. Remember thinking that was odd.

Quiet day at work. Caught up on the typing and the filing. Good thing to have days like that every so often.

After work took the final clean copy of *AofP* to Master Gronow's office. Of course, the door was closed, so had to slide it through the slot in the door. Once again, leaned head against door and recited prayer about story. Went back to room, began rereading Issue 5 of *Der Schwarze Kater*. Still shiver and get serious gooseflesh when reading *Pigeons from Hell*. Little background sketch of author says Master Howard committed suicide at age 30. One wonders if he wrote many stories like this, if there was a connection.

Recited evening prayers—three times. Now to bed.

From the Journal of Philip Fröhlich
20 August 1635

> **Tuesday**
> **Breakfast–**
>> *1 cup morning broth 1 pfennig*
>> *1 cup berries 1 pfennig*
>> *1 mug beer 2 pfennigs*
>
> **Supper–**
>> *1 sausage 2 pfennigs*
>> *1 cup sauerkraut 1 pfennig*
>> *1 wheat roll 3 pfennigs*
>> *1 mug beer 2 pfennigs*

Dreams were dark last night. Dark in setting. Seemed like storm clouds overhead, little light coming through. Walking corpses around, but not like Scripture risen dead. More like Master Howard's story. Was running to get away. Don't remember where I was running to. Turned corner, street was full of them. Woke up just as they grabbed me. Glad I woke up.

Spent most of day copying trust agreement documents for Master Kamerer. Know more than Ella does now about her business. Feels weird. Shouldn't know, I think. On other hand, working for Master Wulff, going to learn and see a lot of things about a lot of people's business. Better get used to it. Better keep my mouth shut, too.

No response from Master Gronow yet. Worried. Usually never takes this long. Know the Submission Requirements says allow six months, but never has taken this long before. Not sure if that's good or bad. Told Christoph and Frau Grubb, so get asked every day. Have to say no response every day. Frustrating.

Nervous.

Recited evening prayers. Now to bed.

From the Journal of Philip Fröhlich
22 August 1635

Thursday
Breakfast–

1 cup morning broth 1 pfennig
1 mug beer 2 pfennigs

Supper–

1 sausage 2 pfennigs
1 wheat roll 3 pfennigs
1 mug beer 2 pfennigs

No dreams that I remembered last night. Woke up tired, though.
Wasn't hungry this morning.

Quiet day at work. Bad. Needed to be busy, to keep from worrying about Master Gronow. Didn't happen. Fretted all morning and into afternoon.

Late in afternoon, messenger stepped in door, brought envelope to me, nodded, left.

Letters From Gronow

Is that it, Christoph asked. Nodded. Looked at it, couldn't move. Master Wulff appeared in the door. Is that from the publisher, he asked. Christoph said yes. Will you please open that so I can tell Portia what he said, Master W said. I swear she is more concerned about your being a writer than you are, if that's possible.

Still sat there just looking at it. Open the letter, Master W said firmly. Hands moved, opened the envelope, took out the pieces of paper inside.

22 August 1635
Master Philip Fröhlich

Congratulations on your story *The Apotheosis of Portia*. I intend to publish it in *Der Schwarze Kater*. A contract will be sent to you in the near future.

When I consider that first story you submitted so many months ago, I would never have believed at that time that you could arrive at this position this quickly. You worked very hard to improve, and it shows.

You are not the first down-timer to submit something that I will publish. You are one of the first, though, and at this point your story is, I would say, overall the best story I've yet to receive. Congratulations again.

Now, write me another one.

It is now with great anticipation that I say I look forward to seeing your next works.

In conclusion, congratulations again. You deserve it.

Johann Gronow

Editor and Publisher

Der Schwarze Kater

Epilogue

Philip Fröhlich felt his throat begin to tighten as he approached the office door that was open for the first time in his experience. He sidled up to the door, enough to see a tousled head of hair bent over a large table desk facing the door. He noted absently that there were a few strands of gray in the hair.

He tugged at his jacket to make sure it was straight, swallowed, and gave a diffident knock on the frame of the open door.

"Yes?" was the growled response. The bent head didn't move, but the pen that had been in motion paused.

"Master Gronow?"

"Yes," came another growl, but now the head raised. Dark brown eyes bored into him from under lowered brows.

"I'm . . . I'm Ph-Philip Fröhlich," Philip stammered. "I . . . uh . . ."

Gronow's countenance lit up and realigned itself into a beaming sun of a face as he threw the pen down on the tabletop and thrust himself to his feet. He stuck his hand out over the table. "Master Fröhlich!" the editor exclaimed. "Come in, come in!"

Philip entered the office and placed his hand in the editor's clasp, to find it firmly gripped and pumped like a machine. Gronow smiling was a younger man than Philip had expected or even than he had first appeared.

"It is so very good to meet you, my friend. Come, sit down." Gronow dropped back into his chair, and waved to a chair sitting across the table. "What can I do for you?"

Philip settled onto the edge of the chair. He was still somewhat nervous about this. "I, ah, wanted to come by and thank you for buying my story. I . . ." He ran out of words.

Gronow smiled. "Philip, my friend, to paraphrase an up-time saying, this is the beginning of what I foresee to be a long and beautiful and profitable relationship."

David Carrico

Episode 7

Magdeburg
From the Journal of Philip Fröhlich
29 August 1635

Thursday
Breakfast–
1 wheat roll 3 pfennigs
1 sausage 2 pfennigs
1 mug beer 2 pfennigs

Supper–
1 wurst 2 pfennigs
1 wheat roll 3 pfennigs
1 mug beer 2 pfennigs

Sleep was peaceful last night. If I dreamt, don't remember them.

Got a message from Master Gronow today asking me to meet with him tomorrow night after work is done. He didn't say what for, but has to be something to do with my story. Returned a message saying I'd be there. Good thing work was quiet today. Just had some filing to do most of the day, which was good. Mind was a bit preoccupied.

Still very happy to know that my story will be published in *Der Schwarze Kater*. Wake up most mornings, see the letter on the wall. Starts day off with big grin.

Funny, Frau Portia is even more excited than I am. She told me she had told Frau Simpson. Don't know why, but that makes me a bit nervous. Don't know if Ella Kamererin has heard yet. Would like to know what she thinks.

Spent part of tonight rereading *Pigeons from Hell* again in Issue 5. Might be the tenth time I've read it. Still get shivery. Wonder if this Master Robert E. Howard wrote any other stories. Will have to ask Master Gronow tomorrow.

Also finally started reading the copy of *Table Talk* I bought at Syborg's Books recently. Only two pages tonight. Reading German instead of Latin like *The City of God* was relaxing.

Even though didn't do much today, still tired.

Recited evening prayers, and now to bed.

∞ ∞ ∞

Master Wulff came out of the inner office, adjusting the sleeves of his jacket as he did so. He looked up as he got the last one set to his satisfaction and grinned at Philip. "You meeting with Gronow tonight?"

"Yes, at Walcha's Coffee Shop." Philip managed to not sound like a child responding to a father. Christoph Heinichen, Master Wulff's assistant, grinned at Philip from behind the attorney's back.

"Good. And what's the rule?" Master Wulff raised his eyebrows.

"Don't sign anything until you've had a chance to read and approve it." Philip didn't—quite—sigh.

"Good. Have fun tonight. Good night to the both of you. Christoph, lock up when you leave." And with that, the attorney waved goodbye and was gone.

The two young men looked at each other, and Christoph gestured at the door. "Go on, get to your meeting. I'll be leaving very soon."

"You're sure?" Philip asked. Christoph nodded and pointed at the door again. "All right. I'll see you tomorrow, then."

"Right. Go talk to your editor." Christoph made shooing motions.

Philip grinned. A few moments later he walked out the door at the bottom of the stairs, took a deep breath of the evening air, then turned and walked in the door to Walcha's Coffee House. The hum of many conversations washed around him as a couple of well-dressed merchant types brushed past on their way to the door. Anna the server waved him over as she finished clearing off a table. By the time his rump had settled onto his chair, she was back.

"By yourself tonight, Philip? Want your usual?"

"I'm meeting someone, so I'll…" Philip saw Master Gronow loom up behind Anna, "never mind, here he is now."

"Him?" Anna expostulated as Gronow took the other seat. "You're meeting with him? I thought you had better taste than that." She shook her head, but the smile that pulled her lips up belied her feelings.

"Nice to see you, too, Anna," Gronow said with a wide grin on his face. His Hamburg accent was noticeable but not overpowering.

"So where's the rest of that disreputable pack of over-grown urchins you usually join up with?"

"Tonight is a night for business," Gronow proclaimed, adopting a serious mean, "not B S." He emphasized the initials that had crossed over into Amideutsch from Grantville English early in the process of the pidgin forming.

"Uh-huh." Anna crossed her arms. "And that and a thaler will get me a beer at the Green Horse."

"You wound me," Gronow proclaimed, splaying a hand across his chest and leaning back in his chair, trying to remain serious even though another grin was forcing its way onto his face. "Seriously, you see before you a hard-working publisher and his newest author, met to discuss their joint endeavor."

Anna's eyes widened and she straightened. "Seriously?" She looked at Philip, who nodded back. She did smile at that. "Well, all right, then. You be good to him, though," she pointed a finger at Gronow. "He's a nice guy, and he works for the toughest attorney in Magdeburg. You really want to be nice to him."

She pulled her pad from her pocket. "Now, what do you want?"

Gronow looked to Philip and raised an eyebrow. "What do you like?"

"One café au lait, please."

"A man after my own taste," Gronow proclaimed. "Make it two large ones, and bring us a half dozen of those delectable oatmeal raisin cookies. Veritable ambrosia of the gods, those are."

"Two large café au lait, six cookies. Got it." Anna whirled away.

"Pack of overgrown urchins?" Philip couldn't help asking.

Gronow chuckled, then said, "I have several writer friends, and we frequently get together here for loud arguments and much recitation."

"Do I know any of them? Do they write for you, Master Gronow?" Philip was really curious now.

Gronow laughed now. "Call me Johann. We're going to be working together for a long time, I hope. No, they're all a bit older than I am, and although they support *Der Schwarze Kater*, none of them contribute to it. They all make fun of the kind of stories we're publishing. That's okay. I'm selling more books than the three of them combined. You might know Friedrich von Logau—he does some writing for the newspapers."

"The epigrammist?" Philip asked as Anna appeared to set two large mugs of steaming coffee on the table before them, followed by a saucer piled with cookies. Gronow nodded as he took up a mug and took a careful sip.

Philip was impressed. He had recently discovered Logau's needle-pointed wit and razor-sharp satire. Frau Portia had showed him several articles and reviews by Logau to give him examples of word crafting to consider and emulate. She'd also shared anecdotes, his favorite of which illustrated Logau's expert command of the ability to damn with faint praise. According to Frau Portia, his review of a showing of an artist's works as 'fairly well done' had left the poor man in disconsolate tears.

"Wow. I like what he writes, even if he does get sharp sometimes." Philip picked up his cup and blew on it. "He makes me think."

"Friedrich would probably consider that the ultimate compliment," Gronow said as he picked up a cookie and took a bite. "Umm, this borders on divine."

Philip lifted his mug, took a careful sip, and followed it with a bite of cookie. He had to agree with Master Gronow. He wasn't sure how anything could be better than that.

"Told you," Gronow mumbled around the remainder of cookie he'd shoved in his mouth.

Philip sipped some more of his coffee. He still didn't know what this meeting was to be about.

Gronow sighed, picked up his cup with both hands, and leaned back in his chair. "So, you're probably wondering why I asked you to meet with me."

"Well," Philip acknowledged, since that very thought had just crossed his mind, "yes. I assume it has something to do with my story…"

"Of course it does." Gronow took a noisy slurp of his coffee. "I want to give you some understanding of what's going to happen next. First, your story will be edited."

"And you're the editor, so you'll be doing the…editing?"

"Correct." Gronow beamed at Philip.

"So what is editing? What does it mean to be edited?"

"I read through the story looking for misspelled words, grammar errors, and such that may have slipped your eye before you submitted the story. And look for places where the story may fail or break down."

Philip felt confused. "Why would you buy a story if it was broken?"

"The publisher is a hard taskmaster, who insists that we put out a magazine every three months with at least forty thousand words in it. Sometimes that means, if we're short of good stories, we buy one that's almost good and either work with the author to fix it or fix it for him." Gronow shrugged. "Part of the job."

Now Philip felt even more confused. "Wait a moment…aren't you the publisher?"

Gronow shifted position in his chair, sitting up straighter and adopting a serious expression. "Why, yes, I am."

"So why would you say you're a hard taskmaster?"

Gronow frowned. "Who said that? You've been talking to that lazy lout of an editor, haven't you? Fellow doesn't work any more than he has to, buys the worst stories, spends my money like water, and eats at the fanciest restaurants and expects me to pay for it." He picked up another cookie and took a bite, giving a wink to Philip.

Philip had felt his jaw drop open when Gronow began his last statement, but now he closed it firmly. "You jest."

"Do I?" Gronow shrugged. "Perhaps I do. Yet being both publisher and editor makes me feel like two different men at times. The publisher has to keep track of the most mind-numbing details and schedules and money, while the editor—who is also a translator and at times a writer as well, you must remember—must tend to the souls of weary writers and nurture and encourage them to grow and blossom and put forth great works. Those two priorities don't always get along, and often create friction. Indeed, you should hear some of the arguments I have with myself at times." He took another bite of cookie and winked at Philip again.

Forced to smile at last, Philip shook his head. He reached out and took another cookie himself, but paused before he bit into it to ask, "So, who usually wins the arguments?"

Gronow laughed. "That's the spirit, my friend. Enter into the game with us. And the answer is, usually the publisher. Of course, he cheats, because if it looks like he's going to lose an argument based on the reason or logic of it, why, he simply refuses to pay the editor's expenses until he gives in. A low fellow, the publisher." He popped the rest of his cookie into his mouth and chewed it with vigor, tilting his head at Philip. That elicited another grin out of Philip.

The next few minutes were spent in providing appropriate attention to the remnants of the acme of the baker's art before them. After he swallowed his last bite, Philip was giving serious consideration to licking his finger to chase the crumbs on the plate, only to see Gronow do exactly that and pop the laden fingertip into his mouth. His own mouth quirked as he resolved to move faster the next time…if there was a next time.

Gronow drained the last of the coffee from his cup, and set it aside with a sigh. "But enough of sybaritic delights. To business, so I can charge this as a business expense." He pulled a document case into his lap, took out a wad of papers, and started leafing through them. "Not this one, not this one, definitely not this one, where is it…a-hah!" He pulled a small sheaf of papers out of the wad, and stuffed the remainder back into the document case, which he set aside.

Anna came by and picked up the empty plate. "Just in time," Gronow remarked as he set the papers in the space previously occupied by the plate. "Now, Philip, I need to talk to you about two things today. The first is the actual edit." He spun the papers around so that they were right side up to Philip, where he recognized his final submission copy of *The Apotheosis of Portia*—his story.

Gronow's expression was now very serious. "The purpose of an editor is to make sure that a story—your story—is as good as it can be. Fortunately, your command of the German language is more than adequate. You've also learned—admittedly, with some help from me—to tell a good story. There are a few misspellings in your manuscript, and a very few grammar errors." He shrugged, as Philip frowned a little. "It happens. Everyone makes mistakes. Sometimes they are minor, and sometimes they are terrible. I still shudder when I think of Robert Barker." And he twitched his shoulders.

"So who is Robert Barker?" Philip asked.

"He's the printer in England who a few years ago reprinted their King James Bible, but made a typesetting error that stated the Seventh Commandment as 'Thou shalt commit adultery.'"

"What?" Philip almost jumped up at that horrific thought. "That happened? You're not jesting?"

"I would not joke about something like that," Gronow replied. "Publisher's errors are very common, but that one was especially bad and attracted notoriety. The stories and rumors spread very quickly."

"I can see why," Philip said, settling back in his chair. "Please don't do something like that in my story, Johann."

"We're not likely to," Gronow said with a twisted smile, "but we'll try not to make any mistakes. It helps that your hand is clear and very legible, and there won't be many corrections needed. And ordinarily any changes or corrections we make will be straightforward. But there is one word in your story . . ." he leaved through the pages of the story until he arrived at the one he wanted, " . . .there. That word—*sauber*." He pointed at the word. "It almost makes sense as it is. But I don't think it's the word you meant. I think you want *zauber* there instead."

"You can read upside down?" Philip was surprised at that.

Gronow grinned. "A very useful skill when there is only one copy and there are two readers. Now reading the set type, that's challenging. You have to read mirror imaged and from right to left. I'm not very good at that yet."

Philip shook his head, then read the sentence in question as he had written it with *sauber*, twice. The word meant 'clean', and it seemed to work, but it also didn't feel right. So then he read it, substituting *zauber*, which meant 'spell'. "I think you're right. *Zauber* makes more sense in the story. It feels right." He shrugged. "If you're asking my opinion or permission, I'd say change it."

"Right. That settles that easily enough." Gronow gathered the story pages together and restored them to his document case, from which he then pulled a folder which he held in his hands. "On to the second thing. Anna said something about you work for a lawyer. Who would that be?"

"Master A. N. D. Wulff," Philip recited with some pride, "of the firm of Grubb Wormb and Wulff."

Gronow's eyes widened a bit. "Indeed. And what do you do for them, if I may ask?"

"I clerk in their office, and manage their files. I'm learning more about law, and eventually may go to university. And Master Wulff told me not to sign anything until after he reads it."

The editor nodded, said, "We won't need these, then," and pulled a couple of pages out of the folder and put them back in his case. He then handed the folder to Philip. "That is the contract to publish your story in *Der Schwarze Kater*. I need it signed and one copy returned to me within two weeks in order to move forward with publishing your story."

Philip asked the most burning question in his mind. "When would the story be published?"

"If I get the contract back in two weeks, probably in Issue number 7, which would be in about…" he leaned back and started at the ceiling for a moment, "…call it five months."

"Why so long?" Philip was disappointed.

"Editing, setting the type, printing the pages, designing and printing the cover, folding and binding the pages. It all takes time. In fact, it might be Issue 8, just to have enough lead time to get everything done."

That was even more disappointing to Philip, and it must have showed on his face. "Don't worry," Gronow continued. "I want your story out as soon as possible, because I want to proclaim you as a local writer. And speaking of that, do you have an idea for another story?"

"Umm, no." Philip hadn't even thought about that yet.

"As soon as you finish the last story, you should start another one. Keep in the feeling and rhythm of writing, you see. So come up with another idea and get after it. If you can't think of one, come talk to me and I'll see if I can help you come up with one."

The publisher pulled a pocket watch out and looked at the time. "I have to be at another appointment in a few minutes." He waved at Anna, who brought the tab. He took one look at it, muttered, "I need to buy a share in this place," and pulled a few bills out of his pocket and handed them to her.

"I can pay for mine," Philip said, reaching into his own pocket.

"No," Gronow insisted. "It's a rule from the up-time. When an editor and a writer go out together, the editor buys."

"But . . ."

"No." Gronow was serious, Philip saw.

Anna brought a few coins to the table. Gronow took the largest one, and left the rest. "I'll be back in touch with you soon. And get that contract to me as soon as you can." A moment later, the door was closing behind him.

Well. That had been an eventful conversation. Philip looked down at his cup, and realized there was still some coffee in it. He swallowed the last of it, then grimaced because it had cooled to not much better than tepid temperatures.

"You're supposed to drink it while it's warm." He looked up to see Anna smiling at him. "You want another cup?"

"Not tonight," Philip responded. He stood, then kind of cocked his head and asked Anna, "Is he always like that?"

She grinned and shrugged. "He's always been a bit funny from what I've seen. Why?"

"Just trying to decide whether to take him seriously."

"I'd say when he's serious, be serious; otherwise, just watch him like he's an actor."

Philip decided that was good advice. "Right." He left the coffee shop and started west down the street toward his rooming house.

He hadn't even made it as far as Syborg's Books before he came to a sudden stop in the street, which caused someone to brush by him with a muttered imprecation. "Blast!" he said with some force. "I forgot to tell Johann that I really really like *Pigeons from Hell*." After a great sigh, he shoved his hands in his pockets and moved on.

From the Journal of Philip Fröhlich
31 August 1635

> Saturday
> Breakfast–
>> *1 wheat roll 3 pfennigs*
>> *1 cup broth 1 pfennig*
>> *1 mug beer 2 pfennigs*
>
> Supper–
>> *1 cup fish stew 3 pfennigs*
>> *1 barley roll 2 quartered pfennigs*
>> *1 early apple 2 pfennigs*
>> *1 mug beer 2 pfennigs*

Dreamt last night. Max showed up. First time in a long time. Was dreaming something not rememberable, when he came strolling in from the left. Still carries his big black rifle. Wings still blue, but look bigger now. Told him that I thought he'd gotten rid of all the demons, that I hadn't seen anything like that in a long time. He said that that just meant he had to be even more on his guard, that the ones you don't see right away are the ones that are more dangerous. More I think about that, the more uncomfortable that makes me. Decided that having Max around is a good thing. Hope he's not just a recurring dream.

Otherwise, sleep was calm.

Stopped at Mama Schultz's for breakfast. She smiled. That was almost scary. She called me a good boy and told me to eat more. Early apples are starting to show up a little bit. Glad. Like apples.

Master Wulff finished reviewing Master Gronow's contract for the story today, had Christoph type up an acceptance letter with a change to one of the terms, had me sign both the contract and the letter, and sent me off early to deliver them. Told me to take the rest of the day off and be in early on Monday. He's the boss.

Letters From Gronow

Had the original contract and the acceptance letter in an envelope. Stopped by Master Gronow's office. Wasn't there. Wasn't surprised. Dropped the envelope through the slot in the door, left the building. Decided I hadn't been to Syborg's Books recently, so took myself that direction.

Old Master Syborg was there, Master Matthias. He smiled when he saw me come in, asked me what I was reading now. Told him I had finally started *Table Talk*. He said that was good, and that it never hurt to know the words of Martin Luther.

Browsed around the store for a while, didn't see anything new that I wanted. Asked Master Matthias when the next issue of *Der Schwarze Kater* was due out, he said not for a while. Then he told me that the store was going to offer a subscription service on the magazine. He said that for everyone who paid for the magazine issue at least a month ahead of the delivery, Syborg's would guarantee delivery of a copy of the issue when it was delivered. I told him to put me on the list. He laughed and said he'd already done that. I said I needed to tell Frau Grubb. He said if I meant Master Wulff's wife, her name was right ahead of mine on the list. We both laughed.

Wandered around the store some more. Was looking at a book of poetry by someone named Göthe when a voice behind me asked what was I looking at. Turned to see Ella Kamererin standing there. Her father was talking to Master Matthias, but I could see that he was still keeping an eye on Ella, so said good morning to her, and showed her the book. That's an up-timer, she said. Turns out her tutor has that same book. It's a new edition of a book that came back with Grantville in the Ring of Fire. She said she liked it, but her father wouldn't let her have a copy of her own. Said it was too mature, or something. Decided I wanted to get it, if it caused that reaction, but put it back on the shelf because I didn't have enough money to buy it right then.

Ella asked me how my story was going. Told her that Master Gronow had bought it, and would publish it in *Der Schwarze Kater* before too long. Her eyes lit up and she smiled. Made me feel good inside. She said she wanted to read it. Told her I would bring my copy to the office, and she should come with her father the next time he visits Master Wulff. She smiled again, and nodded. Felt warmer.

They left soon after.

Before I left, Master Matthias called me over to show me a special book. It was an up-timer book printed in English. Couldn't read it, of course, but really wished I could when he told me what it was: the collected sermons of a famous up-time preacher named Charles Haddon Spurgeon. Or actually, just volume two of five of the collected sermons. Carefully opened the book, looked inside. Could recognize a few words, but couldn't make sense out of anything. Frustrating. Really wanted to read them, compare to Luther. Asked him what he was asking for it. He said he had already turned down an offer of one hundred groschen for it. About fainted, and very carefully returned the book to the table.

Asked him how he had acquired it. He said that he has an agent who frequents these things called garage sales in Grantville and buys up any books they offer. He said by now there aren't many left in Grantville that people are willing to sell, and the competition for them gets pretty stiff, but that sometimes even this long after the Ring of Fire he gets something really good, and this one is very very good indeed. He expects to make a lot of money selling it to a university or a publisher.

Went home thinking I need to learn English. Have thought that before. Really think I need to do that now. There is so much to learn from the up-time that I will need English to learn.

That thought was in my mind the rest of the night, even when reading the Bible and reading *Table Talk*.

Said evening prayers. Now for bed.

∞ ∞ ∞

Philip stepped up his pace up the stairs to the office, as he could hear the steps of his boss coming up behind him. Master Wulff's rapid pattern was unmistakable. Philip stepped onto the landing and immediately moved to one side, just in time to let Master Wulff brush past him. A moment later the door to the offices was unlocked, and he followed Master Wulff into the office. He started to shut the door, to find that its progress was blocked by Christoph Heinichen's hand. The other clerk followed him into the office and closed the door.

Master Wulff looked around. "It's Monday, and I've slept since we were last here. What's on the schedule for today, Christoph?"

The older clerk was already standing behind his desk, looking at the large schedule calendar he kept on his desktop and changed and annotated as needed. "At 9 a.m., a Frau Sarah Diebes verwitwet Bünemann is due to discuss matters from her late husband's estate."

Master Wulff looked as if he had bit into something sour. "Ah, yes. I remember that one. Nasty business, not helped out by the misfeasance of Frau Diebes' husband's previous attorney, Jacob Köppe." He shook his head for a moment. "What else?"

"Master Brendan Murphy sent a note saying he will be in right after lunch to pay off his account, and wants to know if there is any more information about the matter with Malcolm Kinnard and Margarethe Becker. He says his wife Catrina is 'bugging him' to find out."

Master Wulff laughed. "When he comes in, tell him that Malcolm Kinnard is now working for Meister Becker, and will be for some time. Kinnard may actually end up marrying Margarethe Becker, but if they don't get married, Kinnard will undoubtedly have made a serious contribution to her dowry fund.

"Anything else?"

Christoph moved his finger down the calendar page. "There is a consultation with Master Kamerer at 2 p.m."

"I remember that. Routine business, I think. Time-consuming, but not critical. Not yet, at any rate. What else?"

"The only other thing on the schedule is a note that Meister Jacob Lentke wishes to consult with you at 4 p.m."

Wulff's eyebrows rose. "What about?"

"I don't have that information," Christoph said. "It wasn't in the note he sent requesting the meeting."

Wulff snorted. "Well, when the de facto head of the *Schöffenstuhl* asks to meet with the newest attorney in Magdeburg, said attorney had best be available to him. So make sure nothing else tries to take that time frame."

Christoph nodded, and picked up a pencil to make a note on the calendar.

Wulff looked over at Philip, who stood beside his desk. "I'll need the Paulus Bünemann file for the morning meeting, Philip, and the Kamerer work notes file for the early afternoon meeting. Also, be ready for the 9 a.m. meeting—I may want you to take notes. Christoph needs to get the monthly report to the partnership done."

Philip nodded, although he was a bit nervous at the thought of taking shorthand notes. He'd been practicing, but he wasn't sure he was very good yet.

Wulff dug around in a pocket, pulled out a money clip, peeled off a bill and passed it to Philip. "But before you do that, I need some coffee. Run down to Walcha's and bring back a large coffee for me. They know how I like it. Get whatever you and Christoph want as well."

With that, the attorney pulled off his outer coat and hung it on the coat tree before entering the inner office. Christoph grinned and pointed at the outer door. Philip grinned back, and headed for the stairs.

∞ ∞ ∞

The morning went well. Frau Diebes proved to be a short woman, neither thin nor plump, who dressed well, which helped to offset a very plain face. This was in contrast to her companion, Anna, who was taller, thinner, and although dressed in a plain manner was somewhat prettier. She said nothing, simply sat beside her mistress with her hands in her lap, but she seemed to be following the conversation as it flowed around her.

Frau Diebes was also accompanied by her bookkeeper, Johan Dauth. He was young—didn't seem to be much older than Philip. He was quiet, but when he spoke it was with assurance and confidence. Philip admired that.

Philip was able to follow most of the conversation, although parts of it got so complicated he had to make side notes on his pad to keep track of some of it. When the meeting concluded, Master Wulff escorted the clients to the front door in an uncommon show of courtesy. He had waved Philip to stay, so Philip remained standing in front of his chair to one side until the attorney returned.

"So, did you catch all of that?" Wulff asked after he threw himself into the chair behind the desk.

"I think so." Philips nervousness returned.

"Good. Read it back to me."

Wulff leaned his chair back with a squeak of springs while Philip read from his notes. The attorney's eyes were closed and his hands were interlaced across his stomach. When Philip finished, he sat up and opened his eyes, placing his hands on the desk.

"Good," he repeated. "You caught almost everything." Wulff spent a minute or so giving Philip two additional items to add to the notes. "That should do it," he said, then bellowed, "Christoph!" The sudden noise made Philip jump. The other clerk appeared in the doorway almost instantly. "Have I explained to you the background of Frau Diebes' issue?" When Christoph shook his head, Wulff waved him into the office and pointed at a chair. "You'll both need to know this. Mind you," he said with lowered eyebrows, "this is client confidential. You don't discuss this with anyone other than our staff, and then only in the office or somewhere that you know is fully private. Understood?"

Wulff steepled his fingers before his mouth for a long moment, then lowered his hands. "Let us begin by saying first of all that Frau Diebes is a good woman, certainly better than her husband deserved. She is, however, as you could see, rather plain of face. It was, in fact, her dowry that achieved her marriage, rather than her appearance. And her father wrote a superb piece of contract work for the marriage agreement, in which she not only retained rights to the dowry interest in the event of annulment or divorce or other termination of the marriage, she received significant rights to the business of her husband, the not-too-recently-deceased Master Bünemann. I wish I could have met her father. He might have challenged me." Wulff's mouth twisted in a wry grin.

"Master Bünemann, on the other hand, was a reputable member of the community, a well-thought-of merchant and corn factor, who seemed to be reasonably honest. Yet in his private life, he seems to have been, shall we say, less than honorable to his wife. The accounts are that he had established many mistresses over the years, and frequented prostitutes, all in search of the son that his wife had been unable to give him. He died last year, murdered by the father of a young woman he had attempted to seduce. There's more to the story than that, as you might imagine, but that's all you need to know right now.

"Frau Diebes came to us because her husband had no associates or assistants in his business, only a couple of bookkeepers, so there was no one there to step into his place and run the business after he died. And then the head bookkeeper died not long afterward, so she was left with the young man you saw—a good bookkeeper but not one to be the man of business . . .at least, not yet. So she followed the advice of her husband's attorney, Meister Köppe, and contracted with Meister Andreas Schardius to manage her husband's accounts…for an appropriate consideration, of course." That last was said in a very dry tone, which prompted a smile from Philip. He was starting to understand his new boss' sense of humor, and was finding that he rather liked it.

"With her father and her husband dead, Frau Diebes relied on Köppe's advice and signed the contract. Things seemed to go well for a few months, but then they missed several status reports. When they approached Schardius for clarification of the condition of Frau Diebes' assets and how much of her funds were available, she and Meister Köppe were informed that her assets were not available. Then right after that, Meister Köppe had an apoplexy and dropped dead in his home. So things were getting desperate for her.

"Frau Diebes had encountered my wife Portia at one of Frau Mary's salons, and they had become good acquaintances, if not friends yet, so she called on Portia, and as soon as Portia heard what had happened, she brought her to me. And we're just getting started. I think we can recover her assets. We may not recover any of her profits. But that may depend on how hard a game of hardball Schardius and his attorneys want to play. Frankly, I'm looking forward to it." The attorney's face had taken on a hard-edged grin at that point.

Wulff took note of what must have been a look of confusion on Philip's face. "Sorry, I forget that not everyone has lived among the up-timers like I did for a couple of years. You know that there is a game called baseball the Americans play?"

Philip nodded. "I've seen a game—or part of one, anyway."

"It's played with a hard ball, so they sometimes refer to it as hardball, as opposed to a similar game called softball."

"Ah. And the hardball game is harder?"

"In almost every sense, especially if you get hit with the ball."

Philip nodded. He understood the expression now.

"So that's where we are with Frau Diebes' case."

They heard the outer door open. Christoph immediately stood and headed for the outer office, Philip on his heels. It was a messenger delivering a sealed envelope. Christoph took charge of that, so Philip moved to his desk and began transcribing his notes from the earlier meeting. It took until close to noon to write them out. After a quick break for something to eat, Philip returned and typed up the file copy of the notes. He pulled the typescript out of the typewriter, grinning at the pure joy he felt at operating the machine.

It took a couple of minutes to read the notes again, making sure that he hadn't made any errors in the typing. Once that was done, he filed the notes and returned the file to its particular spot on the shelves, patting the shelf in satisfaction once that was done.

The mantel clock chimed. Philip looked to it, and saw that it was a quarter hour before two p.m. Master Kamerer would be here shortly. He moved down the shelf to find the Kamerer work notes file, then slipped through the open door of the inner office to place it on the right edge of Master Wulff's larger desk. Master Wulff looked up from the document he was reading long enough to glance at the file and smile at Philip, then returned his gaze to the page in his hand.

Philip returned to his desk. The thought of Master Kamerer coming made him wonder if Ella would come with him. He hoped so. It would be nice to see her again.

He busied himself with sorting the other filing that had accumulated during the morning's activities. Just as he finished that, the outer door to the office opened and Master Kamerer entered. Philip's eyes moved to the space behind the client, and he was rewarded to see that Ella had indeed accompanied her father today.

Ella gave Philip a small smile from where she stood behind her father. Philip glanced at Master Kamerer, who was following Christoph through the door of the inner office, then returned the smile.

"Ella," Master Kamerer had paused in the doorway to look back, "this shouldn't take long. Don't bother the young men—they have work to do." And with that, he entered the inner office to receive Master Wulff's greeting.

Ella rolled her eyes, and Philip almost choked as he suppressed a laugh. He did hear something like a snort from Christoph. Apparently he needed more practice in the art of laugh suppression.

"Honestly," she said in a very low tone, "you'd think I was five years old." She walked to a nearby waiting chair and settled herself in it with grace. Philip admired how smoothly she did it. Of course, that wasn't all he admired about her, but he banished that thought from his mind.

"I actually do have a lot to do for this monthly report to the partners," Christoph said with a grin, "so I'll leave you in Philip's care." He resumed his seat at his own desk, picked up a pen, ran a finger down a page to a point, and started writing.

Philip stepped to his own desk and pulled open a drawer, from which he pulled a folder, which he turned and offered to Ella. Before he could say anything, he heard Master Wulff call out, "Philip! Bring your notepad."

"For you to read," Philips whispered as he dropped the folder with his copy of *The Apotheosis of Portia* in Ella's lap. Then he whirled, grabbed his pad and pencil from his desk, and hurried to the inner office, hearing the mantle clock chime the hour as he closed the door at Master Wulff's direction.

∞ ∞ ∞

It was a full hour later when Philip opened the inner office door again, stepping through and over to his desk quickly to get out of the way of the other two men. He set his notepad on the desk, carefully aligning his pencil alongside it, then interlaced his fingers and inverted his hands, pushing his palms away from him to stretch his tired and cramped fingers. The two men had talked almost non-stop, covering many aspects of the business, and Philip had made notes all the way. His poor fingers felt like they were about to fall off his hand from gripping the pencil so hard.

Ella rose from the chair she had been sitting in and stepped over to face Philip across his desk. She precisely placed the folder in the exact center of the desk with care, then looked up at him with a broad grin.

"I like this!" She tapped on the folder. "I really do. Is this the one that you sold to *Der Schwarze Kater*?"

The fact that Ella liked the story triggered a wave of happiness that flowed through Philip in a moment. He felt a similar grin form on his own face, and stared into her eyes for a long moment. "Yes," he finally replied.

"When will I be able to buy it?"

Philip's smile faded away. "I'm not sure. According to the publisher, it won't be the next issue, and maybe not the one after that. He says it takes time to do all the editing and what he called 'putting all the pieces together.'"

Ella's mouth quirked. "Hmm. Well, when you find out, tell me. I'll want a copy as soon as it comes out."

Philip nodded as Master Kamerer ended his final exchange with Master Wulff, and approached his daughter.

"Come, Ella. We've handled everything I needed to discuss with Master Wulff, so we should leave and let these young men get on with their work."

Ella rolled her eyes again, and Philip looked down to keep from laughing. After a moment, once he felt his face was under control, he looked up again to see Ella looking at him. He gave her a definite nod, which she returned before turning and moving toward the outer office door.

Master Kamerer paused for just a moment beside Philip's desk; just long enough to give him a very direct look, followed by a very slight nod. Philip returned a much deeper nod, going so far as to move his shoulders slightly. The merchant followed his daughter through the outer door, which Christoph closed behind him. Philip released his breath and turned to see Master Wulff looking at him with a quizzical expression.

"Do you know Master Kamerer, Philip?"

Christoph chuckled, and Master Wulff looked at him.

"More like he knows Ella," Christoph explained. "He spent a lot of time talking to her at Frau Mary's salon."

Enlightenment dawned on Master Wulff's face as Philip felt his own face heat in embarrassment. "I...met them at Syborg's Books a few weeks ago, too. I like Ella. She reads." He could tell his face was getting redder. "She likes my story."

"Oho!" Master Wulff said with a chuckle. "This sounds serious, if you let her read your unpublished manuscript. Portia had to practically threaten you to see it. Wait until Portia hears about this!"

The following chuckle rolled on for quite a while. Philip's embarrassment continued to climb, although he didn't see how that was possible. He was already so flustered and self-conscious that he felt as if he was about to explode.

The laughter died away, and Philip began to feel the heat recede from his face. He took a deep breath, releasing it slowly.

"Back to work," Master Wulff said. "Philip, bring your notes and let's go over them." Philip grabbed his notepad and followed the attorney into the inner office, where he sat in the chair indicated by Wulff. "Do you know why I'm reviewing these notes with you?"

"Umm . . .to make sure they're correct, I'm sure," Philip responded.

"Well, yes," Wulff said, leaning back in his chair. "But I expect them to be substantially correct."

"Then . . .why?"

"To help you see what my thinking process is. The more you understand about how I approach the work and the individual cases, the more you can follow what I'm doing and why, which in turn will help you fit in to the work here better, but will also start to help your critical thinking."

"Critical thinking?" Philip was confused by that phrase. He'd never heard it before.

"Your ability to look at a problem or issue and analyze it—break it down into its various parts, and begin to develop solutions or approaches to solutions. The thought isn't new, but that descriptor is from the up-time, and I like it. That's a necessary skill for someone who wants to assist an attorney. It's also a necessary skill to be a lawyer."

Wulff stopped there, and just looked at Philip for a long moment. Philip had several thoughts run through his mind; two of which stayed with him.

"I never seriously dreamed of being a lawyer," Philip said slowly. "I mean, from my family, the most we've ever been is clerics or clerks, and not many of those. I have a cousin at Jena now, but he's just getting the standard classes. He expects to be a tutor when he finishes his studies. When I entered the job as a bookkeeper with Master Gröning, my family thought I had reached a peak." He tilted his head. "So did I." He paused for a long moment. "Do you honestly think I could be a lawyer?"

Wulff leaned forward and clasped his hands on his desk. "Yes, I do. You have the mind for it. You have the ability to focus and put forth the effort. You take it seriously. There is no doubt in my mind that you would be a good lawyer. How old are you, anyway?"

"Eighteen."

"Hmm. You look a bit younger than that." Wulff smiled at him. "You put in two years with me, learning everything you can learn, and my firm will sponsor you to Jena to study law officially. I expect by that point you could probably teach the classes, but you'll definitely go through them in short order. I expect you could take your exams in a few years and come back to us a recognized lawyer thereafter. Christoph will have his degree before then, and if he stays here and you join us, we'll dominate Magdeburg."

Philip could see that lupine grin on his boss' face. This time it was exciting to see. "Yes, Master Wulff," he responded, a smile on his own face.

"So, that's understood," Wulff said, unclasping his hands and setting them flat on the desk. "Ready to read the notes now?"

"Could I ask one more thing?"

"Certainly." Wulff was affable, but Philip could tell he was wondering what else Philip could possibly have to talk about now. "What?"

"I want to learn English," Philip said. "Up-time English," he hurried to clarify.

Wulff leaned back a bit at that. "Why?"

"I want to read up-time books and understand them. The theology books they have, and now I presume their books about laws."

Wulff nodded slowly. "I see." He leaned forward again. "I can see that, and it would probably bring some value to the firm as well. I can read it to some extent, although Portia does better than I. None of my partners or the younger lawyers who work with them, or even Christoph, have acquired the skill. The more I think about it, the more I think it might prove to be valuable to have someone who can read the up-time texts. Plus, if you can read the up-time texts, you can probably read the current English works. The reverse is not necessarily true." He nodded his head. "I'll speak to Portia. She can probably get you started; then when it's needed, there are up-timers in Magdeburg who might be able to tutor you in the skill. If nothing else, some of the teachers at the Duchess Elisabeth Sofie Secondary School for Girls might be willing to earn some extra money by tutoring in the evenings."

Philip smiled at that. Wulff nodded, and said, "Okay, read me your notes."

Philip flipped to the first page, and started reading.

From the Journal of Philip Fröhlich
25 September 1635

> **Wednesday**
> **Breakfast–**
> > *1 wheat roll 3 pfennigs*
> > *1 apple 2 pfennigs*
> > *1 mug beer 2 pfennigs*
>
> **Supper–**
> > *1 sausage 2 pfennigs*
> > *1 wheat roll 3 pfennigs*
> > *1 mug beer 2 pfennigs*

Dreamt last night that Masters Poe, Howard, and Lovecraft had invited me to join them at Walcha's Coffee Shop. Remember that both Poe and Lovecraft wanted coffee with milk, like the café au lait I usually get, but Howard said he wanted his coffee straight and black. He offered me a taste. Hot, bitter, almost made me spit it out. He laughed. Don't remember what we talked about after that, but remember it was a good time. Another dream I wish I could remember all of it, instead of just pieces.

Broadside sellers were calling out Extra Extra today. Didn't buy one, but overheard someone reading one to his friends. According to the broadsheets, Elector Johann Georg of Saxony was killed several days ago by some of the rebels who rose against him after he abandoned the cause of Gustavus Adolphus. Not well informed on the affairs of princes, but if one doesn't keep his word, and abandons the cause of the proper church as well, then he deserves such an end. Sorry for his family, but he made his choices.

Work was work today. Typed letters, filed papers. Christoph showed me the bookkeeping ledger they use for this office. Think I can follow it. Should be able to learn it. Don't know if the plan is for me to take it over, or if Master Wulff just wants me to know it.

May have a glimmer of an idea for another story. Just a hint of one. Almost just like a hint of a nice smell—know it's there, but when I try to bring it into my thinking it just fades away. Frustrating.

Recited evening prayers, and now to bed.

From the Journal of Philip Fröhlich
30 September 1635

>Monday
>Breakfast–
>>*1 wheat roll 3 pfennigs*
>>*1 sausage 2 pfennigs*
>>*1 mug beer 2 pfennigs*
>
>Supper–
>>*1 wurst 2 pfennigs*
>>*1 wheat roll 3 pfennigs*
>>*1 apple 2 pfennigs*
>>*1 mug beer 2 pfennigs*

Max was in my dreams again last night. Nothing big going on. He just kept floating through, would wave at me every once in a while. Didn't say anything. One of the dreams was weird and funny both. Dreamt I was listening to an up-time preacher preaching in English. Heaven instead of Himmel, God instead of Gott, Tcheeses instead of Jesus. Every time I heard one of those words, especially any word starting with the English j sound, I laughed. Laughed so much Max wrinkled his brow and put his finger before his lips. Made me laugh harder.

Guess what Frau Portia told me is true—I'll know when I start getting better at English when I start dreaming in it. Guess I'm getting there.

Quiet day today at work. Some typing, lots of filing, bit of note taking in one meeting. Master Wulff didn't even go over the notes with me. First time. Guess he figures I am fitting in, or something.

Got a letter from Master Gronow today. He wants to meet me after work tomorrow. Sent a response back to tell him yes. The messenger had been told to wait.

Frau Portia's trick of reading an up-time English Bible and comparing it to the German Bible is really helping learn to read English faster than I thought it would. However, that doesn't help my pronouncing the words. English is weird. I mean, tough, through, though, enough, bough are five words that should rhyme but are pronounced four different ways. Just weird. She said she would come by on Wednesday to hear me read. Guess I can deal with that. It will be better than last time, anyway.

Reading the Gospel of Johannes, or John as the English would say it. In the fourth chapter. Starting the story of the Samaritan woman. At least she doesn't have a name in the story. Names are hard.

Finished the evening relaxing by reading again a story from *Der Schwarze Kater* Issue 5, *All Soul's Eve*, by Pieter Arcangelus. Another story that I didn't like the first time I read it, but now seems to be improving the more times I read it again. That night is supposed to be dangerous for encountering evil creatures, but suppose that one met old gods like Old One-Eye or The Thunderer. What would that be like? More scary every time I read it.

So, recited evening prayers, and again, and again. Now to bed—and sleep, I hope.

∞ ∞ ∞

Philip looked up from where he was transcribing notes getting ready to type them up. It was the middle of the afternoon, and so far Tuesday had been a repeat of Monday until the door opened and Frau Portia walked in. Master Wulff's wife was a unique woman: short, petite, slender, with dark hair and regular attractive features. Her nose was a bit aquiline, and one of her lower teeth wasn't quite straight, but when she smiled, it seemed the room would light up and no one noticed. She had a larger than life presence, Philip thought as he watched her close the door. In that, she was a good match for her husband. She also had a quick mind, which also made her a good match for Master Wulff.

"Hi, guys," she called out in the local version of Amideutsch. "How are you?"

Philip's "Fine," response followed on the heels of Christoph's "Well."

"So, Philip," Portia said with a grin as she leaned against the edge of Philip's desk, "Andy tells me that you have a girlfriend." She crowed with laughter as he blushed. "It's true! It's true! How delightful!"

"Not a girlfriend," Philip protested. "Just…I like to talk to her…"

"And?" Portia tilted her head and peered out at him from under lowered eyebrows.

"She likes my story," Philip muttered, ducking his head and feeling his cheeks heat more.

"Oho!" Portia straightened and her eyes got big and round, like she was impressed. "This is serious, then. Should Andy start writing up a marriage contract?"

Philip could see the laugh lines deepen at the corners of her mouth and eyes, for all that her expression was still pretty sober. He just looked down at his notepad and shook his head.

Master Wulff appeared in the doorway of the inner office, donning his outer jacket as he came through. "Portia, stop tormenting the staff." Philip heard a muffled sound that must have been a choked off laugh from Christoph's desk.

"You're no fun." Portia pouted for a moment, then dropped the expression and gave a smile to Philip. "That really is good to hear, Philip. It's good to know that you have things in your life other than this job."

"I have church," Philip responded with something like a protest.

Portia's smile changed a little, almost like it got sad. "Of course you do, and that's good too. But I think the good Lord has more in mind for you than dull dusty papers and preaching."

"Come, Portia, or we'll be late." Master Wulff crooked his elbow, and Portia tucked her hand into the angle of it. He looked at Christoph and said, "You can finish what you're working on, but if no one else comes in this afternoon, lock it up when the clock chimes four. See you lads tomorrow."

And with that, they swirled out of the office.

"But I like my job," Philip almost whispered as the door closed behind them

Christoph laughed. "She knows that, Philip. She's just wanting you to have more enjoyment in life, to find more fulfillment. It's a woman thing, I think you'll find."

Philip thought about that in the back of his mind while he finished transcribing the notes and then typed them up. As he filed them away, he decided that while it probably made sense, he didn't understand it.

And with that, their work day was done, and he followed Christoph out the door and down the stairs. When they exited to the outside, they waved to each other and Christoph turned toward his rooming house. Philip just stepped down the way a couple of paces and entered Walcha's Coffee House.

Letters From Gronow

"Philip!"

He heard his name called, and looked over to see Master Gronow at a table with three other men. Master Gronow was beckoning to him with vigor, so he headed toward them.

"My friends," Gronow announced as he stopped between a couple of the chairs, "this is one of my latest finds in the literary arts, Philip Fröhlich, who has written a wonderful story that I will be publishing in my little magazine soon. Philip, here you see my oldest circle of writer friends: the two scurrilous rogues flanking you are Karl Seelbach and Johannes Plavius, and this surly lout to my right is none other than Friedrich von Logau. They all have some claim to being men of letters, but don't let that reputation fool you—they are all a low sort."

The men all nodded to him, and Logau actually lifted a hand in greeting. Philip grinned. "Are they the sort that the editor or the publisher would share a drink with?"

"Oh, the editor is much better than this." Gronow's grin increased. "He would have nothing to do with this lot. The publisher, however, finds them to be very charming fellows, which tells you just how low a character he is."

Plavius lifted his nose and gave an ostentatious sniff. "It seems the mire is becoming a bit deeper than usual."

Seelbach sniffed as well. "And a bit riper, as well. A good thing that I have an appointment with a patron that I must attend to." The smile on his face belied the haughty tone in his voice.

Seelbach started to rise, and Plavius joined him. "I shall keep you company, my friend." They each gave a bow to the other, joined arms and made their way toward the door. Philip followed them with his eyes, still grinning, then turned back to the table. Logau was shading his eyes with his hand, and Gronow was chuckling.

Logau lowered his hand and sighed. "Hopeless. Just hopeless." He stood as well. "But, I think on that note I will also withdraw from the field. Good evening Johann, nice to meet you, Philip. Hopefully the next time we meet will be more regular." He nodded to them both, and followed his friends out the door.

"So, sit down," Gronow said, waving at a chair. Philip settled into the chair across the table from Gronow.

Before either of them could speak, Anna appeared at Philip's elbow. "See what I meant about overgrown urchins?"

Philip laughed.

Gronow made a face. "That wasn't kind. Fitting, perhaps, but not kind." Anna smirked. Gronow looked at Philip. "Usual?" At Philip's nod, he turned to Anna and said, "Two large café au laits, please, and a half dozen of the oatmeal raisin cookies."

"Sorry, we've sold out of those cookies today," Anna said. She said it with a straight face, so Philip was sure—mostly—that she wasn't teasing Gronow.

The editor reacted dramatically, pressing one hand to his chest and sitting back in his chair with a stricken expression on his face. "No oatmeal raisin cookies? How can that be? Did I not have one earlier?"

"The bakery didn't produce as many as usual today. I think they're about to run out of raisins, or something. You and your friends ate the last of them an hour ago."

"Those gluttons," Gronow muttered.

Philip laughed again.

"Well, I am crushed and cruelly deprived," Gronow said with a sigh, "but what might you recommend to replace them?"

"It's been a busy day," Anna replied. "About all we have left are a few chocolate brownies from yesterday."

"What is the world coming to?" Gronow said with a shake of his head. "Ah, well, if that's what you have, that's what we'll order."

"Got it," Anna said, and she spun away.

"So," Gronow picked up the conversation thread, "thank you for returning the contract so quickly, and with so few changes. I reviewed your requested changes, and feel we can accommodate them. That being the case," he pulled a folded paper out of an inside jacket pocket, "here is a signed copy of the amendment letter."

Philip took the proffered paper, unfolded it long enough to verify that it was indeed the letter in question and that it was indeed signed, refolded it and put it in an inside pocket of his own jacket. "Thank you," was all he said in response.

Before either of them could speak again, Anna appeared and set before they their drinks and a plate with two large squares of a thick dark brown . . .something. That had to be the 'brownies' that Anna had mentioned, and they were indeed brown, but Philip had never seen anything like them before. He looked at Gronow, with his eyes raised, and the editor chuckled.

"You drink the hot chocolate sometimes, yes?" When Philip nodded, Gronow chuckled again, reached out and picked up one of the 'brownies', and took a bite. "You should like this, then." He beamed at Philip, and as soon as he swallowed took another bite.

Philip had to chuckle a bit himself at the expression on Gronow's face. He picked up the remaining brownie and took a small bite of one corner. Dense, intense flavor reminiscent of the hot chocolate he had had before, somewhat sweet, although no overpoweringly so. He chewed and swallowed, washing the bite down with a swig from his coffee cup. And the taste of the coffee complemented the brownie so well, that he just closed his eyes and savored the flavors for a moment. But only for a moment, because he popped his eyes open almost immediately and took a larger bite of the brownie.

The brownie didn't last long. And he beat Gronow to the crumbs on the plate. Gronow laughed when he saw him swoop down on them. "You learn quickly, my friend! My father always said it was the quiet ones who bore the most watching, and I see that he was right." He was chuckling as he raised his cup to drain it, and resumed the chuckle as soon as it left his lips. Philip had never met anyone who laughed as much as Gronow. It was infectious—he found himself grinning in reply and wanting to laugh along with him.

At length, the hilarity died away. Gronow pushed his empty cup to one side. "To get back to your story, it looks like it will be published in Issue number 7. The printer says he can get the type set in time to print the necessary pages. Fortunately, the magazines are small enough as to size and number of pages, and we only print in one color, so we only need to handle the pages once before folding, binding, and cutting. Good thing the publisher made that decision."

"You mean the editor might want the magazine to be more fancy?"

"The editor would print the magazine in six colors if he could get away with it," Gronow said after a snort. "Silly fellow has no idea of the cost of things. Each additional color would require another run of the pages through the presses. Just adding one color would double the print time, and we barely make our schedule as it is. And the price of good colored ink?" Gronow waved a hand before his face several times. "Absolutely out of the question. Can't afford it without raising the price of the magazine a lot, which would probably kill it."

"Too bad the editor doesn't understand that," Philip said.

"Oh, the editor understands it just fine," Gronow replied after shifting position. "He just thinks the publisher is a miser and cheapskate who doesn't work hard enough to make the magazine great. Tiresome bore, always harping on the cost of things."

There was a hint of a smile around Gronow's mouth, and Philip felt the corners of his own mouth starting to curl up in response. He said nothing, simply placed his elbows on the table and rested his chin on his clasped hands.

After a moment, Gronow shifted position again. "So you'll be in good company. Master Poe and Master Lovecraft, of course . . ."

"Not Master Howard?" Philip queried. "I really liked Pigeons from Hell."

"So did I," Gronow professed. "But I'm behind on my translating, and Master Howard uses language a little differently from either of the other two up-timers, and I haven't worked all his turns of phrase like I have with Poe and Lovecraft, so it will be a while before I have his next story ready. But it's a good one, the first in a series of stories about Solomon Kane, an English Puritan adventurer who supposedly was born in the middle of the last century."

"A real person?"

"No, just as made up as everyone else who has appeared in the magazine. But I will be able to build a following for Master Howard's writing with the few stories in this series, and then I will unveil a much larger series with an even more impressive character. And that will catch everyone's attention, sell lots of magazines, and make money—hopefully lots of money."

"Which will undoubtedly make both the publisher and the editor happy," Philip pronounced.

"I'm not certain it would make the publisher happy, sour individual that he is." Gronow produced another grin. "The editor, however, is dancing gavottes and gigues at the thought." He lifted his hands a bit above the table and waved them as if they were wings.

Philip giggled. He couldn't help himself.

The door to the coffee shop flew open, and a flood of brisk evening air blew in as a young woman holding a large piece of paper stepped through the doorway.

"I've got one copy of today's Battle Cry from the CoC left," she called out. "Anyone in here want it?"

"What's the headline?" Gronow called out. She stepped over and handed the broadside to him. As he glanced at the front, Philip looked at the back of it. His eyes were caught by a title above a particular box.

Without thought, his hand reached out and snatched the broadside out of Gronow's hand. He caught the editor's eyebrows shooting up in surprise out of the corner of his eye, but his gaze focused on the box and read the brief article. "How much?" he said as he read the article again.

"A dollar or a pfennig, whichever you've got," she said, holding out her hand.

Philip pulled his money clip out of his pocket, peeled off a dollar bill, and held it out without looking up. The CoC vendor deftly took it from his fingers, turned, and left without another word. He finally looked up at Gronow, who had his head tilted slightly, as if he was examining something curious.

"I know this man." Philip turned the broadside around and pointed to the box on the back. "I used to work in his office. He was my old master."

MERCHANT ATTACKED BY OWN CLERK
Master Lorenz Gröning was treated at hospital yesterday for injuries he claimed were received when his clerk Thomas Schmidt assaulted him. When contacted, Schmidt indicated that "I could tell he was going to hit me, so I hit him back

first." The Magdeburg Polizei are investigating. The Committees are watching to see if this is a matter of a master treating his employees unfairly.

From the Journal of Philip Fröhlich
1 October 1635

Tuesday
Breakfast–
> *2 barley rolls 1 pfennigs*
> *1 apple 2 pfennigs*
> *1 mug beer 2 pfennigs*

Supper–
> *1 bowl fish stew 3 pfennigs*
> *1 wheat roll 3 pfennigs*
> *1 mug beer 2 pfennigs*

Mostly a good day today, until the very end. Routine day at work. Met with Master Gronow after work, got the word that *The Apotheosis of Portia* will appear in Issue 7. Excited about that.

Found out from a CoC broadside that Thomas apparently attacked Master Gröning this week. Haven't been able to think of much else since then. Feel like if I had been there, might could have stopped it. At the end, didn't care much for Master G, but he didn't deserve that.

Mind has been busy thinking about it. Tried to go to bed an hour ago. Mind was still running like one of those steam engines, around and around and around. Knew Thomas was weird and getting weirder, but to physically attack a master, especially one as old as Master G? That's not weird. That's beyond weird. That's . . .don't know what to call it. Something is not right about Thomas.

Recited evening prayers again—twice. Very tired. Can't keep eyes open. Will try to sleep now. Hope it works.

∞ ∞ ∞

Philip waited until Master Wulff had drunk at least half of his cup of coffee before pulling the broadsheet out of his pocket, unfolding it, and putting it on the desk before the lawyer.

"What's this?" Wulff asked as he raised his cup to his mouth again. Philip said nothing, just put a finger at the top of the story box about Master Gröning. The cup paused just before it reached the lips, then was set down on the desktop with a *clack*.

"Christoph!"

"Yes?" The older clerk appeared in the doorway to the outer office.

"Are we clear of the matters of Master Lorenz Gröning?"

"Yes, Master. All drafts paid, all funds received, all work either completed or returned."

"So no active connection with the man or his affairs at this point?"

"To the best of my knowledge, no."

"Good. That's all I needed. Sorry to disrupt your work." Christoph nodded, and returned to the outer office. Wulff looked at Philip. "You have some reason for showing me that?" He raised his eyebrows.

"I . . .am not sure," Philip began. The words barely crawled out of his mouth, it felt like.

"Do you know something about this event?"

"No. But . . ." Even slower coming out.

"You know something?"

"I worked for Master Gröning for over two years, and worked alongside Thomas for several months, at different times. I . . ."

"You think you know something about them." That was a statement from Master Wulff. Philip nodded. "What kind of people they are."

"That . . .and Thomas attacked me in the office."

Master Wulff sat up straighter. "You mean that?"

"Yes. And I lost my job because I hit him back."

Wulff stiffened for a moment, then leaned back slowly, bringing his hands to interlace fingers and rest upon his stomach as he did so.

"Is there more to that story?"

Philip nodded.

Wulff was still for a long moment before breaking the silence.

"Christoph!" When the other clerk appeared in the doorway, Wulff continued with, "Send a note with my compliments to the Polizei informing them that we have someone here who may have information that bears on the matter of the assault on Master Lorenz Gröning, and it might be to their benefit to send the investigators of the matter to discuss this."

Now Christoph's eyebrows rose, which almost triggered a nervous giggle on Philip's part. "Your compliments to the Polizei, and they should send the investigators of the assault on Master Gröning here because we have someone who may have information that may bear on the matter."

"Right. See to it, please."

"It will only take a moment to write the note," Christoph said. "Finding a messenger may take a bit longer." He turned and left again.

"I would like to hear the story," Wulff said in a quiet voice, "but it would probably be better if you spoke first to the Polizei. Why don't you go try and work on your papers while we wait?"

Philip wasn't sure he could, but he didn't want to just sit here in Master Wulff's office, so he got to his feet and went back to his desk in the outer office. There was quite a pile of papers on his desk that had gathered there in the late afternoon on the previous day, plus a few more that Christoph had apparently generated that morning. He started sorting through them, all the while pushing Thomas to the back of his mind. He did focus well enough that he barely noticed when Christoph returned.

It took some doing, but Philip settled into his routine, and was actually a bit startled when the outer door opened and four very serious looking men entered together. He was filing the last of the papers in their folders, and paused when the door opened. Three down-timers and one up-timer, he judged them. He wasn't sure why—they were all wearing mix and match of up- and down-time styles. The one he thought was an up-timer opened his mouth and proved him right.

"Lieutenant Byron Chieske, of the Magdeburg Polizei, along with Detective Sergeants Hoch, Peltzer, and Honister," he said in passable German, not Amideutsch, but with a marked up-time accent. "We're here in response to a request from a . . ." he consulted a paper in his hand," . . .Master A. N. D. Wulff."

Wulff stepped through the inner office door. "That would be me, Lieutenant."

The up-timer shifted his gaze to him. "Good. You indicated you have some information for us?"

"Actually, Philip has some information you might need." Wulff nodded at Philip, who suddenly found himself the focus of six pairs of eyes. He swallowed, put the pages in his hand in their folder, and straightened.

"Philip . . .?" Chieske's voice ended on a rising tone.

"Fröhlich, Lieutenant Chieske."

Philip saw that all three sergeants had pulled notebooks out of their pockets and had pencils making notes. That caused him to smile for a moment.

Lieutenant Chieske nodded to Philip, then looked back to Wulff. "Is there some place we can talk?"

Wulff walked forward, pausing by Christoph's desk. "Things are clear this afternoon, right?"

"Until 3 o'clock, yes."

"Good. Hold down the fort, as they say in Grantville." He looked to the polizeimen. "If you'll come with me."

Philip saw Wulff beckon, so he followed him through the outer door and down to another door near the end of the hall, where Wulff pulled a key from his pocket to unlock it. Throwing the door open, he entered, Philip on his heels and the polizeimen following.

Philip saw a largish room with a long plain table in it flanked by chairs. Wulff took him by the arm and guided him to the chair at the nearest end. "Sit here." He looked to Chieske. "Will this be acceptable?"

"Absolutely," the up-timer said. "This is not an interrogation. Master Frölich is not under suspicion. This will be an interview. We will ask questions, and we will be appreciative of anything you can reveal to us." He was looking at Philip, then shifted his gaze to Wulff. "Since Master Fröhlich is not a suspect, an attorney is not required. Are you his attorney of record?"

They both looked at Philip, who was a bit confused. "What?"

"Do you want me to be your official attorney while they ask your questions?" Wulff asked.

Philip thought for a moment. "Do I need one?"

"Probably not, but it would give you some protection if something unusual or weird comes up." That was Chieske.

"It can't hurt, and it might help," was Wulff's response.

Philip nodded. "I think I'd like that."

Wulff smiled slightly, and pulled out the chair at Philip's right hand. He seated himself as the detectives took chairs on both sides of the table, leaving an empty chair on each side between Philip and his attorney and themselves.

"Let me get us started," Chieske said. "You contacted us and said you might have information of use to us. What would that be?"

"I, uh . . .I worked for Master Gröning as a clerk for almost three years," Philip began. "Thomas Schmidt was another clerk in the office for part of that time."

Four sets of detective eyes riveted themselves to Philip's face.

"So you know both men, then?" That was from the one named Honister, Philip thought.

"Yes."

"Well?"

Philip shrugged. "Maybe. We hardly saw Master Gröning. I saw enough of Thomas to know that he was no good."

"Why do you say that?" asked Sergeant Peltzer in Polish-accented but understandable German.

"He was lazy, skipped work a lot. Made lots of stupid mistakes in his arithmetic and his account entries. Wasn't very pleasant to work with, either."

"So you weren't friends?" That was Sergeant Honister again.

Philip shrugged again. "Never had a chance. Everything he did was right, everything we did was wrong, we were all against him, and he'd show us. Kind of hard to befriend someone who is like that."

There was a moment of silence as three pencils made notes in three sergeant notebooks. Philip noticed that Lieutenant Chieske wasn't taking notes . . .but then, with three sergeants doing so, he probably didn't need to.

"May I make a suggestion?" Wulff spoke up before the questions resumed. Lieutenant Chieske passed a hand above the tabletop, palm up, which Philip assumed was a gesture of assent, as his employer continued with, "Let Philip make his statement of his experiences. I think that will give you the basic information you need, and will help you refine your questions."

The detectives looked at each other, and the sergeants one by one either nodded or shrugged. Chieske gathered them in, then looked to Philip and gave a nod and another hand gesture.

Philip took a deep breath, and then told his story. It took quite a while—longer than he had expected, anyway. Part of that was because he kept forgetting things and backtracking to add them in.

Once he had finished recounting the part of the story that dealt with his last day in Master Gröning's office, there was a brief pause while the sergeants reviewed their notes, then the questions began again. Honister and Peltzer did most of the questioning, for the most part taking turns. They didn't badger him, but they also weren't shy about trying to pin him down if his answers were weak or uncertain. Every once in a while, Sergeant Hoch would pose a question. Philip noticed that seemed to happen after he and the lieutenant would exchange whispers.

The session finally dragged to an end. Philip was exhausted, and soaked with sweat. Even though he wasn't the one being investigated, being under the focus of the four very serious investigators had not been either easy or enjoyable. On the other hand, while he wasn't especially fond of Master Gröning even now, if it came down to the master or Thomas Schmidt, he'd take the master every time.

"Thank you for stepping forward," Lieutenant Chieske said after the questions had dwindled to an end. "And thank you for your help and patience."

"What will come of this?" Wulff asked in return. Philip was glad he did; he wanted to know, but hadn't had the presence of mind to ask the question.

Chieske shrugged. "Since Mr. Fröhlich wasn't a direct witness to the alleged attack, everything he's said today is basically background information which helps establish a context for the assault, and may help establish things like motivation."

"Will I have to testify in court?" Philip asked the thought that was foremost in his mind.

Chieske shrugged again. "Right now, I doubt it, but that may depend on whether this proceeds as a civil case or a criminal case. You could be called to testify either way, but if it goes as a criminal case, that might depend on what else we discover and on what the judge calls for. Again, either way, it's certainly possible."

Philip nodded.

The lieutenant stood, the sergeants following a heartbeat later. "Our thanks, *Masters*. We'll be in touch if we need to follow up on anything. Good day to you."

Philip and Wulff stood as well, and moved a bit to make it easier for the polizeimen to leave the room. Once they were gone, Philip dropped back into his seat like a sack of turnips and put his hands over his face.

"Weary?" Wulff asked from where he had resumed his own seat.

"I feel like an axe that was used to split rocks—dull, dented, and even bent."

Wulff chuckled. "Actually, you did well. This is the kind of thing that is done at times when a deposition needs to be prepared. I'm actually a bit surprised that they didn't ask for one to be done. Ah, well, if they decide later they need one, they'll be back." He chuckled again, then turned serious. "You did well."

"Thank you . . .I think," Philip replied, pulling his hands down to rest on the table. "That was harder than I expected . . .but then, I had no idea how this kind of thing would work, did I? Thank you, by the way," he looked at Wulff. "I know you didn't say much, but it was a comfort to me having you there. I felt like you would keep me from saying or doing the wrong things."

"I'd have tried," Wulff said with a grin, "but you're welcome. Now that I've heard the full story, I really doubt you have much to worry about from the Polizei or whoever will be in charge if they elect to go to court over this matter. Whoever ends up prosecuting will make a decision about that."

"Well, no offense to you or the other attorneys out there, but I really hope I don't end up facing a judge to testify on this," Philip said.

Wulff just laughed, but said nothing more about it.

Philip looked around. "Nice room. I didn't know we had this."

"We didn't, originally," Wulff said. "But after we handled Brendan Murphy's case, I decided I wanted my own conference room here in Magdeburg. So when we got back to Magdeburg, I checked with the agent for the building, and made arrangements to lease this space for that purpose. This is the first time we've officially used it, so I'm glad we had it to use."

Wulff stood. Philip rose slowly, and Wulff laid his hand on Philip's shoulder. "You've had a long day. Go home, get some rest, come in tomorrow."

Philip nodded, preceded Wulff out the door, and paused at the top of the stairs to look back. Wulff made a "move on" gesture with his hand with a smile. Philip turned and headed down the stairs.

From the Journal of Philip Fröhlich
2 October 1635

> Tuesday
> Breakfast–
> > *1 wheat roll 3 pfennigs*
> > *1 sausage 2 pfennigs*
> > *1 mug beer 2 pfennigs*
>
> Supper–
> > *1 wurst 2 pfennigs*
> > *1 wheat roll 3 pfennigs*
> > *1 mug beer 2 pfennigs*

So tired. Don't remember anything about dreams last night. Just want to go to bed now, but it's early.

Talked to four polizeimen today because Master Wulff said I should tell them what I know about Master Gröning and Thomas Schmidt. A lieutenant and three sergeants. Detectives, they were. Spent over an hour talking to me and asking questions. They got more out of me that I thought I knew. Asked more questions than anybody should be able to think of. Had more ways of asking the same question than anybody should be able to do. Exhausted by the end of it. Head really hurt. If that's how they treat people who are trying to help, don't want to be someone they're "investigating".

Master W sat with me during the questions, then sent me home early. Guess he could tell I was spent.

Ate supper early. Too tired to read, way too tired to try and write.

Can't keep eyes open.

Recited evening prayers, almost went to sleep in middle. Now for bed.

∞ ∞ ∞

Philip was the last one to arrive at the office the next morning. He was still chewing his last bite of bread as he topped the stairs. He obviously wasn't far behind the others, as Christoph was standing in the open doorway still with his jacket on.

"Heard you coming up,1" Christoph said as he held the door open for Philip to take before he stepped into the office himself. Philip entered behind him, and closed the door. By the time he had his jacket off and hung on the coat tree, Master Wulff and Christoph were conferring over the schedule for the day. The afternoon was busy, but the morning looked to be fairly light, with nothing scheduled before 10 o'clock.

Once they were done, Wulff straightened. "Philip." A sidewise motion of his head brought Philip into the inner office.

"You look better today than you did yesterday afternoon." The attorney leaned back against his desk and crossed his arms, smile on his face.

"I feel better," Philip replied. "I'm still a bit tired from it, but not like I was. Do they always do that?"

Wulff shook his head. "I had expected only one polizeiman to show up, maybe two, so I was just as surprised as you were to see four. And then who they sent. Those four are pretty much their top detectives, Chieske and Hoch especially. They're the ones who solved that case of the deranged pastor last month."

Philip felt his eyes widen. The case of the pastor who had murdered three women from the poor part of town and cut the eyes out of their heads had sent shockwaves through the entire community of Magdeburg. The news of who had done it had produced a shock almost as strong as the original crimes. Philip hadn't known Pastor Agricola well, but he had seen him preach at St. Jacob's Church more than once. To know that he had committed the grisly crimes while serving as a pastor still nauseated Philip. It seemed there were monsters in real life as much as in books.

Wulff continued. "I figured they'd ask a few questions, then leave, so I was just as surprised as you were at how much they worked on it. I talked to someone last night at one of the salons who is in a position to know. According to him, after that case with the pastor, Captain Reilly and Lieutenant Chieske decided that all the detectives need some additional tutelage in how to properly question or interrogate witnesses. So apparently Chieske came along to critique Honister and Peltzer, and that meant his partner Hoch came also."

"So I was an object lesson?"

Wulff laughed. "If you want to think of it that way, yes."

"I thought maybe someone was pushing them for results, and this was how they were showing how they were working hard." Philip smiled at his own joke.

Wulff laughed again, but said nothing.

"What will happen now?" Philip asked.

"Maybe nothing, maybe a lot." Wulff shrugged. "I think it's going to depend on whether they want the government to prosecute it as a crime, or if they're going to sue for damages."

"What do you think?"

"I suspect they'll try to make a criminal case out of it." Wulff started counting on his fingers. "First, the merchants in town probably would like to have that established so that clerks and assistants will be more careful and respectful of their masters. Second, given the young age of the offender, the chances of being able to collect much in the way of damages from him are, I would say, pretty slim. And," Wulff pursed his lips for a moment as he ticked off the third finger, "Master Gröning may well be in a punitive frame of mind. It may depend on whether or not he's finally come to his senses about dealing with Georg Schmidt."

Philip shook his head.

"What?" Wulff said.

"Doesn't sound very fair."

Wulff sighed, crossed his arms, and looked soberly at Philip. "One thing you need to get clear now is attorneys and courts aren't about fairness. Not even me. We're about the law, about how the laws that have been written can be applied to a situation or a specific charge or case. Sometimes fortune smiles, and we are able to resolve a case with a modicum of fairness and equity. But almost equally as often, the reverse is true—we are able to resolve a case, but only in a manner that leaves one or both of the parties involved disadvantaged. Laws, whether civil or criminal, are not about fairness. They're about keeping society working with a minimum of disruption and violence.

"Regardless," Wulff uncrossed his arms and stood straight, "unless Master Gröning drops the matter altogether, I suspect they will be coming back to you and your friend Martin for depositions, at least, and perhaps actual testimony before the judge. It's all going to depend on Master Gröning's frame of mind."

"What about Master Schiller?"

Wulff shrugged. "Unless you or Martin can say where he was living here in Magdeburg so he can be tracked down, he probably won't be a factor in this mess."

The door to the outer office opened. Wulff straightened and waved outward. Philip turned and made for his desk.

The rest of the day was routine as far as Philip was concerned, filled mostly with filing and preparing some routine correspondence at Christoph's direction. He got to use the typewriter, which, as always, left him lusting for one of his own.

Wulff called Christoph in to take notes for the afternoon client sessions, which left Philip to man the outer office by himself. That made him a bit nervous . . .it was the first time he had been trusted with that.

He swore inside that he would prove himself trustworthy, but underneath that was a hope that nothing would go wrong.

At the end of the day, Philip took a certain sneaking satisfaction in the fact that nothing had gone wrong. He bounded down the stairs ahead of Master Wulff and Christoph and burst out into the evening light, almost running over a broadsheet seller who snarled at him. He dodged the cuff that the seller swung his way and set off for Syborg's Books.

Master Matthias was in the shop when Philip got there.

"Philip! It's good to see you, lad."

"And it's good to see you, Master Syborg. Anything new come in?"

The older man shook his head. "Nothing you'd be interested in. And the next issue of *Der Schwarze Kater* won't be available until next month. But then, you probably know the schedule better than I do."

Philip returned the shopkeeper's grin. "Maybe not better, but probably as well." He dug into his pocket. "I'm ready to buy my subscription now."

"Are you now?" Matthias beamed at him. "That's good news."

"Why? Not selling many?"

"No, they're selling well enough. But the more we sell, the better. Come to the table, and let me write you a receipt." Matthias settled himself in a chair and drew a pad of paper to him with his left hand as he dipped a pen in an inkwell with his right. "How many issues are you subscribing to?"

"Four," Philip said as he pulled his money clip out of his pocket. He had been so impressed with Wulff's clip that he had acquired one for himself.

"Aha," Matthias said. "A full year's worth. Very good. That will be . . .eight dollars or the equivalent in coin."

Philip pulled his bills free and placed a five and three ones on the table before Matthias. "Eight dollars, as requested." He folded the remainder of the bills back into the clip and restored it to his pocket.

"So it is, so it is," Matthias replied as he tapped each bill with a forefinger. "Eight dollars for four issues of *Der Schwarze Kater*, or one year worth at the current schedule." He was writing as he spoke, and a moment after he finished the final sentence, he pushed the pad to one side. "We'll just let that dry while I enter you in the book." He pulled over a hard bound book that when he opened it proved to be comprised of printed line sheets, the first few of which were covered by handwriting of different styles. "And, received from Philip Fröhlich," he dictated as he wrote in the book, "eight dollars for Issues 6 through 9, 2 October 1635, and my initials."

Matthias picked up the pad, blew on the top page, then pulled and tore it out of the pad. He handed it to Philip. "There you are, my lad. Signed and delivered." Making sure the ink on the receipt was dry, Philip carefully folded it and placed it in an inside pocket.

"What else can I do for you this evening?" Matthias asked.

"Do you have any of the up-time books?" Philip was certain that if the shop did actually have some, he wouldn't be able to afford them, but he could at least look at them for a few minutes.

"Only the same one you saw the last time you were in, the sermons of the preacher Spurgeon." Matthias mangled the name, but Philip knew who he meant. He wandered toward the table where the book had been last time, only to come to a sudden stop when he realized it wasn't there. He looked back at Matthias, who beckoned him over to a locked cabinet. The shopkeeper produced a key to unlock the cabinet. He opened the front of the cabinet. Philip could see several books inside. Matthias took one of them out and handed it to Philip, then closed the cabinet and locked it again. "Someone tried to steal it a couple of days ago. We keep it locked up now."

"If it's worth a hundred guilders, I'd lock it up, too," Philip said.

"We're asking a hundred and twenty-five guilders for it now," Matthias said with a bit of a raffish grin. "Doctor de Spaignart, pastor at St. Ulrich's Church, has entered the bidding for it, and between him and two universities, the price has gone up."

"A pastor?" Philip had trouble believing that.

"His family has money," Matthias said.

"They must have, if he can afford that much for a single book," Philip muttered.

Philip cradled the book gently, and walked over to where he could get better light on the pages. He opened it with care, turning to the first sermon in the book, and began reading it—slowly and laboriously—but reading it.

Engrossed in the reading, Philip wasn't sure how much time passed. He was understanding more than he had expected to, actually, if by no means all of it. He was beginning to pick up things from the context that helped him figure out what some of the unknown words had to be. He turned another page, and focused on the words at the top.

"What are you reading?"

The question sounded from right beside Philip's elbow, and he jumped, bumping into the person who spoke with his elbow.

"Sorry," he exclaimed as he looked over to see Ella Kamererin standing beside him, rubbing her chest. He immediately flushed, and ducked his head. "Sorry," he repeated. "I didn't see you standing there."

"Of course you didn't," Ella replied, dropping her hand. "How could you, as enraptured as you were? That was my fault, for getting so close and surprising you. But what are you reading? You were blind and deaf to the world around you."

Philip closed the book on his finger, and showed Ella the cover. "It's a book published in the up-time that came back through the Ring of Fire."

Her eyes got wide, and she reached out a gloved hand to gently touch the book. "Wow. And you can read it?" Her eyes shifted to his face, and seemed to take on a bit of a glow.

"I'm learning to read American up-time English, so I can read it," Philip replied. "Parts of it," he corrected himself. "I'm not very good at it yet."

"But still, to read up-time books," Ella said, crossing her arms to hold her elbows.

"Can you really read them?" came another voice from behind them. They turned to see Ella's father standing behind them with raised eyebrows.

Philip suppressed a swallow before responding. "Yes, Master Kamerer, I can. At least, as far as the words I have learned. But since this is a book of sermons, and I am learning to read by reading an up-time Bible, I can read a bit more than if I was reading, say, a history or a book of philosophy."

Kamerer nodded his head, then adopted a quizzical expression. "But why? Why bother? There aren't that many up-time books, and anything of any value will eventually be translated. Why put yourself out when someone else can do it for you?"

Philip thought about that for a moment. "I expect it to prove useful in my work with and for Master Wulff, the lawyer. We will be dealing with the...what did Master Wulff call it...the ramifications of the Ring of Fire for generations. He says that it would behoove anyone who works in law or merchanting to understand the up-time viewpoints, especially if we are dealing with them in person. I think he's right. And if that's true, I would rather do my own translations than rely on someone else's."

He shrugged. "I also expect it to prove useful in my studies in theology and the law. And then, there is simply the joy of learning it." A smile crossed his face as he realized that he meant that. There was a joy in learning the words, and unlocking the meaning of someone who wrote hundreds of years in the future.

"Well said," Master Kamerer replied. He turned back to Master Matthias and gestured at a nearby shelf. They moved that direction, but Philip heard Master Kamerer mutter, "…unusual to meet a young man who can think, and who can look to the future, take the long view…"

"I've always liked Philip," Master Matthias murmured, and then they passed beyond Philip's ability to hear. But he did feel a certain thrill to understand that Master Kamerer might view him as more than just a boy filing papers.

Philip turned his gaze back to Ella, catching her in the act of moving her own focus from her father to him. He tilted his head at her and grinned, then opened the book and showed Ella the page he had been reading. She looked at it, then looked up at him with a frown. "I don't see anything I know."

"There are some words that are similar, and a lot that are different."

She pointed to a short word on the page. "There—that one—ar-eh?" She pronounced it as two syllables. "What does that mean?"

"Are, not ar-eh" Philip corrected. "One syllable. And it can be translated to be several different words, depending on how it's used: bist, seid, sind."

"That's crazy," Ella said with a moue of her mouth.

"Ja," Philip said. "That's English, especially the American version. Even the Americans say so. How do they put it? 'English is the result of Norman French soldiers trying to bargain with Anglo-Saxon barmaids,' or something like that."

Ella had a gloved hand up before her mouth, apparently trying to suppress a smile, with only middling success. Her lips were hidden, but the outside corners of her eyes were crinkling.

Master Kamerer was suddenly by them again. "Come, Ella, we must leave." He looked to Philip and nodded. "It was nice to speak with you, young Fröhlich."

That stunned Philip. He barely managed a slight bow before the older man turned away. Ella managed a wave of her fingers when she took her hand from before her mouth as she followed her father. Philip watched them leave, and sighed.

He looked down at the book in his hands. Suddenly he wasn't interested in reading it.

"Thank you for allowing me to look at this." He closed it with care and carried it over to hand it to Master Matthias.

"You're welcome to read it as long as we have it." The shopkeeper took out his keys and returned the book to the safety of the locked cabinet. "And I'll keep an eye out for any other up-time books that may come available."

Philip nodded at that, and left the store. He was hungry, he decided, and Mama Schultz's fish stew sounded good, so he headed toward the little booth where she and her iron ladle held sway, licking his lips as he went.

From the Journal of Philip Fröhlich
17 October 1635

Wednesday
Breakfast–
1 wheat roll 3 pfennigs
1 apple 2 pfennigs
1 mug beer 2 pfennigs

Supper–
1 bowl fish stew 3 pfennigs
1 barley roll 2 quartered pfennigs
1 mug beer 2 pfennigs

Dreamt last night. Seemed like Portia was waiting for me. Didn't see her when the dream started. Heard her clear her throat. Turned around to see her standing there, arms crossed, frowning, toe tapping on the…not sure if it's floor or ground in a dream. Whichever it was, was hard, because I could hear her toe tapping. Wanted to know when her story was going to be published. Told her in Issue 7, in four months. She wasn't happy with that answer, and proceeded to let me know that. More she talked, more she ranted, more other people began to appear until it seemed like we were surrounded by a crowd. Unhappy crowd. They took her side. Being stared at by a hundred eyes is not fun. Even if they were dream eyes, which were less than ghost eyes.

Finally got done, said I'd better make sure it got published, and turned around and stomped off. Stomped. Could hear her footsteps in the dream. Crowd turned around and drifted off and faded away. Pretty soon only one left was Max with his big black rifle carried in one arm. Grinning. Told him he wasn't much good if he couldn't protect me from crowds like that. Grin got bigger, and he said that wasn't his job. Those were all things that came out of what was inside my mind, and he was only responsible for protecting me from things that came from the outside. I said I needed to see the contract, because that was less than I was entitled to. His eyes got big, then he started laughing. Was still laughing when he faded away, too.

Sergeant Brendan Murphy came in today to pay on his account. Christoph took his money. While he was in the office, he told several jokes. Wish I could remember them. Laughed a lot, I know that. He said to come to the Green Horse Tavern tomorrow and see him do his routine, whatever that is. Said I'd go.

Later, got a message from Master Gronow wanting to meet tomorrow at Walcha's. Sent message back to him to meet me at The Green Horse. Hope he comes.

Saw Martin Niemoller this evening on the way home after work. Asked him if the Polizei had talked to him yet. He said yes, but they didn't ask a lot of questions. Told him they might come back, depending on what Master Gröning decides to do, or if they think it should be a criminal case. He frowned and shook his head.

Asked him if he knew where Master Schiller went. He said no. Talked a bit more, said goodbye. Before we left, though, he asked if I'd ever sold my story. Admitted I had. He smiled a little, and said that was good, even though it wasn't something he thought he'd read. Nice of him.

Spent some time tonight thinking about what story I should try to tell next. No ideas yet.

Recited evening prayers. Now for bed.

Thursday, October 18

As it chanced, Philip saw Gronow approaching from the other direction as he neared The Green Horse's door, so he waited. It was a brisk autumn evening, and he shivered a bit under his jacket. A couple of men pushed by him to enter the tavern.

"Philip!" Gronow exclaimed as he drew near. "Inside, man. There's no sense in you getting colder because I'm lagging."

Philip still waited until Gronow was only a couple of steps away before he set his hand on the door handle and pulled. He tried to wave Gronow ahead of him, but the editor put his hand on Philip's shoulder and impelled him through the doorway first.

Inside, the tavern was about half full, but there were still seats at tables that were open. Philip headed for a small table near the performer's platform, and dropped into a seat there just ahead of a stocky burly man in laborer's clothes. Philip looked up at the man and shrugged, but the laborer just laughed and waved a hand before he moved on to another table.

Gronow dropped to a chair beside him. Before he could speak, one of the serving girls stopped and looked at them expectantly.

"Beer," Gronow said with a thumb to his chest.

"Beer," Philip said with a nod.

The serving girl nodded herself, and headed for the next table over.

"So," Gronow said, "the coffee at Walcha's isn't good enough for you?"

Philip laughed. "No, I was invited here tonight to see a . . ." he had to think back to the conversation, " . . .a 'comedy routine', whatever that is."

"Ah, Master Murphy is talking tonight?" Gronow said with a smile. "Good. If you haven't heard him, you should enjoy this. His Deutsch isn't perfect, but sometimes that makes the jokes funnier."

The beer mugs landed on the table in front of them with a thump, and Gronow passed over a few coins to the server. By now, Philip was so used to the editor buying that he didn't even try to protest or pay himself.

Gronow took a pull at his mug, and smacked his lips. "Good stuff. So, down to business before Murphy gets here." He pulled a large brown envelope out from under his coat and handed it across the table.

Letters From Gronow

Philip opened it and pulled out the contents, which turned out to be printed pages. He looked down at them, and saw a title at the top of the first page: The Apotheosis of Portia. Below that was the byline: By Philip Fröhlich. He sat stunned for a moment, concentrating on not clutching the paper too hard so it wouldn't crease or crinkle.

Looking up, he saw Gronow with a huge grin on his face. "That's the proof copy of your story. I had him run two copies of it. You can keep that one. I won't do that for every story, but since this is your first, I thought you might want that as a memento."

"You thought right," Philip husked. The words on the page seemed to swim around a bit before he blinked a couple of times to clear things up. He very carefully returned the pages to their envelope, and tucked it away under his own jacket.

The crowd in the tavern had continued to increase in size, and the resulting noise level made it hard to hear. Thus Philip was surprised when a very large up-timer appeared at his elbow and bent down between him and Gronow. It was Brendan Murphy.

"Hi, guys," Murphy said loudly about three inches from Philip's ear. That penetrated even the rising din. "You've got about the only empty chair in the place. Mind if my wife Catrina sits with you during the performance?"

"Not at all," Gronow replied at the same volume level. Philip nodded strongly and pushed the empty chair at his left elbow a few inches away from the table before Murphy's large hand grasped the back of it and drew it back far enough for a young red-headed woman to seat herself and draw up to the table. A moment later, the server girl swirled by and deposited a glass of red wine before her.

Philip was impressed. That was the fastest service he'd seen yet.

"Thanks, guys," Murphy said in that loud tone before he turned sideways and edged between the tables to get to the cleared area and the performer's platform at the end of the room. It wasn't anything as pretentious as a stage. It was barely a hand's width high, but it was enough to let a performer stand and be visible to most of the audience in the room.

Murphy stepped up on the platform and turned to face the tables. He swung a guitar that Philip hadn't noticed hanging down his back on a strap so that it was before him, and cradled it in his arms. At least, Philip thought it was a guitar. It looked sort of like one, but it was larger than any guitar he'd seen before, and either had too many strings or not enough. Then he snorted. Murphy was an up-timer, so that was probably an up-time guitar. That wasn't hard to figure out.

The up-timer didn't say a word—just started playing the guitar, strumming softly through the strings as he picked a melody out. Philip didn't recognize it, but it was pretty. He guessed it was another up-time work…made sense, since Murphy was an up-timer and playing what was probably an up-time instrument.

After a moment, Murphy looked up at the crowd, and smiled. "For those of you that this might be your first time to see me up here, my name is Brendan Murphy. My family was from Ireland originally, but I was born and raised in Grantville before the Ring of Fire happened. So, yeah, if you can't tell from my accent, I'm an up-timer. And I'm here tonight to tell some jokes, maybe sing a few songs, and hopefully help you leave in a better frame of mind than when you walked in."

"And sell some beer," someone called from the back of the room.

"And sell some beer," Murphy agreed, his smile becoming a little brighter. "Nothing wrong with that, is there, friends? That would certainly improve the frame of mind of our host Ernst, whose voice you just heard."

A ripple of laughter rippled around the room. Murphy continued playing, looking around with that grin, waiting for the laughter to die.

Philip had laughed; now he was watching Murphy. He watched him square his shoulders.

"Folks, there's been a lot of music come out of Grantville. You've heard a lot of it in this tavern, a lot of it from Marla Linder and her group. Well, I'm not claiming to be as good as her..."

"That's good, because you're no Marla Linder," somebody said loudly from off to Philip's left. He looked that direction, but couldn't tell who had spoken, especially with the wave of laughter that followed the comment.

Murphy kept playing, and as soon as the laughter died down again, he said, "That's right, friend, I'm not as good as Marla. Never claimed I was. But there's plenty of room to be pretty good at the music and not be as good as her, so don't hold everyone up to her standard.

"But what I was heading toward saying was, I've got a new song for you tonight. How many of you have heard some of the country and western music?" Murphy looked around the room. Philip followed his gaze, and saw a few hands go up and quite a number of heads nodding. "That's good. How many of you liked it?" A few yells and whistles responded, and Murphy's grin grew again. "That's good, too, because this here song is a country and western song. But it's not a good country and western song. It's not even a mediocre country and western song. It's a bad country and western song. In fact, it may be the worst country and western song ever written. And here it comes."

Murphy's playing style changed, moving to short choppy strumming in a hard driving rhythm. Philip heard the harmony cycle through twice, and them the up-timer opened his mouth.

Well, I had aspirin for breakfast
And I chased it with a beer.

My girlfriend, she don't like me,
So I guess I'm out of here.
My dog, he likes her better,
So I guess I'm out of luck.
I went outside to leave her,
Someone stole my pickup truck.
Movin' on.

Murphy shifted back to his earlier style of playing, looking around the room as he did so. "That's the first verse," he said. "Say, did I ever tell you about . . ."

Several minutes later Philip was weak with laughter from the three jokes that the up-timer had told. He was holding his arms across his belly, pressing on his diaphragm and trying to get a deep breath. The thought crossed his mind as he gasped that Gronow had said Murphy's command of Deutsch was rather imperfect. Philip thought it was pretty good, actually. The few times a wrong word or wrong word form was used, it usually made the joke even funnier.

Murphy was merciful, because instead of another joke, he shifted playing styles again, and started singing.

I went down to the cop shop
To tell 'em about my truck.
The sarge he listened to me
And said "Man, that's gotta suck."
Then I told him all about my dog
And he tried hard not to laugh,
Then he shook his head from side to side
And said, "Dude, you got the shaft."
Movin' on.

"Second verse," Murphy drawled. His hands had returned to the earlier playing style. "Hey, did you hear the one about . . ."

By the time the up-timer was done this time, Philip was about to slide out of his chair and his voice was hoarse and raspy from laughing so much. The jokes were so funny . . .especially the one about the pig and the one about the mule. He almost sighed in relief to hear Murphy shift the playing style back to the song pattern. A moment later, he began to sing.

> *Well, I got myself a new dog,*
> *And I got myself a truck*
> *I haven't found a new girlfriend*
> *And that may be my good luck.*
> *This thing called love amazes me*
> *And I find it kind of weird.*
> *But all I know is all I need*
> *Is my dog, my truck, and beer.*
> *Movin' on.*

"Last verse," Murphy said almost unnecessarily right before another roar of laughter went up. That one took quite a while to die down. "And that was the World's Worst Country and Western song. Listen, thanks for being here tonight, hope you enjoyed yourself, and tell your friends about this. The more folks come in, the more beer Ernst sells, the more he'll let me stand up here and make you all laugh." He brought the guitar to a final chord, then damped it with his hands. "Thanks again, and good night."

Philip joined the applause that broke out as Murphy slung his guitar to hang down his back on its strap as he stepped off the platform. Everyone was on their feet, and several of the men at the front tables stepped forward to shake the up-timer's hand and slap his shoulder. Voices were loud around them, even after the applause died down. Catrina Murphy moved to join her husband, smiling at Philip and Gronow as she went by. Gronow tapped Philip on the shoulder, and jabbed a thumb toward the door. Philip drained the last few drops of his beer, and followed his friend.

Once they were outside, the quiet of the evening descended on them, and Philip found himself relaxing shoulders that he hadn't even realized were tense.

"Well, that was fun," Gronow said, wrapping his coat a little closer and shoving his hands in his pocket. "I'll have to come in on his nights more often."

"Jah," Philip replied. "A very funny man."

They walked on down the street. Gronow looked over at Philip, and said, "One bomb."

Philip laughed, and replied with, "You don't eat a pig like that all at once."

They both laughed, and continued on down the street, trading punchlines from the evening's jokes.

From the Journal of Philip Fröhlich
27 October 1635

Saturday
Breakfast—
1 wheat roll 3 pfennigs
1 cup morning broth 1 pfennig
1 mug beer 2 pfennigs

Supper—
1 bowl fish stew 3 pfennigs
1 barley roll 2 quartered pfennigs
1 mug beer 2 pfennigs

Hard to write tonight. Hard to work today. News from abroad is horrible. Have to wonder what God is doing to allow these things to happen.

First, not sure exactly when it happened, but sometime in the last few days the queen of Sweden was killed. I heard the word assassinated in one of the broadsheets being read. I think her name was Maria. And that has everyone upset and worried about the safety of Princess Kristina, the heir to both the Swedish royal throne and the USE imperial throne.

Second, as if that's not bad enough news, Gustavus Adolphus was injured in battle within the last couple of days. Rumors are everywhere. No two broadsheets agree on what happened or what his condition is. Sounds like he got hit in the head really hard. If that's so, surprised he's not dead. But most of the rumors and broadsheets say he is alive, so having to assume that's right. Praying that it's right. If the emperor is dead, do we have any hope? Can even the up-timers save us if the emperor is gone? Don't know.

Hearing all kinds of stories. Don't understand a lot of them, don't know if I should try to understand them. Just wish the emperor would return to us.

Praying for healing. Praying for wisdom in leaders. Praying for Princess Kristina, who has lost her mother and may be close to losing her father.

Dear God, why? Why this? Why now?

Recited evening prayers. Three times. Need to go to sleep. Not sure I will. Will probably spend much of the night on my knees.

From the Journal of Philip Fröhlich
7 November 1635

>**Wednesday**
>**Breakfast–**
>>*1 wheat roll 3 pfennigs*
>>*1 sausage 2 pfennigs*
>>*1 mug beer 2 pfennigs*
>
>**Supper–**
>>*1 wurst 2 pfennigs*
>>*1 cup cabbage soup 1 pfennig*
>>*1 mug beer 2 pfennigs*

Dreams were quiet last night. Nothing momentous or tumultuous. Think Max floated by once, but not sure. Memory isn't very strong.

Frau Diebes came in to consult with Master Wulff today. Took notes. Can't say what the conversation was about, but it sounds like she might be getting some at least sort of good news soon. Hope so. She's a nice woman who's had some awfully bad luck.

Sergeant Peltzer came in today. Didn't expect that. Nervous. He said he needed to speak to me and Master Wulff together, so Master W took us back into the inner office. Said that a decision had been made to treat the assault on Master Gröning as a crime rather that a civil matter, that the court's investigation would begin next Monday, and that I should be present as a witness to testify. He handed me a folded paper. Master

Letters From Gronow

Wulff took it from me, unfolded it and read it quickly, then handed it to me. Official summons. It basically told me to report to the Rathaus on Monday 12 November 1635 at 9 o'clock in the morning to provide testimony in the matter of City of Magdeburg vs. Thomas Schmidt. Master Wulff asked if there was any risk of my being charged with anything. Sergeant Peltzer said as long as I answered truthfully, no. It was his understanding that since I was not a direct witness to the alleged assault I would only be asked to testify as to the general nature of the business and on what I had observed of the relationships of the two principals in the case. So have that to look forward to next week. Can't say I expect this to be fun.

On other hand, stopped in at Syborg's Books after eating. Master Matthias was there this evening. As soon as he saw me come in the door, he waved me over and placed a copy of Issue 6 of *Der Schwarze Kater* in my hands. Was very glad to see it. Had to sign for it before I could leave because of the subscription thing, but wasn't long before I had it stuffed under my coat and was headed for home dodging horses, mules, and people.

Got to my room, scrambled to light a candle, didn't even take off my coat, started reading. New story from Master Lovecraft, but other up-timer story isn't a Poe story, but from Master Howard. Read it first. Title is Red Shadows. Different from either Poe or Lovecraft. Different from the story in the last issue, too. Actually feels bit more real to the down-time now. Liked it a lot. Hero was Solomon Kane. Remember Master Gronow talking about those stories. Guess this is the first one. Ready to see more.

Late now, work tomorrow, will save the rest of Issue 6 for tomorrow. Helped me forget the news for a while, anyway.

Read a few pages from Table Talk. Helped clear mind.

Recited evening prayers. Now for bed.

12 November 1635

Philip was ushered into a high-ceilinged room that looked to be not much larger than the space used as a conference room at the Grubb Wormb and Wulff offices. There was a table at the far end with three well-dressed men seated behind it who were conversing together softly. To one side was a table at which he could see Thomas Schmidt seated, with another well-dressed man beside him. Suddenly he was glad to know that Wulff was behind him. As he moved forward a little, it shocked him to see that Thomas was wearing fetters.

Wulff nudged him and gave a small gesture at the few rows of benches beside them. Philip sidled into one of the rows, and moved over far enough to leave room for Wulff before he sat down.

Neither of them said anything. The atmosphere in the room was a bit repressive, which didn't help the state of Philip's nerves.

After a few moments, the sound of the cathedral bells ringing the hour could be heard. The men at the table ceased their conversation and the one in the center pulled out a pocket watch to confirm the time.

"It is 9 o'clock," the central figure said, restoring the watch to its pocket. "We will commence. I am Jacob Schweighart, presiding judge for this investigation. Seated here are Johann Möritz Hoch," he gestured to his right, "and Peter Eichhorn," a matching gesture to the other hand, "who will be the *Schöffen* and will be hearing and judging this matter along with me. We will be investigating an assault upon the person of Master Lorenz Gröning, who was allegedly assaulted by one of his employees, one Thomas Schmidt, bookkeeper."

Judge Schweighart looked over at the other table. "The court sees that the accused, Thomas Schmidt, is present. Has he been properly secured?"

"Manacles on both hands and feet, Judge," came from behind Philip. He looked over his shoulder to see a burly individual with a truncheon thrust through his belt standing against the rear wall. Obviously a guard either for a gaol or for the court.

"Indeed," Schweighart said with a nod. "And you are . . ." He looked at the other man at the table with raised eyebrows.

"Advocatus Oswalt Bieger, Judge Schweighart." The younger man—to Philip he didn't look much older than Christoph Heinichen—gave a slight bow.

"Are you here as a witness or as an attorney?"

"Attorney, Judge Schweighart." The younger man pulled a folded parchment out of the document case on the table before him, and stepped around the table to hand it to the lead judge.

Philip watched as Schweighart perused the diploma carefully, then handed it back to the young attorney. "A newly fledged attorney. Very well. Shall we assume by your presence at the side of the accused that you have been engaged to represent him?"

"Yes, Judge Schweighart."

"Humph. You should have asked around first." Schweighart chuckled at the expression on Bieger's face. "There are a number of very competent attorneys in Magdeburg, Master Bieger." Philip could hear a bit of a sardonic tone in the judge's voice. He wondered if that was part of legal training. He had heard the same tone in Master Wulff's voice more than once. "You should ask yourself why one of them did not take the charge." From the expression that now crossed the young man's face, apparently he hadn't thought of that. "Exactly. Take your place, young man."

Bieger slowly resumed his seat, and Schweighart looked at Wulff. "Are you here in an official capacity, Master Wulff?"

Wulff stood. "No, Judge Schweighart. I am here solely as an observer and as moral support for my employee and friend, Philip Fröhlich." He laid a hand on Philip's shoulder for a moment. Philip was almost as warmed by the touch as he was by Wulff calling him 'friend'.

"Your employee?" Schweighart's bushy gray eyebrows rose. "Are you involved in this mess, Master Wulff?"

"Only peripherally, Judge," Wulff replied. "Only to the extent that I was consulted by Master Gröning about a few contracts some time before the event you're investigating, and only to the extent that I hired Philip as soon as I realized that Gröning had discharged him."

"Hmm." Schweighart lowered his head and stared at Wulff from beneath lowered eyebrows. "Somehow I suspect there's more to the story than that, but we'll let that go for the moment. Take your seat, Master Wulff." His gaze shifted to Philip. "And you are the redoubtable Philip Fröhlich, then?"

Philip stood without prompting, and gave a slight bow. He could feel the judge's gaze passing over him, and he was very glad that he was wearing his best clothing and that he had given them a good brushing last night.

"Very well," Schweighart said at last. "Let us commence. Come forward, young Fröhlich."

Philip advanced until he was standing directly before Schweighart with only the width of the table separating them. The judge pushed a book forward.

"Take up the Holy Writ," Schweighart intoned. Philip took the Bible up in both hands. "Do you swear that the testimony you are about to give will be the truth, with no omissions or falsehoods?"

"I do." Philip swallowed.

The judge pointed. Philip raised the Bible and kissed it before returning it to the table.

"If you would sit there," Schweighart gestured at a chair. Philip stepped to it and sat down.

"I am informed that Master Gröning will not be present this morning. Some matter of ill health, I understand. However, inasmuch as this is a criminal investigation rather than a civil action, his presence is not necessary."

Schweighart looked down at the papers before him for a moment. Everyone else in the room, including the two *Schöffen*, waited. Eventually he looked up.

"Very well, young Fröhlich, let us begin. What exactly was your relationship with Master Lorenz Gröning?"

"I was a bookkeeper and clerk for him for a bit over three years."

"When did you begin and end work for him?"

"I started working for Master Gröning in late March 1632, I believe, and he discharged me on the 8th day of June, 1635."

"So you were not employed by him on the date the alleged assault occurred?" Schweighart's tone was level, as if he was asking questions for the form of it, as if he probably knew the answers. Which, if he had read the *Polizei* interviews, he probably did.

"No, I was not." Philip felt himself relaxing a bit.

"Why were you discharged?"

That question came from one of the *Schöffe*, Master Hoch. Philip thought about it carefully before responding.

"Because on that day I was assaulted by Thomas Schmidt."

"You were discharged because you were assaulted?" Master Hoch's voice carried a note of surprise, and his eyebrows raised a bit.

"No," Philip said, forcing himself to remain calm, "I was discharged for defending myself. He said something about he couldn't have his clerks brawling, but instead of discharging Thomas for starting it or discharging both of us, he only discharged me."

There was a muffled sound from Thomas' table, but Philip managed to avoid looking at his old adversary.

"Are you angry with Master Gröning for discharging you?" That came from the other *Schöffe*, Master Eichhorn, who was twirling a pencil in his fingers.

Philip thought about that one for a short while, answering only when Eichhorn opened his mouth to speak again. "No," Philip said, "I probably should be angry with him, but I'm not."

"Why not?"

"Because up until then he'd always treated me pretty fairly . . .hadn't beat me, hadn't forced me to work extra time without paying me, hadn't cheated me, had always paid my wages as he had promised."

That got a reaction out of all three judges; varied expressions of surprise. "How would you characterize your feeling about Master Gröning, then?" Eichhorn said.

"Disappointed that he wasn't fair there at the end. And . . ." he paused for a moment, " . . .I guess I feel sorry for him."

That got another reaction out of the judges, this time a bit of a frown, as if he'd said something disparaging. Which, looking back at it, Philip guessed he could see where they got that.

"So you think you had a good relationship with Master Gröning until the very end of your employment?" Judge Schweighart said.

"Yes," Philip said with a nod.

"Hmm." That was all Schweighart said in response. He shuffled a couple of papers, then looked up. "Very well, then, how long did you work with Thomas Schmidt."

"I don't remember exactly when he came to work for the master, but it was less than a year."

"So you know Master Gröning better than Schmidt?"

Philip shook his head. "No, I wouldn't say that. The master wasn't in the office very often, and when he was in, he was mostly talking to Master Schiller, the manager of the office. He probably didn't say more than a dozen words to me every few months. Thomas was with us every day the office was open—or he was supposed to be."

"Ah," Schweighart said, with a bit of a twist to his mouth. "That sounds . . .no, let us do this correctly. What was your relationship with Thomas Schmidt?"

"I was the senior clerk, working under Master Schiller."

"Did Schmidt report to you? Was he under your authority?"

"No. Master Schiller was the manager, we all reported to him, and he reported to Master Gröning. But I was responsible for showing Thomas how to do the work, and for checking his work for errors."

Schweighart tapped the pages before him a couple of time. "Was he a good employee?"

"At first, he was . . .not good, but not bad."

"Mediocre?"

There was another sound from Thomas' table. Philip made himself ignore that as well.

"Perhaps a bit better than that. It's expected that new employees will make mistakes. Martin certainly did."

"Martin?"

"Martin Niemoller, who was hired just a few months before I left."

"The office was busy enough to need three clerks?"

"Well," Philip began with a bit of reluctance, but honesty compelled him to continue with, "we could have done it with two good clerks."

"By which you mean to indicate that Schmidt was not a good clerk. How would you characterize him?"

Philip took a deep breath. "He was more than a bit lazy. Even at the beginning he wouldn't do any more than he absolutely had to. He missed days of work when he would say he had been sick. And he didn't seem to learn. He made the same mistakes over and over again, then would get mad when he was made to correct his own errors. But the worst was the cause of Master Schiller discharging him—he was a thief."

"A thief." All three judges stared at Philip at that statement, pens and pencil held motionless. Schweighart cleared his throat. "Did you observe this?"

Philip nodded. "Master Schiller kept a bottle of wine at his desk, and would occasionally take a small drink from it. Not every day, and never more than once a day, from what I saw. I think it was for stomach trouble, or something. But one day something happened that drew Master Schiller to the door for some time. After he closed the door and turned around, he saw Thomas drinking from his bottle. He shouted, and Martin and I turned to see Thomas with the bottle almost upended, guzzling the wine. The bottle was almost empty.

"Master Schiller called Thomas a thief, thrashed him, and threw him out, telling him he was discharged and not to come back."

There was a moment of silence, then the judges all seemed to blink in unison. "That's a very serious assertion," Master Hoch said. "Are you certain?"

"Yes," Philip said in a level tone, despite the fact that his stomach was beginning to hurt. "You can ask Martin Niemoller and Master Schiller."

"We will," Judge Schweighart said in a similar tone.

There was another moment of silence, then Judge Schweighart said, "So how did Schmidt become employed again?"

"I cannot tell you of my own personal knowledge," Philip began. "All I know is what Master Schiller told me."

"We will take that into account. Continue."

"What Master Schiller told me was that Thomas was related to a patrician in Magdeburg with whom Master Gröning wished to at least do business, that he really wanted to form a relationship with this man, and that the price of doing that was he had to rehire Thomas. Master Schiller told me that he had protested to the master that this was a foolish action, and that Master Gröning had told him that not only was Thomas coming back to work for him, but that Master Schiller would not be allowed to discharge him without the master's approval."

The judges' eyebrows all went up in unison at that, remained there for a long moment, then gradually lowered as the pens and pencil scratched across their note pages.

"And did your opinion of Schmidt improve any after he returned?" That from Master Eichhorn, pencil poised motionless above his notes.

"No. He was still sloppy, he was still careless, he still made stupid errors. Only now, now nothing we said would make him do it right, and he knew he couldn't be discharged, so his behavior was openly rude and disrespectful even to Master Schiller, much less to Martin or myself . . .when he bothered to arrive at the office. He was absent much more than before, and there were a number of days toward the end of my time there that he came to work at least partially drunk at opening time. "

There was another muffled sound from the direction of Thomas' table, then Thomas started shouting, "Lies! It's all lies! You hate me and you're making up these lies!"

The sound choked off, and Philip finally looked over at the table to see the guard had one very large hand firmly over Thomas' mouth, while the other hand pinned both of Thomas' to the table top.

Brows contracted at that. "Master Bieger, remind your charge that his presence is not required for this investigation." Judge Schweighart's voice was quite cold, and Bieger flushed in response before bending over and urgently whispering into Thomas' ear.

Pens and pencil scribbled a lot.

"Are you certain of that?" Master Eichhorn said, resuming the questioning.

"Cheeks and nose flushed, eyes red. Some days he smelled of cheap wine, some days he smelled of genever." Philip bit the inside of his cheek to keep from saying anything more than the bare truth.

After another long moment of silence while the judges made their notes, Judge Schweighart looked up. "Is there any more that you can tell us about either Master Gröning or Thomas Schmidt and their relationship with each other?"

"Only what happened the day of my discharge."

"Proceed."

Philip licked his lips and wished he had a cup of water. His throat was starting to feel dry and scratchy.

"It was the 8th of June, earlier this year. Thomas was restless that day. He kept getting down from his stool and walking around. He walked by my desk and saw that I was correcting some errors he had made on one of his account sheets. He got really angry, started calling us all names and said we were out to get him when he didn't do anything wrong. After that he picked up my inkwell and threw the ink at me. It got all over two account sheets on my desk and soaked into my shirt. Ruined it. Then he grabbed me and hit me."

Philip stopped there for a moment, to take a couple of deep breaths because his voice was getting shaky. The judges waited until he was able to continue.

"He hit me twice, and I hit him back, but only after he hit me first."

"Did you hurt him?" one of the judges asked. Philip wasn't sure which one.

"Probably. I did hit him square on the nose, and I knocked him down the second time. He got up, blubbering about how we'd all be sorry we treated him like that, and ran out the door. We were able to clean the account sheets off well enough to copy them to clean pages, and about the time we were finished with that Master Gröning came in with

Thomas and another man. The master announced that he wouldn't countenance fighting between his clerks, and I was discharged effective the end of the day."

"What did you do?" That was Schweighart.

"I tried to explain that Thomas started it and hit me first, and all I did was defend myself, but the master said that didn't matter, and if I didn't stop arguing I would have to leave right then and I would lose the day's pay as well. I saw the master wasn't going to be fair, so I closed my mouth. The three of them left together. At the end of the day, I collected my wages and belongings and left."

"And you found employment with Master Wulff not long after that?"

"Yes."

Philip suddenly felt weary, as if every bit of life had drained out of him.

"Were Martin Niemoller and Anton Schiller also present at this event?"

"Yes."

The pens and pencil of the judges made more notes. Philip sat in his chair, almost drooping.

There was a sudden clatter as Thomas surged to his feet, knocking his chair over backward and pushing the guard to sprawl on the floor.

"No! That's not right! He's lying! That's not what happened! They all hated me and they were making things up to get me in trouble!" Thomas lunged forward and tried to climb over the table, only to have the guard jump back up and thump him with his truncheon. Thomas collapsed, moaning. The guard stood over him breathing heavily, hefting his truncheon as if he wanted to lay into him some more. Philip's eyes were wide, and he could feel his heart racing.

"Take the accused back to confinement," Schweighart ordered in a hard tone of voice. The guard reached down and grabbed Thomas by one arm and pulled him to his feet, then pushed him stumbling out of the room. "Don't give me any more trouble or you'll get more of that," Philip heard through the door to the hallway before it closed.

Schweighart turned his hard gaze on Oswalt Bieger, who was standing beside the table with an appalled expression on his face. "Master Bieger, your charge will not be returning to this room today. We will hear him another time. And he hasn't made your task any easier." The judge's tone was more sardonic this time. "Resume your seat."

Bieger sat down. Philip took a deep breath and held it for a moment, then released it slowly. He could feel his heartbeat start to slow down. He looked to the judges, but they were all looking at their notes. One by one they finally raised their eyes to focus on him again.

"An interesting narrative," Judge Schweighart said. "And yet you can truthfully say that you don't harbor ill-will for either Master Gröning or Thomas Schmidt?"

Philip shook his head. "No. Like I said, I'm disappointed in Master Gröning, and I feel sorry for Thomas, but I don't hate either of them."

"Not even after he attacked you?"

Philip shrugged. "I gave as good as I got. Better, actually."

Schweighart shook his head with a small smile on his face. "You may be a better man than I am, young man." He looked to one side and then the other, collecting nods from Masters Hoch and Eichhorn. "Very well, then, we have your testimony. You may leave now. If we need anything further from you, we will send a summons. Thank you for your time."

Philip stood, gave a slight bow, and turned to leave. About the time he reached the door, he heard Judge Schweighart say, "A moment, if you would, Master Wulff." He looked back over his shoulder, to see Wulff standing in a similar posture right behind him.

"Yes?" Wulff replied.

"You are not under oath, Master Wulff, but I would be interested in your opinion as to whether young Fröhlich is an honest man."

Philip was offended by that statement, but held his peace as Wulff spoke immediately. "Yes, painstakingly so, sometimes painfully so, and all too often to his own detriment."

"Ah. Thank you, Master Wulff. That is useful to know. Good day to you both." And with that, Philip left the room, followed closely by Wulff.

A few moments later they found the exit and were outside walking down the steps. Once they reached the street, Wulff placed a hand on Philip's shoulder. "You did well in there. Good job."

That sparked a bit of warmth in Philip that counteracted the chill in the air. He cherished that.

∞ ∞ ∞

The rest of the day was calm and quiet, which was a very good thing as far as Philip was concerned. He sat at his desk and transcribed notes and filed papers all afternoon, thankful for the more or less mindless routine. Christoph didn't ask anything of him except to type a couple of response to query letters, and Master Wulff used Christoph the two times he needed notes taken.

Near the end of the day, Philip's spirits seemed to rise a bit, or maybe it was that his energy was beginning to restore itself. He finished the filing he had in his hand, stood straight, and looked around, only to discover that Wulff was watching him from the doorway of the inner office.

"You back with us now?"

Philip blushed, and said, "I think so."

Wulff beckoned to him, and Philip followed him to the inner office. Wulff turned and leaned back against the front of his desk. "I know that was hard on you, but there was nothing I could do to prepare you. And now you have some idea of what that kind of investigation and court work is like. And they were easy on you."

"If that was easy," Philip muttered, "I don't want to see hard."

Wulff chuckled. "The main judge leads the investigation, the *Schöffen* assist. As young Schmidt found out, they are not particularly concerned about the welfare of the accused. They are interested in the truth, and there are few constraints on what they can do to find it." He shrugged.

"So can a judge . . . ?" Philip wasn't sure how to word his question.

"Can a judge go wrong? Can a judge make a mistake? Can a judge have an agenda and pursue it rather than the truth?"

"Well . . .yes."

Wulff crossed his arms. "Yes, yes, and yes. And that's one of the reasons why there are some laws about what they can and cannot do, and that's one of the reasons why anything very serious is supposed to be judged by three men, not just one. These men are all good men, so it is doubtful they would do anything other than make the right judgment. But young Schmidt didn't do himself any favors today."

Philip winced as he remembered what had happened at the end of the session. "How do you think they will rule?"

"From what I saw, they're not very impressed with Master Gröning. I would have wagered they would be lenient on Schmidt, until his fit of temper. I think Schmidt may have a disease of the brain or mind, but that won't stop the judges from ruling strictly after what he did today."

"Flogging? Scourging?"

"At least."

Philip felt a bit nauseated at that thought.

From the Journal of Philip Fröhlich
12 November 1635

Monday
Breakfast–
> *1 wheat roll 3 pfennigs*
> *1 sausage 2 pfennigs*
> *1 mug beer 2 pfennigs*

Supper–
> *1 barley roll 2 quartered pfennigs*
> *1 cup cabbage soup 1 pfennig*
> *1 cup small beer 1 pfennigs*

Long day today. Had to testify at investigation about Thomas assaulting Master Gröning. Judges were polite, but no doubt who was in charge. Treated me fairly, but really wouldn't want to be in the accused chair before them. Like Thomas.

Always knew Thomas wasn't very smart. After his outburst in court today, I'm beginning to think that Master Wulff is right—he's not right in the head. Either that, or he's really really stupid. The judges are probably going to judge him harshly, and I may have helped put him there.

All I did was tell the truth. Is that worth a man being flogged for being stupid?

Not sure I want to be a lawyer now.

Wasn't hungry tonight. Didn't finish the soup or the roll.

Spent a lot of time tonight reading in Psalms. Some comfort there.

Recited evening prayers, but still disturbed. Feel distant from God. Don't like that.

Recited evening prayers again, slowly this time, really thinking about the words. Helped.

Hope I sleep tonight. Right now, not sure I will.

21 November 1635

Philip opened his eyes, rolled to his side and sat up on the edge of his bed. For the first time in days, he didn't feel weighted down. He stretched his arms up, rolled his head around on his neck. Still good.

After a moment, Philip rose and shuffled to the table, where he poured some water into the basin and used his hands to bathe his face. He dried hands and face on a scrap of toweling that he threw back on a peg set in the wall.

He stared at the wall for a moment. He couldn't figure out why today was different from what had come yesterday, or the day before, or the day before that. But something was different. He felt clear-headed for the first time in days, and the dull ache at the base of his skull was gone.

The mystery continued to fill Philip's mind while he dressed. At the end, he walked back over to the table and picked up his Bible. It fell open to Deuteronomy chapter 24. His gaze passed down the page, only to stop, arrested, at one verse:

> *The fathers shall not be put to death for the children,*
> *neither shall the children be put to death for the fathers:*
> *every man shall be put to death for his own sin.*

Verse 16, it was, and it so resonated with Philip at that moment. It dawned on him that, sometime during the night, his mind had decided that whatever happened with Thomas, it was neither his fault nor his responsibility. Thomas had made his own choices, and would pay accordingly. The burden of guilt, or shame, or grief, whatever it was, had been released, and Philip felt well and light for the first time in over a week.

Minutes later, he was whistling when he walked into Grandma Schultz's little cookshop. Her eyebrows climbed her forehead at the sight of him in such a mood. The large two-tined roasting fork she was holding almost slipped out of her hand, but she caught it at the last moment. The sight of her gap-toothed smile as he paid for his food almost made Philip laugh.

Philip's appetite was back full force, and it didn't take long to ingest a large piece of sausage, not one but two wheat rolls, and a mug of beer. With a wave to the old woman, he was back on the street. He started whistling again as he marched along, dodging around slower pedestrians until he arrived at Walcha's building, where he bounded up the stairs.

"Good morning," Philip sang out as he passed through the doorway into the outer office. "Lovely day, isn't it?"

Both Master Wulff and Christoph looked at Philip with looks of mingled surprise and incredulity as he took off his coat and tossed it to hang on an arm of the coat rack. He started shuffling through the papers on his desk, starting to get ready for the day.

"Philip?" That was Master Wulff. He looked around to see Wulff beckoning to him. A moment later, he was standing before Wulff, with Christoph to one side. "Are you all right?"

"Yes, I am." Philip couldn't help grinning.

Wulff's eyes narrowed. "Are you sure?"

"Yes, I am." The grin continued

"You seem somewhat . . . . . . different."

"Oh, that." Philip nodded. "While I was asleep last night, I decided that Thomas' troubles were Thomas' own doing, and I can't take responsibility for them. When I woke up this morning, the decision had been made. And here I am." He spread his arms wide.

Wulff nodded, slowly at first, then faster a couple of more times, and a smile appeared in response to Philip's grin. "Well done, lad, well done. There are men three times your age who haven't learned that lesson. You can only be responsible for you, not for anyone else. And if you stay in the lawyer business, this won't be the last time you'll find yourself dealing with something like this. Best you learn this now, so you can be prepared for any future events." He clapped Philip on the shoulder. "Good man. Now, enough of the silliness. Get to work."

"Right away," Philip said.

From the Journal of Philip Fröhlich
1 December 1635

> **Saturday**
> **Breakfast–**
>> *1 wheat roll 3 pfennigs*
>> *1 apple 2 pfennigs*
>> *1 mug beer 2 pfennigs*
>
> **Supper–**
>> *1 wheat roll 3 pfennigs*
>> *1 wurst 2 pfennigs*
>> *1 mug beer 2 pfennigs*

Lots of dreams last night. Don't really remember any of them, though. Just remember them floating through my mind. Weird. Think Max was in one of them, but don't remember for sure. Don't know if I really like or dislike not remembering many of the dreams. Would like to remember the good ones, the important ones. Would probably get some story ideas from them. Other hand, from what I do remember, suspect that a lot of them would not be pleasant. May be a good thing I don't remember most of them. Do like horror stories, but wouldn't want to have them rolling through my mind all night and wake up remembering that. Euggh.

Der Schwarze Kater Issue 7 comes out next month. Getting really hard to wait. Last time I was in Syborg's Books they asked me if I knew when it was coming out. Jokers. Gave them a fig. They laughed. Was rude of me, so apologized later. They laughed some more.

Still haven't come up with an idea for a new story. Not sure why. Can't really write another story about Portia. I mean, after an Apotheosis, where could a character go? Can't think of anything to do with one of the other characters from her story, either. Frustrating.

Still haven't heard what the judges decided about Thomas. Expected them to rule before now. Even Master Wulff is surprised at how long they are taking. Other hand, not looking forward to hearing.

Read some from Table Talk tonight. Luther's discourses are varied and interesting. Would have really liked to have been able to talk to the man. Although probably wouldn't have been able to say a word if I had met him. How do you talk to one who walks with the apostles?

Recited evening prayers. Now for bed.

4 December 1635

It was late in the afternoon when the outer door to the office opened. Philip looked up, only to have his heart almost stop when Detective Sergeant Peltzer stepped through, followed by Detective Sergeant Honister. "Is Master Wulff available?" Although Peltzer led, it was Honister who spoke.

Before Christoph could respond, Wulff appeared in the doorway to the inner office. "I am to you, Sergeants. What transpires?"

"Judge Schweighart instructed us . . ."

"Asked, really," Peltzer interrupted.

"Well, yes," Honister continued with a bit of a sour look at his partner, "asked us to deliver to you the judgment in the matter of Gröning and Schmidt."

Wulff straightened, and Philip's heart fell to the floor. He took a deep breath.

"So what judgment did the court render, then?" Wulff asked.

"Thomas Schmidt was found guilty of felonious assault."

Philip released his breath, and leaned on his table. Wulff nodded. "And what was the punishment?"

Peltzer responded to the question. "A dozen strokes with a rod." He paused for a moment. "Sentence was carried out immediately."

Philip sucked in his breath at that, then released it slowly. That wasn't much worse than what Thomas' behavior would have earned him in the grammar schools Philip had attended.

"Only a dozen, then," Wulff said. "I thought the judges would be more severe than that after what we saw Schmidt do in the court the day that Philip testified."

"Sergeant Honister agreed with you," Peltzer said. "He was sure he'd get at least two dozen strokes. He lost." Honister said nothing.

"Lost?" Wulff's eyebrows went up.

"Nothing," Honister muttered, looking down for a moment, then back up. "Judges' decision, in any event, not ours."

"Indeed." Wulff's voice was very dry. "Thank you for bringing the news."

"Word on the street is that young Schmidt will be sent to visit distant relatives after his back heals." Peltzer gave a bit of a twisted smile, to which Wulff responded in kind.

Philip wasn't sure what he felt. It was good that Thomas had been found out, and that he had received at least some punishment or discipline for all the trouble he had closed. And he had to admit that the thought of never seeing Thomas again didn't exactly disturb him. But somewhere in the back of his mind he was still wondering if what had happened was fair. Then he shook his head as he remembered Wulff's comments the day he was first interviewed by the Polizei—the law wasn't about fairness.

"Thank you for bringing the word." Philip held his hand out to Peltzer first, then Honister. They shook hands with him, exchanged nods with Wulff, then turned and left.

Wulff looked at Philip. "Satisfied?"

Philip shrugged. "I guess so. As satisfied as I can be, given that we can't make another Ring of Fire happen and go back to June and make some changes." Wulff's eyes widened, and then he burst out in laughter, with Christoph joining him a moment later. "What?" Philip demanded. "What? It could happen, couldn't it?"

Wulff tapered down to chuckles before responding with, "It is remotely possible, I suppose, since no one walking the face of the earth, not even the most learned of the up-timers, has even a crumb of a clue as to what caused the first one to happen. But at the same time, I wouldn't give very good odds on it happening again. Other than miracles of healing, God doesn't seem to repeat his miracles."

"Hmmph." Philip frowned for a moment, then his face moved to a grin. "Speaking of odds, do you think the sergeants had a bet on how the case was going to end up?"

Wulff returned the grin. "I'm certain that they did. But it was bad manners to talk about it before us."

"Wonder how much Honister lost?"

"From his expression, I'd say enough that it hurt." Wulff's grin turned wicked.

"Hmm. Remind me not to wager with Sergeant Peltzer." Philip gave a definite nod.

"Smart man."

19 December 1635

Philip stared at Frau Portia in horror. "A salon? You want me to attend another salon?" His gut tied itself into knots. "I almost ruined the last one I went to. Why would I want to go to another one?"

Frau Portia gave a lady-like snort—if there was such a thing—and said, "You did no such thing. You were calm and well-behaved. Frau Mary was impressed with you."

Philip felt his stomach lurch. Frau Mary Simpson, the Lady of Magdeburg, one of the most preeminent of the preeminent up-timers, knew who he was? She remembered him? She was impressed with him? His mother would be astounded, Philip knew. He just felt sick. He had no business in the upper ranks of Magdeburg society. He had no desire to be someone who was known by those types of folk. It could only lead to trouble.

"You don't know," he said in desperation. "I almost puked twice. That would have been a disaster. I'd have had to leave Magdeburg if I had puked on the shoes of someone like Frau Mary, or Herr Gericke, or…or…"

"Or me," Frau Portia said with her wicked grin.

"Or you!" Philip said. "God forbid!" His stomach knots spun themselves into Gordian magnitude at the thought of what Master Wulff would have said if Philip had bathed his wife's feet with the contents of his stomach.

Frau Portia relented. Her wicked grin softened into her sweet smile; the one that softened her face and seemed to emit a glow. She patted his upper arm, and said, "Philip, you were nervous, but you did fine. You didn't vomit then, you won't do it now."

"But…but my clothes…"

"The suit fit you fine, didn't it?" Philip's mind went to where the suit was handing from a peg on the wall of his room, and he nodded with some reluctance. "Good. I'll bring another shirt by for you to wear. You'll do fine." She patted his arm again, then linked her arm with Master Wulff's. "Let's go, dear." She looked back at Philip. "Saturday upcoming, Philip. Be ready."

Master Wulff winked at Philip over the top of his wife's head as they headed out the office door.

"Why is she doing this to me?" Philip muttered after they left.

"Maternal instinct, maybe," Christoph said with laughter in his voice.

Philip looked at him. "What maternal instinct? They have no children."

"Which may be why she's taking it out on you." Christoph uttered a real laugh.

"Not fair," Philip muttered. "Why should I go to the salon? I'm not one of those people. What would I get out of it?"

"Ella Kamererin will probably be there," Christoph said in a sly tone, needling Philip slightly.

That thought settled into Philip's mind, and for the rest of the afternoon wasn't far from the front of his thoughts. And he didn't complain any more about the salon.

21 December 1635

The door to the inner office opened. "…and I can tell you that Gröning has certainly lost some respect in our circles as a result of the trial." That fragment of a statement preceded Master Kamerer as he exited, followed by Master Wulff.

"I'm not surprised at that," Wulff responded. "I am a bit surprised at how quickly the word spread, though."

Master Kamerer snorted. "Oh, come now, Andy. You know that the only group more likely to spread gossip around than old ladies in church is master merchants when the brandy has been served. I dare say that the words of your young clerk were being quoted at Walcha's and at the Green Horse the very night of the day he gave testimony. And there he is, as we speak of him."

Philip stood still as he found the gaze of the master merchant fixed on him.

"You, young man," Kamerer pointed a finger at him, "are to be commended."

"Umm, all I did was tell the truth," Philip said, trying to prevent a defensive tone from entering his voice.

"Indeed. You told the truth plainly and clearly, and revealed to the court and to anyone who reads the court's notes the nature of both Master Gröning and young Schmidt. And neither one of them came off very well. Schmidt is a buffoon, a lout, a wastrel, and that reputation now is dogging the heels of his cousin, Georg Schmidt. Gröning is revealed as a once honest dealer who appears to be slipping into his dotage."

"He was a good master," Philip protested.

"Was," Kamerer returned. "Was. But not now. And the way he treated you is the proof of it. No, the only ones who come off with any merit in this matter are you and your fellow workers. And those of us who had an interest in the case are thankful that you were there, and you told the truth. Trust me, young man, your name is known in Magdeburg now, and not least because you work for this wolf in lawyer's clothing." He flashed a wicked grin at Master Wulff, who returned it in kind.

"But seriously," Kamerer continued to Wulff, "that jackal Schardius is already sniffing around both Gröning and the elder Schmidt. There may be more repercussions from this than we had imagined."

"Schardius." Wulff worked his mouth as if he was about to spit. "Calling him that is an insult to jackals, to all carrion eaters."

"You've met the man, then?"

"Once. Mostly I've been dealing with him on behalf of Frau Diebes."

"Ah. Enough said." Kamerer pulled a pair of gloves out of his pockets and put them on. "Shall we see you later tonight, then?"

"When have you known Portia to miss one of Frau Mary's salons?" Wulff was now sporting a broad grin.

"Very good. Until then." Kamerer said. He nodded to Philip before leaving.

And the thought began circling in Philip's mind that if Master Kamerer would be at the salon, possibly—maybe even probably—Ella would as well. His own mouth curved in a smile.

∞ ∞ ∞

Philip hovered outside the main doors to the Brewers Guildhall. He could have gone on in, but he was nervous as it was. Entering alone would have made it worse. So he stood, waiting for Master Wulff and Frau Portia so that he could enter with them. If he could ride in on their coattails, as it were, they would attract all the attention and he could slip away to the sides of the room and hopefully just be a shadow in the room to everyone. He could hope, anyway. He still thought it was a rotten thing that Christoph had managed to beg off attending with an excuse that he needed to go to Halle and make sure his parents were doing okay after they both had fallen and suffered injuries. In his darker moments, he wondered if the event had truly happened or if Christoph was simply fabricating an excuse to avoid the salon.

He straightened and stood still as he saw Wulff and Portia approaching. (He wondered if he would ever get to the point where he would call the master 'Andy'.) Frau Portia looked him up and down, then smiled. "You look fine, Philip. That shirt looks well on you, and I think the up-time style haircut does too."

Philip felt his cheeks heat as he blushed a little, despite his attempts to suppress it. "Thank you."

The shirt was a rich plum color, albeit faded enough to explain why it was no longer in Master Wulff's wardrobe. Philip looked down at to catch a glimpse of it within his jacket, then ran his hand self-consciously over his head, feeling the shortness of the haircut the barber had talked him into trying that afternoon. He felt the cool breeze playing around his head, more so than he usually would. He was afraid he looked foolish, but if Frau Portia liked it, then maybe it was okay. If nothing else, hair would always grow back.

"Shall we go?" Master Wulff asked. It wasn't really a question, but it served to get them moving again in a polite manner.

"Let's," was Frau Portia's response. Philip followed two steps behind.

They paused inside the door long enough for Frau Portia's long cloak to be taken, and then they moved farther into the room to where there was a very short receiving line—Frau Mary Simpson and Frau Lady Beth Haygood—much like the one Philip had seen at his first salon.

"Andy, Portia," Mary said with obvious delight. "I'm so glad you could come tonight. And what a lovely dress, dear."

Philip hadn't really noticed what Frau Portia was wearing, so frazzled was he by his own presence at the salon. Now he paused to look at her. The dress was velvet, of so bright a blue color that it was almost painful to look at. Her arms were covered by sleeves, unlike the dress she wore to the last salon. She wasn't wearing a collar, and her hair was upswept, which emphasized the black velvet ribbon around her throat with a pendant or brooch or medallion on it—he wasn't sure which. He looked around the room. Every woman in sight was staring at Frau Portia, and most of them had expressions that could have clabbered milk. Philip smiled a bit as he recalled what Christoph had said at the last salon: "And after seeing her, no man here is going to look at any woman but her tonight." Philip suspected that that would be a true statement tonight as well.

"Don't you just love the new dyes that Lothlorien Farbenwerke is coming out with?" Portia said with a smile. "They call this 'electric blue', and as soon as I saw it I had to have a dress done in it." She turned from side to side, allowing the skirt to float a little.

"Very nice, dear," Mary said. Lady Beth said nothing, but nodded in smiling agreement. "And you, Andy . . .I hear you were involved in that recent case involving Lorenz Gröning."

"Sorry to disappoint you, Mary, but I had nothing to do with that matter." Wulff turned and gestured. "It was actually Philip, here, who was involved."

Portia also turned and took a step back, and Philip found himself without cover. Frau Mary's gaze was fixed directly on him. "Ah, yes . . .Philip Fröhlich, is it not? You were the one who was aspiring to be a writer of . . .horror stories, wasn't it?" Philip gulped, amazed at her recall. "Have you sold one yet?

"Ah," Philip began, "ah, one, actually."

Mary smiled at him. "That's more than most people ever manage. Take some pride in that, young man. Now, go enjoy yourself."

Wulff took Frau Portia's hand again and led the way deeper into the guild hall. Philip gave a quick bow to Frau Mary and Frau Lady Beth, then edged around them as someone else came up behind him.

Once he was past the entry gauntlet, Philip looked around for...ah, there it was. He made a direct line for the corner where there was the bulk of a sizable of a growler keg visible through the shifting crowds. This being the Brewers Guildhall, of course there would be beer. Master Wulff and Frau Portia were turning away from the serving table with a glass of wine each as Philip arrived, and he slid into the small gap left by their leaving. As soon as the server looked at him, Philip pointed at the keg. Moments later, Philip turned away from the table himself bearing a mug of beer.

Since Master Wulff and Frau Portia were engaged in lively conversation with Judge Schweighart and another older man, Philip passed them by and moved deeper into the guildhall, sipping his beer as he moved.

Several minutes later, he circulated through most of the rooms, and had yet to see someone that he knew. He was about to return to the foyer area and start over again when he heard, "Philip...Philip Fröhlich."

Philip looked around to see a well-dressed older man beckoning to him. He pointed to his chest and said, "Me?"

The older man nodded, so Philip walked toward him. As he got closer, more lights came on in the room and he was able to see that the summoner was none other than Master Johann Hoch, the man who had served as one of the two *Schöffen* at Thomas' trial. Philip's stomach, which had started to relax and calm down, tied itself in knots again. "Yes?" he managed without his voice cracking. In the back of his mind, he was proud of that for a moment.

Master Hoch clapped a hand on Philip's shoulder. "You are an impressive young man, young Philip," he intoned. Philip caught more than a hint of brandy on his breath, doubtless from the glass in his other hand. "You were calm and well-spoken in the trial of Thomas Schmidt. You impressed all of the judges. I was certainly impressed."

The older man paused for a moment and blinked slowly, then muffled a belch with the hand that had been on Philip's shoulder. "Excuse me," he muttered, although Philip thought there was a certain slur to the words. It dawned on him that Master Hoch might be just slightly drunk. The waves of brandy fumes that were wafting past him certainly indicated that.

Master Hoch turned slightly and tapped a man behind him on the shoulder. "Peter . . ." The man turned around and it was Master Kamerer. Philip almost fainted at that, and the knots in his stomach redoubled themselves. "Peter, have you met young Frölich here?" He gestured toward Philip.

Master Kamerer smiled. "Yes, I have, Johann. It's good to see you, Philip."

Philip swallowed, and dipped his head. "Thank you, Master Kamerer. It is good to see you, as well." He mustered his courage. "Is . . .is your daughter here tonight?"

"Yes," Master Kamerer replied. Philip was encouraged by the fact that his smile was still in place. "She and her older sister are here together. So head toward the music and look for a gathering of young women. She'll probably be in the midst of them." He winked one eye at Philip, who discovered that he was capable of being shocked further.

"What do you think of this young man?" Hoch said, butting into the moment. "Should we try to hire him away from Master Wulff? I mean, is he not wasted as a law clerk?" He made an expansive gesture with the glass-laden hand, and the liquid therein sloshed alarmingly. Philip flinched back a little as the hand passed in front of him.

Kamerer pursed his lips for a moment, then shook his head. "No, I think not. First, Master Wulff is engaged on some work for me. It would be a poor reward to try and poach his assistants from him. And second . . ." he paused dramatically, " . . .would you want Master Wulff angry with you?" Philip saw that shot penetrate the brandy haze and hit home with Master Hoch. Kamerer saw it as well, and chuckled before he concluded, "No, I thought not. Good evening to you, Johann, young Philip." He turned back to the group he had been conversing with before Master Hoch had attracted his attention.

Hoch turned his gaze to Philip and blinked slowly a couple of times before saying, "Umm, yes, the path of wisdom and all that. But let us agree on this, young Fröhlich—if you ever leave Master Wulff's employ, for any reason whatsoever, you will immediately contact me and give me first opportunity to engage your services. Can we agree on that?" He stuck his hand out.

Philip looked at that. His sense of surprise had been exhausted by the evening, he discovered. It seemed like a natural thing that one of the most prominent patricians and merchants in Magdeburg should want to make an agreement and shake on it with a lowly clerk. He shrugged and clasped the older man's hand. They shook solemnly, then Master Hoch straightened and nodded.

"Good even to you, young Frölich." He nodded again, then turned and moved toward the front of the hall. Philip noticed that his glass was empty now. He watched as Master Hoch made his way. He wasn't staggering, but he did seem to be moving with a certain . . .deliberation might be the best word.

"What was that all about?"

Philip turned to see Master Wulff and Frau Portia standing at his elbow. "I think that Master Hoch may have had a bit too much brandy tonight. He talked about hiring me away from you until Master Kamerer convinced him that was a bad idea. He then made me promise if I ever left you that I would contact him about a job."

"Why, that . . ." Frau Portia began in a hard tone of voice, only to stop as Master Wulff placed a hand over her hand where it rested in the crook of his elbow.

"That was the brandy talking, dear," Wulff said. "He has more sense than that." His forehead briefly wrinkled with a frown for a moment. "I do have to wonder just how much brandy he's had. I've seen him drink enough to put most men under a table and still be able to discuss business coldly and sharply. Hmm." He shook his head. "No matter. So, if you leave me, you'll go to him first?"

Philip looked at Master Wulff in alarm. There was a gleam in the older man's eye that he didn't like. "I'm not leaving! I want to stay and learn things and prepare to be a lawyer, like we talked about. I don't want to be a merchant. I want to stay with you!"

Frau Portia slapped her husband's shoulder. "Andy! Don't scare the boy!"

Master Wulff's expression eased to a grin, and Philip relaxed. "So you'd go to work for him if you left me?" he repeated.

Philip shrugged. "If you discharged me or if I left for some crazy reason, I'd need a job. Master Hoch looks like he'd be a good man to work for."

Wulff's smile slipped away, and he nodded. "He would be. Maybe the best of the current bunch in Magdeburg." His smile returned. "But I don't plan on discharging you, so this is all hypothetical and make-believe anyway."

"Is Ella Kamererin here tonight?" Frau Portia changed the subject.

Philip nodded. "According to Master Kamerer, she and an older sister are here together. He told me to listen for music and look for a group of young women."

"Then what are you doing standing here talking to us?" Portia demanded. "Get moving!"

∞ ∞ ∞

It was about a quarter of an hour later that Philip finally found Ella. He managed that by first finding the music. As he made his circles looking for Ella, he could hear some kind of music floating out of one of the side rooms. He drifted that direction until he found a young man perhaps about his age sitting at a cabinet that stood against a wall that had a keyboard protruding from it rather like what an organ or a clavier would have. Not that he had ever seen a clavier. But he had seen organs before, at St. Jacob's Church, and in the Dom itself one time when his mother had dragged him there as a young boy for some special service or mass. He didn't really remember what. But he did remember the vaulted inside of the cathedral and the sound of the great organ.

The sound of the instrument was not that of an organ, nor did it sound like the description of what he had heard about a clavier's sound was like. He moved up to stand beside the instrument and leaned an elbow on the top of it. The young man playing the music with obvious skill and dexterity looked up and grinned before looking back down to where his hands were jumping about like two giant spiders in a hot skillet. The pace was rapid, the notes were flowing like water, and Philip found himself tapping his toe at it, even though it wasn't exactly dance music.

The young player brought the piece to its conclusion, and plucked his hands from the keyboard. "Ha! Played it straight through with no errors. Let's see Christoph beat that!"

"Christoph?" Philip asked.

"Christoph Bach, my next older brother," the player said. "He likes to think that he's a better player than I am." His mouth quirked. "He's better at improvising than I am—at least right now—but an actual composed piece? No." He looked around. "Where is he? He's supposed to be playing next." He put his hands back on the keys and started playing something slow and repetitive.

"So you are . . ." Philip continued his questions.

"Sorry! Heinrich Bach, at your service." The player sketched a bow from the stool he was sitting on as he continued playing. "Fourth generation musician—I think—maybe the fifth generation—of the redoubtable Bach family. We're spread throughout all Thuringia, down into Saxony, and up into Magdeburg province. My brothers and I just moved to Magdeburg the city last year. My oldest brother, Johann, just finished building the organ in the Royal Music Hall and gave a big organ recital." He played a ripple of notes. "Christoph and I helped," he said in an undertone.

"Nice," Philip responded.

"So who are you?"

"I'm sorry," Philip said. "Didn't mean to be rude. I'm Philip Fröhlich. I'm not a musician, but I do like to sing in church."

"Nothing wrong with that," Heinrich said as he ran a ripple of notes up the keyboard. Better that you sing there and enjoy it rather than be a first rank voice in the choir and be sour about what you do . . .which I've seen."

"So have I," Philip said, thinking back to his choirboy days. He shook his head to clear those thoughts away. "What is this instrument? I haven't seen or heard one before."

Heinrich laid his left hand on the top of the cabinet while his right hand kept moving on the keys, evoking melody. "This is a piano. It's an up-time instrument, made according to an up-time design. This one was made by Bledsoe and Riebeck in their factory in Grantville after the Ring of Fire, and they sell them all over the Germanies, maybe even farther. It's got a different sound, but once you get used to the sound and the touch of it, you can do so much with it that you just can't do with a clavier." He brought the left hand back down to the keyboard and did a little flourish that impressed and astounded Philip.

At that point, another young man appeared from the other side of the piano. "Sorry I'm late, Heinrich. What did you end up with?" This must be the next older brother.

"Prelude and Fugue No. 6 in D minor," Heinrich said as he rose. And I'll have you know, Christoph, I nailed it, as Carl Shockley would say."

"Is that so? Well, watch this." Christoph set a glass of wine on the top of the cabinet, set his hands to the keys, and launched into a jangling piece that set Philip's nerves on edge.

Heinrich caught his wince, and pulled him away from the piano. "I agree. Why he insists on playing that Chopin Revolutionary Etude I'll never understand. It's harsh and dissonant by our standards, and most people aren't ready to hear it yet. And there's this one passage late in the work that he hasn't played right yet." Heinrich shook his head. "Just because Frau Marla Linder plays it occasionally, doesn't mean that he needs to try and keep up with her. I think this business of him being the grandfather of Johann Sebastian Bach has gone to his head."

"Who?" Now Philip was confused. Christoph didn't look old enough to be a father, much less a grandfather.

"The up-timers brought back a lot of music by a man named Johann Sebastian Bach. That's who wrote the piece I was playing. Well, with that name, he had to be some kind of relationship to us, but when we had research done at the great library in Grantville, it turns out he was a grandson of Christoph. He takes himself just a bit too seriously now because of that, which is stupid, because the up-timers say that Grantville coming back to the past has changed the future and Sebastian will never be born."

Philip stopped. "What?"

Heinrich shrugged. "That's what all their people of knowledge and learning say. Me, I don't know it for sure one way or the other, but it does make some sense." A wicked grin appeared on his face. "And I love to rub it in Christoph's face every once in a while. So what do you do here in Magdeburg?"

The sudden shift in topic took Philip by surprise. "I'm a clerk and secretary in the office of a very successful lawyer here in Magdeburg. Plus I write stories."

Heinrich's eyebrows went up. "Wow. Who do you write your stories for?"

"My first one will come out in the next issue of *Der Schwarze Kater* magazine next month."

Heinrich's eyebrows stayed up, and his mouth formed an O for a moment. "I love that magazine. My brothers think I'm stupid for spending money on it. But I've only got from Issue 4 onward, and I haven't been able to find the earlier issues anywhere."

"I have them all," Philip said, feeling a bit smug. "You could read my copies."

Heinrich looked at him with an odd look on his face. "Would you really let me do that?"

"Sure. You could come to my room any evening and read them."

"I may take you up on that," Heinrich said. His eyes lifted over Philip's shoulder, and Philip started to turn to see what Heinrich was looking at.

"So when will your story come out?"

Philip completed his turn to see Ella Kamererin standing behind him beside a slightly older woman who looked so much like Ella that it had to be her older sister.

"Early next month is what Master Gronow promised me," he replied with a slight smile. "Good evening, Frau Kamererin and Frau Kamererin," he continued with a nod. "Your father told me you were here somewhere."

"You've seen my father?" Ella's eyebrows drew down. "What did he say?" Ella's tone was a bit dark. Her older sister looked amused.

"Only that to find you I should follow the sound of the music and look for a gathering of young women. I had found the music," Philip gestured to Heinrich and the piano, "but before I could look for the young women, they found me."

Philip smiled at Ella. Her frown deepened, and her sister looked even more amused.

"That's what he said?"

"Yes."

"Nothing more?"

"That's all."

"Hmmph."

Ella looked slightly less disgruntled. Her sister laughed and turned to Philip. "Since my mannerless sister has failed to introduce us, let me introduce myself. I am Maria Kamererin verheiratet Ermann, Ella's older sister."

"My next older sister," Ella interjected. 'I have another older than her."

"And you," Maria continued, "can be no one other than Philip Fröhlich."

Philip gave a slow nod as a bit of a bow. "I'm afraid that I am. You have heard of me, then?" He wasn't sure how he felt about that, especially after he saw a sly look slip onto Maria's face.

"You might say that. You're my sister's favorite topic of conversation…"

"Maria!" Ella exclaimed. She slapped her sister on the arm—hard, if Philip was any judge of blows.

"…and even my father has been heard to mention your name of late," Maria concluded with a gleam in her eye. Ella was blushing, and Philip wanted to look at the floor. The reminder that Master Kamerer know who he was by name was still putting a bit of spin on his knotted stomach.

He felt a nudge and caught a glimpse from the corner of his eye of Heinrich standing up straight beside him. "Lest you think me also mannerless, allow me to introduce my friend, Heinrich Bach." Heinrich gave a bit more of a bow than Philip had, straightening with a wide grin on his face.

"Bach…Bach…" Maria mused. "Are you any connection to the Bach who gave the concert on the new Royal Opera House organ?"

"Indeed," Heinrich said, again with a small bow. "My oldest brother, Johann, who is a superb musician—although I'd never tell him that to his face." His broad grin returned. "You might understand how older brothers are."

"If they're anything like older sisters," Ella said with a glare at Maria, "I certainly do."

"If you were able to attend the concert," Heinrich said, "I was his page turner and organ stop adjuster."

Maria tilted her head. "So you were. I thought you looked familiar."

Heinrich's smile grew brighter, if that was possible. After a moment, he said, "You, Frau Maria, are married, and it's obvious to anyone with sense that you, Frau Ella, are considering my friend Philip, here. But that leaves no one for me with whom to discuss the weather or to offer to share a glass of wine. Is there someone here tonight to whom you can introduce me? So that I don't expire from loneliness and boredom, I mean."

Philip flinched at his friend's forwardness, Ella blushed a little, but Maria laughed and said, "I think you should meet my friend Costanza."

"Is she here tonight?" Both Heinrich's tone of voice and his expression displayed hopefulness.

"She's supposed to be. Come with me." Maria turned and walked away. Heinrich sent a quick grin Philip's direction, and hurried to catch up with Maria.

Ella looked at Philip and shook her head. "Sisters," she muttered. "Especially older sisters."

"I wouldn't know," Philip replied in a sympathetic tone. "But it was good of her to come with you."

"Are you jesting?" Ella's tone was more than a bit sharp and sarcastic. "Miss a chance at one of Frau Mary's salons? She'd have climbed out of her death bed to be here tonight."

Philip shook his head. "I just don't understand that. I mean, yes, it's nice to know that Frau Mary likes you well enough to invite you, but otherwise why is it so important to people?"

Ella's jaw dropped and she stared at him. Philip realized he must have said something out of line, but he didn't know what. His last statement had been the truth.

Ella took a deep breath. "Were you ever hit in the head as a child?"

Philip blinked. "No, not really. Not that I remember, anyway. Why?"

"Just checking. Your question might make one think that you were mazed by the moon, or something. Do you really not see that reputations are made and ruined by whether or not someone is seen at one of these salons? More business deals will be concluded here tonight than in a month at Walcha's Coffee House. There are people who would sell their first-born sons and throw their mothers in for good measure to be invited to one of Frau Mary's salons."

"Oh." Philip felt a bit foolish. "Frau Portia just told me to come along."

"Frau Mary knew of it, you may be sure. I came with my father, and it's understood that I would be here. This is part of the dance for unmarried daughters—being put on display." Ella's voice had softened, but there was a bitter tone to it now. "But you—Frau Mary knows who you are, and welcomed you. Do you have any idea how many people would commit crimes to have that recognition, that acceptance, that presence?"

Philip shook his head. "Why? I'm nobody. I'm just a clerk."

"You're a clerk for one of the most notorious lawyers in Magdeburg. You're a clerk, according to my father, whose testimony just damned with faint praise a major merchant here in the city. And you're a writer . . ." Ella's voice had been gaining in intensity as she spoke, and she now leaned forward and poked him in the chest, " . . .and you're going to be a famous one before you're done."

"Just what I was going to say," a voice obtruded into the discussion. They both looked over to see Johann Gronow grinning at them, a large glass of wine in his hand. Philip was almost stunned. He hadn't expected to see Gronow tonight, although he should have. He recalled Frau Mary saying something about that at the last salon. "Introduce us, please, Philip."

He scrambled after his wits, and stammered out, "El . . .Ella Kamererin, I introduce to you Johann Gronow, man of letters, publisher and editor of *Der Schwarze Kater* magazine, and incidentally the man who bought my story. Johann, I introduce to you Ella Kamererin, daughter of Master Peter Kamerer, the noted merchant and patrician."

Johann swept a bow. "Very pleased to meet you, Fräulein. I know of your father."

Ella's mouth quirked. "Most people know of my father. It makes life a bit awkward at times."

Johann nodded. His expression now was sober. "I can understand that, I believe." His smile returned to his face. "My condolences, Fräulein."

"Don't flatter me, Master Gronow," Ella replied with asperity. "We are not *Adel*, and I have no pretensions otherwise."

"As you wish," Johann said with a slight bow. He turned to Philip. "Two weeks until the new issue comes out, Philip, and your name will be on the cover."

"On the cover?" Philip had trouble believing what he'd just heard. "You hadn't told me that?"

"I hadn't?" Gronow's brow furrowed. "Are you sure? I meant to." He waved his unoccupied hand. "No matter, you know now. The printer and binder will deliver the finished copies within a week or so. I'll give you your author's copy as soon as I have them in hand."

"Wow." That slipped out of Philip's mouth before he even realized it.

"Such good news," Ella said, her face shining as she laid a hand on Philip's arm.

From the Journal of Philip Fröhlich
21 December 1635

Friday
Breakfast–
1 wheat roll 3 pfennigs
1 sausage 2 pfennigs
1 mug beer 2 pfennigs

Supper–
1 wheat roll 3 pfennigs
A few snacks at Frau Mary's salon

Don't remember any dreams.

Good thing today was regular day at work. Was so nervous about tonight I don't think I could have handled any problems.

Met up with Master Wulff and Frau Portia, entered the salon with them. Really felt weird when Frau Mary greeted me and remembered that I want to be a writer. She's only seen me once, how can she remember that about me?

Several people mentioned my testimony in Master Gröning's case. Makes me uncomfortable.

Did get a chance to see Ella at the salon. Met her older sister Maria, too. Seemed nice.

Met a musician who's about my age, maybe a bit younger. Named Heinrich Bach. Nice guy, I think. Likes *Der Schwarze Kater*, so there's something right about him.

Johann Gronow was at the salon, too. Was surprised to see him there. Don't know why. If I can be there, certainly he can be. And afterward I remember Frau Mary saying something about inviting him. He and Ella had a conversation about flattery. Short conversation. Ella basically said don't flatter her.

Ella talked to me for the longest time, mostly about my story, and what my next story should be about. She also talked about what it's like to be a younger sister in a well-off family. I had trouble understanding what she was complaining about. Didn't say anything, though. Could tell she was talking, not looking for solutions.

Really like Ella. Smart. Probably smarter than me. She likes me. Her sister Maria says so. Wonder why? What can a law clerk offer to the daughter of a major merchant house? But the more I see her, the more I talk to her, the more I am drawn to her.

Have to wonder what God is doing with this.

Late. Time for sleep. Recited evening prayers, and so to bed.

From the Journal of Philip Fröhlich
2 January 1636

> Wednesday
> Breakfast–
> > *1 wheat roll 3 pfennigs*
> > *1 sausage 2 pfennigs*
> > *1 mug beer 2 pfennigs*
>
> Supper–
> > *1 wheat roll 3 pfennigs*
> > *1 bowl fish stew 3 pfennigs*
> > *1 mug beer 2 pfennigs*

Dreams last night. At one point Portia came in—the character, not Master Wulff's wife—looked at me and smiled, then waved at me and turned and left. Another time Max floated through, nodded, and moved on, rifle at the ready. Later saw a box that said *Der Schwarze Kater*. Remember hoping it had the new issue in it, but I couldn't get the box open. Frustrating, that was. Really wanted to see the cover.

Read some out of *Table Talk* tonight. Tonight I especially liked "He who will never give a kindness will never experience one." A simple truth, but at the same time both challenging and profound. Beginning to realize just how good a teacher Martin Luther really was. Impressed by not just his knowledge, but how well he explains it.

Just realized I used present tense for that last statement. Luther has been dead for almost ninety years, so really doubt that he's speaking today. Wonder what that says about me, that I think of him that way.

Still don't have a new story idea. Starting to get frustrated.

Recited evening prayers. Now to bed.

From the Journal of Philip Fröhlich
3 January 1636

Thursday
Breakfast–
1 wheat roll 3 pfennigs
1 cup broth 1 pfennig
1 mug beer 2 pfennigs

Supper–
1 wheat roll 3 pfennigs
1 sausage 2 pfennigs
1 mug beer 2 pfennigs

Dreamt last night. Know I did, remember seeing things like clouds flowing as they went by. Kind of pretty, even when they turned dark and gray like storm clouds for a while. The only thing I remember seeing for sure, though, was Ella. She just kind of faded into view, wearing the dress she was wearing at the last salon. She didn't say anything, just stood there smiling at me. After a while, she faded out of view again. Remember feeling glad that she was there, even after she faded out. Glad and sad at the same time. Not sure what that means. May be trying to make something special out of just random chance. But the image was so strong, and I remember it so clearly—and now I think I'm remembering earlier dreams, like in the night before. Did I really dream them, and just not recall, or is my mind playing tricks on me? And why Ella? I mean, I like her, and I think she likes me…her sister says she does, anyway. So…

Gronow sent a note to me at work today, told me that the magazine issue was finished. He promised to bring a copy to me tomorrow. Excited. Not sure I can sleep tonight.

Tried to read in *Table Talk*, quit after reading the same page four times and realizing I didn't remember a single word it said. Tried to read in the

Bible, didn't matter what book I was in, I couldn't focus and read. Too excited.

Finally started reciting evening prayers. Took four times through before I calmed. Going to try and sleep now.

4 January 1636

"Philip?"

Philip looked up from where he was trying to transcribe a batch of his shorthand notes. He must have been asleep when he made them, he'd decided, because they were sloppy and hard to figure out, which was why he'd been concentrating so hard he hadn't realized someone had come in. It took a moment for him to realize that the person who'd spoken was Johann Gronow, who was holding something before him in both hands.

A moment later, Philip managed to reach out to take a copy of *Der Schwarze Kater* Issue 7 in his hand. He felt some small surprise that his hand wasn't shaking, considering how his insides were turning somersaults. It was almost like his hand belonged to someone else, but it reached out and took the book without apparent instruction from him.

He cradled the book in both hands, holding it gingerly. The cover was a simple woodblock cut of a cat, similar to all the other covers that had been. At the bottom of the cover were the words *Containing Stories by Robert E. Howard, Edgar Allen Poe, Philip Fröhlich, and Others*. A sense of light expanding seemed to fill him, and he felt as if he could dance.

Philip looked up after a long moment and saw Gronow grinning at him. He felt a very broad grin of his own spread across his face.

"So how does it feel to be a published author?" Gronow asked.

Philip had to take a deep breath. His feet were shuffling on the floor, and his mind was stuttering, if that was possible. He took another deep breath, then said, "Great! I mean, wonderful! I mean, awesome. I mean . . .I don't know what I mean!"

There was a chuckle behind him, and Master Wulff reached over his shoulder to pluck the book out of his hands. Philip turned to see him examining the cover. "Very nice. Is it at Syborg's Books yet?"

"Tomorrow or the next day," Gronow replied. "The binder is finishing the binding of the final copies today."

"Good." Wulff handed it back to Philip. "Portia will be expecting her copy by tomorrow night, I'm certain."

"We'll try not to disappoint her, then."

The two older men continued with their conversation, but Philip ignored them. Issue 7 was out! Hurrah! He set it on his desk, and gingerly opened it, looking first at the table of contents page, then turned to page 27 to read *The Apotheosis of Portia*. He touched the page to make sure it was real, fingers trembling slightly.

5 January 1636

The door to Syborg's Books slammed shut behind Philip as the chill north wind caught it. He twitched his shoulders under his coat as he walked across the room to where Master Matthias stood. "Did Issue 7 arrive today?"

Matthias reached under the counter and pulled out a copy, which he placed in Philip's hands. "Indeed it did, and a right fine issue it is, too, with your name on the cover and all."

Philip smiled. This brought it home to him. This made it real, in a way that having the author copy hand delivered by Gronow had not done.

"Philip? Is that you?"

Philip turned to see Ella Kamererin approaching from one of the side aisles, her father trailing behind her. He tilted his head a bit, and considered her smiling face. Something seemed to *click* in him, and suddenly he knew what to do. He smiled and handed her the copy of *Der*

Schwarze Kater Issue 7 that he was holding. Her eyes dropped to it, her breath caught as her eyes rounded, and then flew to cling to his face.

"Ella Kamererin, will you accept this gift and allow me to pay court to you?"

He almost laughed as her jaw dropped open, but then it slammed shut and a shining smile graced her face before she replied, "I'd be disappointed if you didn't."

Philip straightened and looked her father in the eye as he approached, intimidating as that felt. "Master Kamerer, may I pay court to your daughter Ella?"

A smile lurked around the corners of the older man's mouth as he replied, "I would be disappointed if you didn't."

The End . . . For Now

Dramatis Personae

Bach, Christoph	Musician playing at one of Mary Simpson's salons
Bach, Heinrich	Musician playing at one of Mary Simpson's salons
Bieger, Oswalt	Attorney representing Thomas Schmidt
Chieske, Byron	Up-timer, lieutenant in charge of detectives for Magdeburg Polizei
Dauth, Johan	Bookkeeper of Frau Diebes
Diebes, Sarah	Client of Andy Wulff
Eichhorn, Peter	Third judge in the Schmidt assault case
Fröhlich, Johann	Philip's cousin, who is studying at the university in Jena and comes to visit occasionally
Fröhlich, Philip	Young bookkeeper who is first attracted to the horror stories from the future, then decides he wants to write stories like that
Gröning, Lorenz	Master merchant who employs Philip when the story begins
Gronow, Johann	Publisher/editor of Der Schwarze Kater
Grubb, Portia	Andy Wulff's wife, encourages Philip in his writing, not to be confused with the protagonist of Philip's stories
Gruber, Moritz	Lutheran pastor who preaches at St. Jacob's church occasionally
Haygood, Lady Beth	Up-timer, not a noble, chief assistant of Mary Simpson
Heinichen, Christoph	Andy Wulff's assistant
Hoch, Gotthilf	Detective sergeant, Magdeburg Polizei

Hoch, Johann Möritz	Patrician, influential merchant, father of Gotthilf Hoch, second judge in the Schmidt assault case
Honister, Karl	Detective sergeant, Magdeburg Polizei
Jotts, Georg	Salesman at Syborg Books
Kamerer, Peter	Influential merchant, from Nürnberg originally, now located in Magdeburg
Kamererin verheiratet Ermann, Maria	Older married sister of Ella
Kamererin, Ella	Youngest daughter of Peter Kamerer
Kierstede, Ernst	Proprietor of The Green Horse Tavern
Logau, Friedrich von	Well-known writer in Magdeburg, friend of Johann Gronow
Lutterodt, Anna	Companion of Frau Diebes
Max the Angel	Inhabitant of Philip's dreams
Murphy, Brendan	Up-timer, client of Andy Wulff, does comedy at The Green Horse Tavern
Murphy, Catrina	Brendan's wife
Niemoller, Martin	New clerk at Master Gröning's office
Peltzer, Kaspar	Detective sergeant, Magdeburg Polizei
Plavius, Johannes	Writer in Magdeburg, friend of Johann Gronow
Rusche, Anna	Wife of Georg Walcha, waitress at Walcha's Coffee House
Schiller, Anton	Office manager for Master Gröning
Schmidt, Georg	Thomas' cousin, influential merchant, brother-in-law of Mayor Otto Gericke
Schmidt, Thomas	Young bookkeeper who works for Master Gröning
Schultz, Mama Ingrid	Old lady who runs a little cookshop that Philip likes
Schweighart, Jacob	Lead judge investigating the case of the assault on Master Gröning by Thomas Schmidt

Seelbach, Karl	Writer in Magdeburg, friend of Johann Gronow
Simpson, Mary	Up-timer, Magdeburg socialite, wife of Admiral Simpson
Syborg, Johann	Younger Master Syborg, son of Matthias, part owner Syborg Books
Syborg, Matthias	Elder Master Syborg, part owner of Syborg Books
Walcha, Georg	Proprietor of Walcha's Coffee House
Wulff, A. N. D. "Andy"	Attorney who hires Philip

Printed in Poland
by Amazon Fulfillment
Poland Sp. z o.o., Wrocław